Earth's greatest adventure begins

Bakker picked up her Coke can, shook it, and then took a drink. "We have nothing in the signal, as yet, to indicate that it is some kind of message. All we have is a new radio source that is acting differently than any other radio source we have ever located. Since it is new, we have to proceed with caution here."

"So," said Hackett, "if I understand you, there is a signal, might be intelligent, might be natural and it is outside the Solar System. How far away is it?"

"Tough question, given that we haven't had all that long for observation, but if I was forced into an answer, I would say between fifty and a hundred light years."

For some reason Hackett relaxed. Something that far away was no threat to the United States or to Earth. At the speed of light, it wouldn't be able to get to Earth for fifty or a hundred years, or more, if it was coming to Earth.

Thinking in a military sense, however, Hackett said, "Then it is no threat to us."

"Why would you even think such a thing?" asked Bakker.

"Because it's my job."

THE EXPLORATION CHRONICLES: BOOK ONE

About the Author

Kevin D. Randle is a captain in the U.S. Army National Guard, an authority on alien abduction, and the author of numerous works of fiction and nonfiction. He has appeared as a guest on many television programs focusing on extraterrestrial activity, including *Unsolved Mysteries*, *Larry King Live*, *Good Morning America*, *Today*, *48 Hours*, *Alien Autopsy*, and *Maury Povich*. He also co-authored the bestselling *UFO: Crash at Roswell*, which later became a popular Showtime movie, and *The Abduction Enigma*.

THE EXPLORATION CHRONICLES

SIGNALS

KEVIN D. RANDLE

2003
50TH
ANNIVERSARY

ACE BOOKS, NEW YORK

THE EXPLORATION CHRONICLES: SIGNALS

An Ace Book / published by arrangement with
the author

PRINTING HISTORY
Ace mass-market edition / April 2003

Copyright © 2003 by Kevin Randle.
Cover art by Danilo Ducak.
Cover design by Judy Murello.
Text design by Julie Rogers.

For information address: The Berkley Publishing Group,
a division of Penguin Putnam Inc.,
375 Hudson Street, New York, New York 10014.

Check out the ACE Science Fiction & Fantasy newsletter!

ISBN: 0-441-01039-3

ACE®
Ace Books are published by The Berkley Publishing Group,
a division of Penguin Putnam Inc.,
375 Hudson Street, New York, New York 10014.
ACE and the "A" design
are trademarks belonging to Penguin Putnam Inc.

PRINTED IN THE UNITED STATES OF AMERICA

10 9 8 7 6 5 4 3 2 1

PROLOGUE

SARAH BAKKER, WHO APPEARED NOTHING LIKE a postdoc in physics, and who looked as if she still belonged in high school, sat at the head of the conference table in the small room on top of the physics building, and said, "I don't know what in the hell we have."

This was a situation that was not unique in the search for extraterrestrial intelligence. Signals, believed to be from an alien world, had been detected almost from the moment that the search began in the 1960s. Those signals, at first thought to be too regular to be natural, were slowly understood, revealing the existence of pulsars and other natural radio sources. SETI had been fooled more than once.

And then there was the detection of signals that suggested intelligence but had never been repeated. The SETI protocols demanded that any signal be repeated so that its existence could be verified by others. The so-called WOW signal of decades earlier seemed to be from an alien intelligence, but no one had ever found it again. It could just as easily have been an aberration.

Now Bakker sat in the small conference room with four others, including the chairman of the Physics Department, Dr. David Avilson, who thought that too much time had been wasted on what he considered fantasy. It wasn't that Avilson wasn't imaginative. It was that he believed nothing good would ever come from the search and even if a signal was detected, it would do nothing other than suggest that intelligent life existed elsewhere in the galaxy. That was, of course, the opinion held by anyone who could think beyond about a third-grade level.

Avilson was a lean man with a shock of gray hair reminiscent of Albert Einstein, and there were those who claimed he cultivated the hair for that very reason. He wore thick glasses and for some reason preferred those with thick black frames. There were those who claimed that he cultivated the nerdish image because it gave him an identity others didn't have. And he wore old clothes and moth-eaten sweaters. There were those who claimed that he thought it made him look scientific, whatever that might mean.

He leaned forward, across the scarred table that held a single ashtray in case Avilson wanted to light his pipe, and pulled the computer printout toward him. He glanced at it, and asked, "Has it repeated?"

Bakker rubbed her lips, and said, "Well, we think it has."

"What does that mean?" asked Steven Weiss, a graduate student who was working on his dissertation and had been for nearly five years. He was approaching thirty but thought of himself as a twenty-one-year-old freshman and often acted like it. He was short and stocky, with thick black hair and a beard that he grew in the fall and shaved in the spring. During the summer he sometimes wore a mustache, but he had no rule. He was dressed as a poor student in a threadbare blue shirt and worn khaki pants, but his bank account contained nearly a quarter of a million dollars and, had he asked, his father would have given him much more.

Bakker looked at Weiss with discomfort and distaste. She didn't like Weiss because too often he was a sharp-shooter. He relished making those with doctorates look bad in front of the department chairman. He thought it enhanced his own position, never realizing that he was creating enemies who would eliminate him just as soon as the opportunity arose.

"It means," she said, "that we have another signal from the same general area of the sky, but that it is not the same message. And the source seems to have shifted too rapidly to be from a planetary source."

"Then you've picked up a satellite again," said Weiss. He fell back in his chair and acted uninterested.

"Well," said Bakker, "we have been unable to identify a terrestrial source."

"Atmospherics," said Weiss.

"Nope, this is clearly something from outside the atmosphere. I thought moon base, but we have isolated that and checked. Even the Martian colony has been eliminated, though there are a couple of deep probes, one inside the asteroid belt and one nearing Saturn, that might account for this if their programming has been corrupted."

The last man in the room, Richard Kelly, leaned to the right and looked at the computer printout. He was just under forty, had been at the university since his undergraduate days, and rarely left the campus even to walk into town. He enjoyed his work and saw no reason to do anything else. He was balding, tending toward fat, with a fleshy face, large nose, and large eyes, but a small mouth. He might have been put together with spare parts from a half dozen other people.

He said, "Well, I think this looks promising."

Avilson said, "I'd rather look at the display. I don't like these paper representations."

"We'll be coming up in about two hours for another look at this thing."

"What have you got from the VLA?" He was asking about the Very Large Array between Magdalena and Datil, New Mexico.

"They're scheduled to take a listen tonight. We should be getting some confirmation from Australia if they picked up anything. I asked them to give a listen."

Avilson lit his pipe slowly, making the ritual last as long as possible while the others waited. He then said, "There really isn't anything for us to do until later this evening."

"You could take a look at the computer," said Bakker, "and let me know what you think."

"This all seems a bit premature," said Avilson. "Until we have some independent corroboration we really have nothing."

Bakker rubbed her face again and took a deep breath. "Actually, this signal has not faded, and although it has not repeated, as far as we can tell, it is still there. If we pick it up tonight, I think we've got the corroboration that we need to verify."

Avilson shrugged. "I want someone else to confirm before we get too excited here. This isn't the first time something like this has happened." He looked at the others and arced an eyebrow. "Anything else?"

Bakker shook her head. "No."

Avilson stood. "Keep me advised."

CHAPTER 1

[1]

RACHEL DAVIES HAD GRADUATED WITH A DE-
gree in journalism two years earlier and now she sat in a
darkened editing bay, the glass door closed behind her, and
watched the small color monitor where another young
woman sobbed because of the horror she had been forced
to endure. Although Davies was glad that the woman had
cried because it made for good television, she thought the
woman deeply disturbed. That didn't mean that Davies
wouldn't exploit her for the minute thirty she could get out
of her.

Davies was a young woman, which made her perfect
for television journalism. She was short but proportioned
to her height so that on television no one could tell. Someone had suggested that she bleach her hair so that she was
blond, but she believed that a reporter, if she was good,
could have hair of any color. She had green eyes that at

times looked more gray and washed out than at others. Her features were fine, with a small nose, and the wide pouting lips that were all the rage this month.

She sat with her fingers on the keyboard rather than use the voice activation because she could think better that way. Her attention was focused on the flickering on the screen directly in front of her. She leaned back and reached over to stop the disk and freeze the image. Using the new keypad, she slowly rewound the image and froze it again. She made a note on the log and hit the play button so that she could review the rest of the interview.

She copied one section to another disk, then looked at her script. Picking up a stopwatch, she began to read her voice-over. "They say that there are millions of planets in our solar system, and that the odds are that some of them would be suitable for human life. Your scientists have been searching for a sign of that life since the middle of the last century. Susan Bachmann says that they no longer need to look because she knows that such life exists. It has visited her."

She punched the button on the watch, found that she was two seconds short but nodded her approval at her own words. She didn't know that she had meant "galaxy" rather than "solar system." Her strong suit in college had not been any of the sciences. Unfortunately, no one else at the station would catch the mistake before it made it on the air. Two people would call to complain about high school students who knew nothing doing the news, but their complaints would be ignored.

Satisfied that she had milked all the humanity out of the story of a woman who claimed that she was repeatedly abducted and abused by extraterrestrial beings, Davies decided that it was time for her lunch. Then she could figure out how to add two seconds to the piece so that she would fill her allotted time. It never occurred to her that journalism was more than just filling the allotted time.

There was a quiet tap at the glass, and Davies leaned over so that she could push the door open. She sat up and looked at the news director, Frank Hall. He was a tall, thin man with dark hair that was rapidly retreating up his forehead. He had closely set, small eyes, a thin nose, and a small mouth. His features seemed crowded together on his face.

Like many of those who had no on-air responsibilities, he was dressed in blue jeans and an old, frayed blue shirt with the sleeves rolled up. He wore sneakers and sometimes, when the mood moved him, or it was cold out, he wore socks.

He asked, "You about through?"

A dozen answers sprang to mind, but Davies said, "Yes. I need just a bit more, but I'll be all ready at six. Just need to add a little . . . polish."

"We might hold it. Not like anyone else is going to break the story before us."

Davies arched her eyebrows. "What's up?"

Hall looked at the notes in his hand. He shrugged, and said, "I don't know what this might mean, but you're our resident expert on astronomy." He pulled the other chair over and dropped into it. He showed her the fax. "Confuses the hell out of me."

It made no sense to her either. Those scientists who searched for alien life, SETI, had announced that they thought they might have detected a signal that could not be explained by natural phenomena. Davies didn't want to admit ignorance because she had already learned that the more they thought you knew, the better your assignments were. Science wasn't a strong area for television journalism, but if they believed she understood science, then she was more valuable to them than another reporter who had the same skills but didn't know science.

To Hall, she said, "You want me to follow up on this?"

"I think that if this SETI thing pans out, it will make a good companion to the other story. Tie the two together in a neat little package."

"I'd need more than a minute and a half."

"Something like this could go to two and a half, maybe three minutes, if it's handled right."

Davies grinned. A three-minute feature on her audition reel would look good and tell other news directors in the larger markets that she was one of the trusted reporters here. They'd be calling for her.

"Where do I go?" she asked.

"University. To the science building. Ask for a Dr. Sarah Bakker. She should have all the details."

[2]

DAVIES FELT COMFORTABLE ON THE UNIVERsity campus. It hadn't been that long since she had been a student, and though she was now dressed better than the undergraduates, she felt as if she belonged with them. A few of them were older than she, and many were about her age.

She walked from the parking lot to a wide sidewalk that led along the river. The water was dark, looking as if it was filled with silt, which might have been the case given all the rain. She came to the pedestrian footbridge, climbed the steps, and crossed the river. On the far bank, facing west, a dozen or so students were sunbathing. A couple of others were sitting on the grass reading.

She entered the student union, walked through it, watching the students swirl around her, some of them looking as if they knew what they were doing. A few of them looked dazed, as if they had been lost in the forest for days and had just made their way back into civilization.

She exited, walked up a hill, crossed a street, and found herself looking at the seven-story physics building. On top were a number of dish-shaped antennae and at the far end, invisible to her now, was a small observatory complete with a reflecting telescope. She had been in that observatory once or twice and knew that the university had built a new one far outside of town, away from the light pollution.

She walked into the lobby of the building, looked at the directory, and learned that Sarah Bakker's office was on the fifth floor. She used the button to call for the elevator and rode it upstairs. She found herself in a brightly lighted but narrow hallway that had institutional tile on the floor, with light green paint halfway up the walls and light gray the rest of the way. Mounted periodically down the hall were television monitors set to display data coming in from one of the many university satellite experiments.

She found Bakker's office. The door was open. She saw a young woman who had long, straight hair. She was thin, almost skinny, and looked as if she could be a reporter on television instead of some kind of physicist.

Bakker's office was small, barely big enough for the desk, which was piled with books, reports, papers, journals, and Coke cans. There was a single chair for a visitor, a window that had closed blinds, some kind of rug on the green tile floor, and a poster on the wall that looked like a map of the universe.

Bakker was sitting at her desk, talking on a cell phone and holding a file in her hand. She didn't look very scientific. Her long dark hair was pulled back in a kind of ponytail. She had a narrow face with a slightly pointed chin, high cheekbones, and large dark eyes. She wore blue jeans and a short white top.

Davies stood in the doorway, half-listening to the conversation in case Bakker said anything that was of news value. When Bakker hung up, Davies tapped on the door, and asked, "Doctor Bakker?"

"Yes?"

"Rachael Davies."

Bakker said, "Ah, yes. I recognize you."

"Can I ask you a couple of questions?"

Bakker said, "Shoot."

Davies sat down, pulled a pad from her purse, opened it, and flipped through some of the pages. When she found what she wanted, she set herself comfortably, looked up, and said, "You received a signal."

For a moment Bakker sat quietly, then grinned, showing plenty of teeth. "Moving right along."

"But you have received a signal?"

"Yes, but the nature of the signal is open to interpretation. You have to remember that."

"So, what was the signal."

Bakker leaned back in her chair, and asked, "What is your interest in this?"

The question surprised Davies. She was used to showing up, being recognized as a TV reporter, and having everyone fall all over themselves to get on air. They would answer the most private questions, reveal the most embarrassing information, all so that they would get their minute on television. She didn't like the subjects to ask questions.

"We heard there had been a signal, and I was sent to learn something more about it."

"What do you know about astronomy?" asked Bakker.

"I know that it is different than astrology. I know that astronomy is a science and that in the last couple of decades we have found lots of new planets." What Davies didn't say was that about shot her knowledge of astronomy, but she knew the crack about astrology would win her some points.

Bakker said, "Well, that puts you ahead of quite a few people. The signal, as you put it, is a radio source that might be of natural origin. We're checking on that."

Davies nodded as if she understood, and asked, "Are there lots of natural radio sources?"

"Yes. The sun is one. Jupiter another. Even the Earth broadcasts, though in our case it's now artificial. There are things all over the universe broadcasting radio noise. We've been trying to find an intelligent signal, an artificial signal, in all that noise. In the last hundred years, we haven't found one that repeated, and there you have it."

"So you have one that has repeated?"

Bakker looked at the reporter, then pointed at the empty chair. "Maybe you would like to sit down. This might take some time."

[3]

RACHEL DAVIES HAD STUDIED JOURNALISM IN college, but she didn't learn much about it. She had come from the interview with Bakker complete with a DVD that she had recorded on the small camera she carried over her shoulder. There had been no cameraman or -woman, no sound person, and no other reporter to find the real thread of the story, so that when she sat down to compose her piece, she missed the real point of it.

Believing that she would have three minutes of airtime, she organized the video from the Bakker interview and examined her notes from the Bachmann interview. Bachmann had made some comments about SETI, and now that SETI was part of the story, Davies wanted to bring that in first. She used the comment made by Bachmann that SETI was unimportant because she already knew that alien life existed out there.

Davies laughed as she cut the piece together, realizing that she was now using the story told by Bakker to support the tale of alien abduction told by Bachmann.

Finished, she stood up and looked back into the bull pen. Hall was standing near another reporter, smoking a cigarette and holding a cup of coffee. Davies found it hard to believe that anyone would drink coffee and smoke cigarettes given all that they knew about those two products, but Hall seemed to thrive on them. Maybe it was because the dangers had been reported in the media, and he knew how thoroughly subjects had been researched. In other words, he didn't believe what he had read.

"Frank? Can you come here?"

Hall glanced her way, crushed out the cigarette, and walked over. "What?"

"Want to see this piece? I cut in the stuff from this afternoon."

Hall pulled a chair around and dropped into it. He sat with his chin in his right hand and his coffee in his left. He stared at the tiny color monitor that was only about two feet from his nose. "Let's go."

Davies leaned forward and touched a button. On the small monitor, the story began with Sarah Bakker sitting in her small office, looking up at a camera, with a chart of the galaxy behind her. She said, "I believe that the signal is just one more example of a galaxy teeming with intelligent life. I believe this signal will end the discussion of other intelligent life in the universe, and we can begin the task of attempting to document it and making contact with it."

The scene cut to Davies, standing with the physics and astronomy building as a backdrop. The students could be seen hurrying to and from classes. Davies said, "Science now suggests that they have found signs of intelligent life. Sarah Bakker believes she has the first message from that intelligent life, but she also says that it will be years, maybe decades for a message from us to reach that far-distant planet and be answered."

Davies looked at the camera seriously, hesitated for that dramatic pause, and added, "But there are those who claim that they have already communicated with alien life-forms. It didn't take years, but only minutes."

Now the story slipped back to Susan Bachmann, sitting in her living room. It was a small room, cluttered with pictures, small statues, vases, a bookcase, television, and DVD, filled with chairs and tables. Bachmann, surprisingly, was a small young woman, with long straight hair, an oval face, and damn near perfect teeth. She looked at the camera with as much sincerity as had Bakker, and told of the small alien creatures that invaded her bedroom on occasion. She told of them gathering genetic material from her, then returning her to her bed.

The cut away showed Davies sitting there, listening intently to Bachmann's words. She nodded and made a show of writing in her reporter's notebook.

They then cut to a collage of random shots of other galaxies, planets in the Solar System, and a close up of Mars. The voice-over was the same one she had used earlier. She said, "They say that there are millions of planets in our solar system and that the odds are that some of them would be suitable for human life. Your scientists have been searching for a sign of that life since the middle of the last century. Susan Buchmann says that they no longer need to look because she knows that such life exists. It has visited her."

Hall said nothing as he watched. When it ended, he turned to Davies, and asked, "Did this Bakker really say that they had an intelligent signal from the aliens?"

"You saw her say it."

"Yeah, but is that taken out of context here? I mean, it sounds as if she was corroborating this woman's story of alien abduction."

"It's not out of context though we really never got into her thoughts on abduction. I just asked her about the signal they had received."

Hall shrugged. "Well, it's not our job to teach people that there are other things going on in the world. I'll make the three minutes for you at six, but you'll have to cut it to a minute forty-five for eleven."

[4]

THE TABLE FOR EIGHT WAS PUSHED INTO A corner where the lights were dim and the noise reduced. Davies sat next to Hall and directly across from another reporter, Cindy Parcell. Next to her was the weather guy, William Self, and next to him was Tiffany Cortes. They had left the station fifteen minutes earlier, after the last of the news broadcasts, and had ordered a round of drinks, a platter of buffalo wings, and a bowl of popcorn. Davies and Parcell, who were weight-conscious, ignored the food while the men, and those not on camera, ate.

Self, a large man, meaning he was tall and big but not fat, held a beer in one hand and part of a wing in the other. He had changed from his on-camera wardrobe into his torn and faded jeans, T-shirt, and light jacket. He took a bite, chewed, and swallowed. He looked right at Davies, and said, "Do you believe that abduction crap?"

She smiled at him sweetly, and asked, "Do you believe you can predict the weather?"

"Seriously? With all the technology that modern science has brought to bear? I can, with great accuracy, tell you what the weather is doing now, and I can tell you, with a fair degree of accuracy, what it will be doing an hour from now, but that's really about it. And you didn't answer my question."

Davies sipped her martini, set the glass on the table, and said, "I do believe her, especially after what I learned from Sarah Bakker. There is life out there."

"Yes," said Hall, "but we don't know that it can get here from there."

"Bachmann seems to believe it can," said Davies. "She believes that it's already here."

"And do you believe that," asked Self.

"Complex question," said Davies. "I have no doubt that she is telling the truth as she perceives it, but I don't know if her truth is grounded in reality."

Hall raised his eyebrows in surprise, and said, "I'm surprised at that comment."

Davies grinned, and said, "I read a couple of things on the Internet before I went to interview her. I wanted to know what to look for, and I didn't want to insult her."

Hall shrugged and drank more of his beer.

"So, this Bakker confirmed what Bachman said?" asked Self.

"No, she just pointed out that they had what she thought was an artificial signal and that if true, that proved, *proved*, that there was intelligent life out there. She seemed to think that the evidence was good enough to draw that conclusion. It just seemed to me that if we knew there was other life, that other life might have figured out how to travel to Earth."

Hall took a drink of his beer and set the glass down on

the table. He reached over casually and dropped his hand to Davies' bare knee. Without looking at her, and giving no indication that he had his hand on her leg, he said, "I grow tired of all this esoteric talk. Let's move it down to Earth."

Davies glanced down and saw the fingers near the hem of her skirt. His fingers were warm. She thought about removing his hand, thought about standing up and demanding he apologize, but in the end, she just sat there knowing that he could be the key to moving on to bigger and better assignments. If he tried anything else, she could always stop him and file suit.

She said, "I think we all have to look at this carefully. I don't think the impact has set in."

Hall said, "People see these sorts of announcements all the time. They figure that tomorrow or next week, there'll be another announcement that takes it all back."

Self ate another wing, tossed the bone on an empty plate, and said, "They just never listen. They think they have all the answers, but they don't."

"So why do we do it?" asked Davies, aware that the fingers had not moved and that Hall had not looked at her.

"Because we get to be on TV, and people will buy us drinks and food."

Hall squeezed her leg, removed his hand, and turned to look at her. He said, "And we get some recognition." He smiled.

Davies, aware of exactly what she was doing, smiled back.

CHAPTER 2

[1]

CAPTAIN THOMAS HACKETT WAS DISAP-
pointed in the Army. He had joined thinking of a great adventure and how he would be trained in combat arms, but
he had made a mistake. Hackett had gotten a degree in
electrical engineering, done graduate work with computers, but had also taken astronomy and physics courses.
When he showed up at the local recruiters with his somewhat thin résumé in hand, the Army was only too happy to
see him, but not for training in the Special Forces or as a
Ranger, but as an engineering officer who worked with
computers. He became, for the lack of a better term, the
resident computer nerd.

Which is not to say that Hackett wasn't an athlete or
couldn't play baseball because he was and he could. He
had played in Little League and he had played high school
ball and had even been recruited by a couple of universi-

ties for the possibility of a baseball scholarship. But the universities that called didn't have strong engineering schools, and he knew the academic load he wanted to take would preclude the practice that was necessary to make a university team. He would soon either flunk out or find himself off the team. He needed to make a decision, and he decided that he would study rather than play.

His personal library, which held the proper engineering books and a couple of the journals to which he subscribed, also held hundreds of science-fiction books, a few true crime, and even some about unidentified flying objects. He told friends and colleagues that he didn't believe UFOs were flying through the atmosphere, but he found the case studies interesting, and, besides, it wasn't all that far removed from science fiction. They didn't believe him.

Hackett was sitting in his office, which was little more than a large closet that had an oversize but battle-scarred desk, a file cabinet with a broken lock, a chair for visitors, a computer with the monitor hung on the wall, and a poster advertising the Army as a great adventure. He was wearing the battle dress utilities in a desert camouflage pattern and sand-colored boots. He hoped to get to the shooting range to qualify with the pistol later in the day, but he wasn't sure that was going to happen until sometime in the next week or so.

He was reading a paper that had been posted to the Internet, not because he needed to read it for professional enhancement but because he found it somewhat interesting. It had nothing to do with electrical engineering, any sort of engineering, and wasn't even a scientific paper. It was about a woman who had said alien creatures had taken her from her bedroom late in the night, dragged her to their waiting ship, and conducted experiments on her body.

His boss tapped on the doorframe and stuck his head in. Lieutenant Colonel Robert Ford was getting close to forty and nearing the end of his military career if he didn't get the magic promotion to colonel. He was a short, stocky man with a fringe of graying hair that was cut so short it was almost a shadow on his shiny, sweat-damp skull. He had hawklike features and, like so many in the military these days, had never heard a shot fired in anger. He had managed to avoid the various conflicts because of the lack of a combat branch assignment.

Ford asked, "You got a minute?"

Hackett cleared the monitor so that Ford wouldn't see the article on alien abduction, and said, "Just catching up on some reading. Nothing that can't wait."

Ford entered the office and dropped into the chair. He glanced out the window, then back at Hackett. "Got kind of a strange call a few minutes ago."

Hackett realized that Ford was waiting for some kind of response, and asked, "What kind of call?"

"You familiar with SETI?"

Hackett shrugged. "Sure. Has to do with a search for an extraterrestrial intelligence. Life on other worlds broadcasting radio signals, or maybe I should say electromagnetic radiation into space and our attempts to find any of those signals."

Now Ford grinned. "I knew you were the right guy. Well, some general heard a news report that some scientist, a woman I think, though that's not really relevant, has found a signal."

"Some general? Some woman?"

"Who has found a signal."

"A signal," said Hackett. "That happens all the time."

Ford looked surprised. "It does?"

"Sure. That's how they found the pulsars. Thought at first it was an intelligent signal, but that was only one of the possibilities. I guess it still is, though the more likely explanation, and the one accepted by science, is that these are collapsed, dense stars spinning at an almost unbelievable speed. Radio sources, natural radio sources, are all over the sky, so they're always finding something."

"According to the general, and according to the story, they think this might be a signal from another star. That this might be the intelligent signal. I guess they're working on the verification."

Hackett rocked back in his chair and wanted to put his feet up, on his desk, but with the colonel in the office, he couldn't do that. He said, "I'm a little surprised that they let the information out. They usually sit on this stuff for a while."

"Why?"

"Well, for one thing, there have been leaks about an intelligent signal a number of times, so when the natural solution appears, someone always ends up with egg on his, or her, face. Then, if it is a scientific discovery, meaning a new natural phenomenon of some kind, the discovery goes to those who made it, but a premature announcement can blur the lines of the credit for the discovery. So they usually gather data quietly. Then they publish in one of the recognized science journals and get credit for the discovery."

"Sounds cumbersome."

Hackett laughed. "You can sit here, having spent so much time in the Army, dealing with the bureaucracy and the chain of command, and talk about cumbersome systems."

"Yeah, well," said Ford. "The general, our general, not the one who started this whole thing by calling us, thought that maybe someone should take a look at this and see if there is anything to it."

Hackett raised an eyebrow in an unconscious gesture, and said, "This fits into our mission how?"

"I could sit here and point out that our mission is anything that the general decides that it is, but I think he was thinking of the impact such an announcement might have on the public at large. Alien creatures out there with ray guns and looking for worlds to conquer. I think he wanted to have a few answers in case someone asked him a question, and he decided that I was the one to find the answers for him. Being the good staff officer that I am, I am now delegating the task to you."

"So where do I go and who do I talk to?"

Ford reached up, into his pocket, and pulled out a piece of paper. He tossed it on Hackett's desk. "Her name is Bakker. She's the scientist who found the signal. Get what you can, give me a report on it without going into too much detail, and nothing over ten pages. I'll boil it down to a page or two and pass it along to the general."

"Wouldn't it be better for me to boil it down and give it to the general?"

Ford shook his head. "No, what's going to happen is that the general will have questions, and I want to have answers. And yes, it will be clear that you did the research and that you provided the data. I give the general what he wants and I get some credit and you get some credit and everybody can go away happy and drink a beer."

As Ford got to his feet, Hackett asked, "When do you need this material?"

"The sooner, the better."

[2]

HACKETT, NOT WANTING TO EXPLAIN TO A half dozen different people who he was and why he was in uniform on the campus, changed clothes before he drove to the university. He walked across the campus, ignoring the students, who now looked so young though he wasn't that much older than most of them. He entered the physics building, took the elevator up after he had read the directory, and found the office of the secretary of the department. She directed Hackett to Bakker's office, and he walked down the hall, glancing right and left. Most of the offices were empty, looking as if they had been abandoned. They were cluttered, filled with books, notes, disks, and in some cases old clothes, but no people.

He found Bakker sitting with her feet up on her desk, a can of Coke in one hand and a pen in the other. She didn't look anything like he thought she would. She was young, dressed more like an undergraduate in cutoff blue jeans and a T-shirt that was cropped short. He could tell that she spent time in the gym. He tried not to stare.

Her attention was focused on a computer screen, and Hackett could see the numbers scrolling across it in a bewildering parade that looked as if it was moving too fast for anyone to comprehend what she was seeing. He wasn't sure if he should interrupt her.

Bakker took the initiative away from him. She looked right at him, grinned broadly, and asked, "You need something?"

"I don't want to take you away from your work."

"Please. Take me away from it. I beg you, stranger, take me away from it."

Hackett stepped inside the office, looked for a place to sit, then leaned back, one shoulder against the cinder-block wall. He said, "I have some questions about the signal."

Bakker laughed. "So it was a joke. You aren't going to take me away from all these numbers but rather question me about my signal."

"I'm confused," said Hackett.

Bakker put down the Coke and pulled a stack of books, disks, and printouts off the other chair. "Please, have a seat. As you can imagine, I have been fielding telephone calls most of the day. I should be angry with that reporter. In fact I was. She certainly screwed this up, making it look as if I was endorsing that tale of alien abduction, but I think it might have helped us."

Hackett just shook his head, "I'm afraid that I don't understand."

"Yesterday there was a reporter here. She asked some questions about the signal, and I answered them. Then she ran off, twisted most of what I said, and created this idea that I was endorsing this story of alien abduction. Reporters, researchers, students, and half the faculty have called me today, so I'm not surprised to see someone else show up here."

"But you have no idea what I want."

"Okay. Okay," said Bakker, nodding her agreement. "I'll stop talking for a while. I'll just sit here quietly and let you tell me what you want."

Hackett sat for a moment, looking out the window, wondering what he had walked into. He had expected

Bakker to be something of a flake, but only because he expected most academics to be flakes, but she seemed to be out by herself, circling the field. She was flakier than a bowl of Kellogg's.

Finally, feeling that he was going to disappoint her, he said, "The signal? How accurate is your information?"

"Oh, we have a signal," said Bakker. "There's no doubt about it. It's been confirmed by other observatories. We have a radio source, and we believe that it is outside of the Solar System, but it seems to be in space, away from a star system, and that has us a little surprised."

"I don't understand," said Hackett.

"Okay. You know what the Solar System is . . ."

"I'm not an idiot," said Hackett sharply.

"Of course not. Sorry. It's been crazy around here, and you'd be surprised how many of these people don't even know the difference between a solar system and a galaxy. Anyway, we expect any radio signal to be associated with a star system of some kind. There are natural radio sources all over the sky, including one in the Crab Nebula, which used to be a star. Well, anyway, we have one that seems to be in the middle of space, away from stars and other such natural radio sources. It's moving rapidly across the sky and that makes some people think that it is really in the Solar System. But, I tell you, we've checked everything there is out there, including that probe the old NASA launched in the mid–twentieth century. This radio source is not ours, and it's acting as if it is artificial."

"Meaning," said Hackett, "that we have found another intelligent race." He said it as if it was the most natural thing in the world. He seemed unaffected by the sudden knowledge.

Bakker picked up her Coke can, shook it, then took a drink. "That would be one interpretation. However, that isn't the only one, and we have found nothing in the signal, as yet, to indicate that it is some kind of message. All we have is a new radio source that is acting differently than any other radio source we have ever located. Since it is new, we have to proceed with caution."

Bakker stopped and looked carefully at Hackett. "Just who are you anyway?"

"My name's Hackett. I'm with the Army. Aren't you being a little loose with the information?"

"The Army? The real Army? The actual Army?"

"Yes."

Now she looked at him suspiciously. "The Army has an interest in this?"

Hackett shrugged. "I don't know. I'm just here to gather a little more information."

"Well, it was on the news last night, and we have contacted others to verify our data. I don't know what more I can tell you about it."

"So," said Hackett, "if I understand you, there is a signal, might be intelligent, might be natural and it is outside the Solar System. How far away is it?"

"Tough question, given that we haven't had all that long for observation, but if I was forced into an answer, I would say between fifty and a hundred light-years."

For some reason Hackett relaxed. Something that far away was no threat to the United States or to Earth. At the speed of light, it wouldn't be able to get to Earth for fifty or a hundred years, or more, if it was coming at the Earth.

Thinking in a military sense, however, Hackett said, "Then it is no threat to us."

"Why would you even think such a thing?" asked Bakker.

"Because it's my job."

[3]

HACKETT RETURNED TO HIS OFFICE TO PUT together a report for his boss. There wasn't much to it. This radio source wasn't close to the Earth and wouldn't be for a half century or more. It, therefore, wasn't a threat. Even if it was a threat, the Army could do nothing about it for another forty years or more. Probably much more. Sort of like a geologist worrying about the big earthquake in California. Everyone knew it was coming, sometime in the future, but no one knew when it would happen, and they couldn't do anything about it anyway. There was no reason to worry about something that was, more or less, a theoretical construct. Theoretical constructs didn't knock down buildings or invade Earth.

While Hackett was trying to organize his thoughts, Ford stuck his head in the door, and asked, "Have you looked into this alien message thing?"

"Yep. I was just writing up the report. Trying to figure out how to say it in fifty words or less."

"Don't write anything then. Just tell me."

"If there is something out there, and even if it is hostile, it couldn't possibly be here for another fifty years. Or more. It's that far away."

Ford laughed. "I should be retired by then, and it will be someone else's problem."

"You and your kids can have retired."

"This is really no problem?"

"Colonel, I don't know what you expected, but this is all very preliminary. They're excited at the university because they have discovered something new, and they don't care if it is artificial or natural. They still have a discovery. At the moment, they just don't know exactly what they have."

Ford nodded, and said, "Well then, I guess we've done our job for the moment."

"Yes, sir," said Hackett because he couldn't think of anything else to say.

Ford said, "Well, thanks. I'll brief the general."

Hackett watched Ford retreat and leaned back. He closed his eyes and replayed the discussion with Bakker. In his mind, he could see her sitting there, relaxed, smiling, as she talked about astronomy and ancient radio signals from deep space. She had a passion that was charming. She loved her work and didn't mind talking about it, though she was annoyed when people misunderstood the simplest of concepts. Hackett had found himself prolonging the conversation just to stay in the room with her. He hadn't felt that way in a long time, and he was now afraid that he wouldn't have a chance to see her again.

[4]

HACKETT TOLD HIMSELF THAT THE UNIVERSITY was basically on the way home. It was, in fact, in the general direction, but there were shorter routes and quicker routes. He had, in the past, driven the long way around so that he could listen to music and watch the scenery. Sometimes he was just interested in the ride before he walked into his empty apartment.

There was no reason to park, but Hackett did it anyway, getting out to walk along the perimeter of the campus, watching the students as they hurried to their early-evening classes. He could never understand those who scheduled classes in the evening, but then, he had been a full-time student and hadn't had to work very hard to pay his bills.

He found himself near the physics building and told himself that he wouldn't go inside. If she walked out and he ran into her, that was one thing. Going up to her office was something else. He didn't want her to think he was stalking her, though he wasn't sure that he could stalk someone if he had only met them once and that had been earlier in the day.

He walked around the building slowly. It stood next to a large, redbrick building that had to be a hundred years old. The contrast between the modern physics building and the older one was interesting. Large trees, some of which had to be as old as the building, shaded that part of the campus, giving it a green and inviting look.

The students hurried along the sidewalks, some of them

cutting across the lawns. A few stood outside the doors, smoking. There were very few smokers, and most of them didn't use tobacco. They smoked an artificial blend of harmless shredded plants, and Hackett couldn't understand it. If there was no chemical benefit from smoking, if smoking didn't alter the brain chemistry, what was the point? Why puff on burning weeds? He didn't realize that "weed" had once had a different meaning.

He stopped at the base of a large tree and looked at his watch. He decided that he would spend another ten minutes, then walk back to the car. Maybe the best thing was just to call the next day. Maybe that would be less intrusive than just showing up at her workplace.

From behind a voice said, "Do I know you?"

Hackett turned and saw Bakker. "We met this afternoon."

"Of course. Was there something else that you needed?"

Hackett rubbed at the back of his left hand. He looked down, then up, and said, "Well, there were some additional questions, and I was on my way home . . ."

She laughed, and said, "You want to do this in my office or would you like to get something to drink?"

"If I have a vote, then I'll take the drink."

Bakker smiled, and said, "If I had known you were coming, I would have dressed a little nicer."

"I think you look fine," said Hackett.

"Well, cutoffs are appropriate in some of the bars, especially those where the undergraduates hang out, but those tend to be loud."

They began to walk away from the physics building, toward a group of stores, restaurants, and bars on the other side of the parking lot. They stopped for traffic, then ran across the street.

Looking around, Hackett could see that he was overdressed for the place. Bakker fit right in with the crowd, looking as if she was still chasing an undergraduate degree. She grabbed his hand, pulled him through a door. She shouldered her way through the crowd, toward another door, then through it. The lighting was subdued, but the sounds of the music were reduced and the noise was more of a quiet buzz than the roar it had been in the first room.

She found a table and sat down. As Hackett sat, she leaned forward, elbows on the table, and said, "A little older crowd in here, and the faculty has sort of staked out this room. The undergrads are afraid to come in. Might see a professor drinking, perish the thought."

"Well, at least I can hear you," said Hackett, suddenly feeling like a tongue-tied teenager.

Bakker sat up straighter, looked around, as if searching for someone or something, then slumped again. "I think we're going to have to serve ourselves. I think I'd like a beer, unless you have something harder in mind."

Hackett tried to smile. "I'm in the Army. We drink beer, sometimes, even if it is warm as soup and as tasty as dirty water."

"Lovely image."

"Well, in the field it's sometimes difficult to get what you need. Should I get a pitcher or just a couple of glasses?"

"Pitcher."

Hackett stood up and walked through the doors into the outer room, where the bar ran its length. He pushed his way through the three-deep crowd of undergraduate drinkers and leaned against the smooth dark wood, worn thin by generations of college students. When he caught the attention of the bartender, he ordered the pitcher, got the two glasses, paid, and, holding both the pitcher and the glasses high, retreated.

When he sat down, Bakker said , "I was about to send reinforcements."

Hackett carefully poured beer into the glasses and set one in front of Bakker. "I think I could have used the rein-forcements." He held up his glass, and said, "Cheers."

Bakker took a deep drink, wiped the foam from her upper lip with the back of her hand, and looked directly at Hackett. "Okay. What are you doing here, really?"

"I'm afraid that I don't understand the question."

"Simple enough. I'm not buying this I stopped off on the way home crap. What are you doing here?"

Hackett rubbed the side of his face, afraid to give the real reason. Instead he said, "We're just a little concerned about this signal." Even to him it sounded lame. There was nothing new that she could tell him. All the information had been laid out for him. There was nothing new to learn.

"There a military project involved in this somewhere?" she asked. "I tap into some kind of supersecret communications deal. I think that happened with that extremely low frequency net the Navy erected."

Hackett had to grin. It was the perfect excuse for him. He wasn't there to see her. He was chasing a secret and didn't want her to find out. He shrugged mysteriously, and said, "I just thought I'd get a beer."

She leaned forward, closer, and lowered her voice. "If I buy the beer and get you drunk, will you tell me all that you know about this?"

Hackett laughed. "Of course. But you have to throw in a dinner, or, at least something to eat."

"I'll buy you a hamburger in a basket, complete with fries, if you'll spill your guts."

"Okay. You've got a deal."

CHAPTER 3

[1]

JASON PARKER HAD BEEN A STATE SENATOR for nearly ten years and had tired of the political turmoil in the statehouse. He relished exchanging it for the turmoil of the United States Senate, which certainly had more prestige and a higher paycheck. United States senators were treated with respect while state senators were seen as flunkies who couldn't make it in the big time.

He held in his hand the morning edition of the newspaper. To his right was a cup of coffee and to his left an ashtray with a cigarette burning. He was trying to quit and often lit the cigarettes, left them burning after one or two drags, and felt better. He thought that he was cutting down, but in reality, he was just spending more money on cigarettes because he needed to keep the nicotine levels up and was burning them without smoking them.

Parker was a fairly young man, with light brown hair

cut very short. He had sharp features except for his nose, which looked out of place. The rounded tip called attention to it, and Parker often found people he engaged in conversation looking at his nose rather than at his eyes.

The story that caught his attention was in the back of the newspaper, where they normally hid articles that dealt with science. It said that there might have been a signal, an intelligent signal, from another world. Parker wasn't sure why it intrigued him, and at the moment he couldn't think of a way to exploit the story for his political gain. It was just something that caught his attention as he read the paper.

There had been something on the news the night before, or the week before, something he hadn't listened to carefully, that mentioned the same sort of thing. Intelligent signals and something about alien creatures. He supposed, if he was interested, he could call the television station, but at the moment he had other things to do.

Parker reached over and touched the button on his intercom. "Susan, can you come in here?"

His administrative assistant, a pretty young woman who refused to have any sort of personal relationship with Parker but did her job exceptionally well, appeared at the door. She stood there, looking across the expanse of carpet.

"Yes, sir."

Parker held up the newspaper, and said, "See what you can find out about this."

She walked across the room, took the newspaper, and asked, "About what?"

"This signal or whatever. I want to know something more about it."

"Yes, sir."

[2]

SUSAN CAIRNES SAT DOWN BEHIND HER DESK and leaned back. She brushed blond hair out of her eyes and set the newspaper on the desk. The story was from the press wire, which meant there was no local contact, and she didn't want to begin searching the various wire bureaus for the writer. Instead, she pulled her telephone directory out, looked up the university listings, then ran down them until she found astronomy and the name of someone she actually knew who worked in the department.

She dialed the number, and, when the phone was answered, said, "Steven Weiss, please."

A moment later a voice said, "Weiss."

"This is Susan Cairnes, Senator Parker's office."

There was a hesitation, then Weiss said, "I know you, don't I?"

"I met you at your father's house a couple of times," she said, "with the senator."

"Yeah. Blond woman with a nice . . . what is it that I can do for you?"

Cairnes shook her head and grinned slightly. Someone must have been teaching him some tact. A year earlier he would have finished the comment.

"I want to know about this signal."

"Well, you came to the right place. Sarah Bakker first detected it, and she was the one who suggested it might be intelligent. I don't agree, but I seem to be in the minority around here."

"Why don't you agree?"

"For one thing, it's moving across the sky a little too fast. To me, that suggests that it's from somewhere in the Solar System rather than from outside."

"I'm afraid that I don't know what that means."

Weiss's voice changed so that it sounded as if he was lecturing a group of students. "If we detected an intelligent signal from a star system, the source would stay, relatively speaking, in the same location in the sky. Yes, as the star moved, the signal would move, but we'd be able to relate it to a part of the sky, and the motion would be the result of Earth's movement rather than the signal's movement."

"Okay."

"If it was on a planet revolving around the star, we'd be able to detect some movement, but again, it would stay in basically the same position, and the motion would be a result of the planetary movement."

Cairnes wasn't sure that she completely understood it, but she believed that Weiss did. She said, again, "Okay."

"Now this signal is moving in the sky much too fast to be either from a star or a planet circling the star. That would suggest to me that the source is inside the Solar System, and that means the signal, if artificial, is probably from a known source, meaning it's really one of ours, and all this attention isn't appropriate."

"Could it be that it's artificial but not ours and be inside our system?"

"Well, certainly, but I think we would have detected it long before now, so I don't think there is much chance of that. Anyway, the debate at the moment is the location of the signal, why it is moving as fast as it is, and can we identify the source."

"Has this ever happened before?"

"Lots of times, and when we track down these signals, we find they belong to us, having been reflected off a planet in the Solar System some way or from one of our own satellites or space probes. One of them reactivated a couple of years ago and got everyone excited until we identified it."

Cairnes had the information she needed and was about to hang up when she thought of another question. "You said you were in the minority."

"Yeah. Bakker and some of the others around here think the signal, though moving rapidly, is outside the Solar System, which means they think it's some kind of alien ship." He laughed. "You should have seen the story on TV about that. The reporter practically had the aliens invading and had Bakker corroborating the idea. Damn. She was mad."

Cairnes now remembered hearing something about that, but had paid no real attention to it. That she could check.

To Weiss, she said, "So some think it is an intelligent signal, might be on a ship of some kind. How far away?"

"Don't know yet. Could be light-years. We don't have quite enough information to make an educated guess. But that's only if it is on a ship and it is artificial and it is outside our solar system. As I said, I think the source is near us and that it's one of ours."

"Yes, you said that. Anything else?"

"Well, if I remember you correctly," said Weiss, "I'd be happy to buy you a drink and maybe some dinner tonight. Bring you up to date on this whole mess."

Cairnes shook her head instinctively, and said, "Sorry. No. I have to work. Thank you." She hung up before Weiss could ask for another night or suggest something else. A young man with money and no real responsibilities often thought that he could be rude, could be crude, and the women would line up anyway. He wouldn't take no for an answer.

She got up and walked back to Parker's office. He was sitting, reading a report, a cup of coffee in one hand. When he looked up, she said, "Got the preliminary information. Some of those at the university think the signal is intelligent, and some think it is on a ship . . ."

"Ship? What the hell kind of ship?"

"Alien spacecraft, I guess. Something about its motion in the sky. Anyway, the guy I talked to thought it might be a little early to be talking about alien ships and intelligent signals. He thought it was from inside the Solar System and belonged to us. He thinks they just misidentified one of our own sources. He said that it happens all the time, but they don't usually announce it."

Parker put his coffee down, took a deep breath, and said slowly, "Okay. I guess we should stay on top of it. Let me know what happens with this."

"You interested in it?" She sounded surprised.

Parker nodded. "Something stirring around in the back of my mind, but I don't have a good idea about it yet. I need to let it vegetate for a while."

"Okay," she said. "When I hear something, I'll let you know. Oh, I guess the local news did something with it sometime in the last week or so."

"Get me a copy of the news report, please."

"Yes, sir."

[3]

HAVING ASSEMBLED ALL THE RELEVANT MATE-rial, having watched the disk of the TV report and read the story that appeared in the newspaper again, Parker grinned broadly. This was a discovery he could get some mileage from. If it turned out to be some kind of esoteric radio noise, then he could talk of vast expenditures of cash, re-alizing, of course, that the shoestring budget given to SETI meant nothing here. They didn't even have the tips of the shoestring. The money was negligible, but the taxpayer would see it as just another colossal waste of his hard-earned cash. Parker could exploit it to get the "face" time he needed.

If, on the other hand, these scientists had found some-thing, then a real threat to the human way of life existed. He nodded to himself. That really was the better scenario. Aliens in space, about to invade, and the Earth ill prepared and virtually undefended. That was a story. That was a real story, though Parker wasn't yet sure how to exploit it.

Or, rather, he wasn't sure until he saw Davies talking to the woman who said that the aliens had already started the invasion. They were here. Parker scratched the back of his neck and wondered if the tie-in would work for him.

Flying saucers and alien invaders were the stuff of sci-ence fiction, but then, in a real world of settlements on the moon, a colony on Mars, and mining in the asteroid belt, people might be ready for a discussion of alien invasion. The science fiction of the mid–twentieth century was the science fact of today. He saw the evidence of it every-where.

He touched the button on the intercom. "Susan, didn't we get, or haven't we gotten, a couple of letters from some guy who says he investigates these alien sightings?"

"I think so."

"Yeah, well could you find those letters and let me take a look at them?"

"Are you serious?"

"Yeah. I want to see if there is anything to this story that's on this disk."

"All right, but it'll take me a few minutes to find the right file."

Parker said, "No rush."

He stood up and walked to the window and looked out. He watched a squirrel run across the lawn and leap onto a tree, seeming to run up the trunk.

He rubbed his chin and thought. This was going to have to be handled carefully, or he would be branded a nut. He'd have to marshal his facts carefully, but if he handled it just right, he would be on TV, not branded as a nut, but as the savior of the human race, alerted to the danger when others just stood around with their thumbs up their butts grinning.

Susan tapped on the door, walked in, and set a file in the center of the desk. She said, "This is all I could find."

Parker turned, sat down, and said, "Thank you."

Parker opened the file and found two letters written by Jonathan Travis. They were both typed on good quality paper and didn't seem to have come from a nutcase. Parker read them carefully, studying the syntax, grammar, and the structure rather than looking at the content. Nothing in the letters seemed to be out of touch with reality. They both asked basic questions and suggested that an impartial investigation into UFOs might provide some scientific insight. Travis even suggested that if the extraterrestrial was not proved, the result of such an investigation might be a better understanding of the natural world around them.

Finished, Parker touched the intercom again. "Susan, do we have anything else on this Travis?"

"You have everything that I can find."

"Okay. Get a telephone number and get him on the line."

"Are you serious?"

"That's the second time you have asked me that in the last hour. It had better be the last."

"Yes, sir."

"I want to talk to this guy, but I want to keep this low-key. Just ask him to hold on and give my name, but don't tell him what I do."

"Yes, sir."

[4]

JONATHAN TRAVIS WAS SITTING IN FRONT OF the computer, his eyes on the screen, where, had he been able to think of anything, he would have written it. The cursor blinked, reminding him that he was behind schedule on his book, but there was just nothing new that he wanted to say. He wished that he hadn't taken the assignment, but the money had been good. He had thought it would take most of a month to complete the book, but at the moment he saw no way ever to finish it, even if he took the rest of the year to write.

Travis was a fairly young man who had prematurely graying hair, a slight limp that he sometimes suggested was the result of war injuries but was, in reality, the result of a late slide into third base in a pickup softball game. The twisted knee, though not severe, ended his softball career, such as it had been. Without the practices and the games, Travis was about ten pounds overweight, but it wasn't noticeable.

He was a tall man, with no bulging muscles. His strength, which surprised many, was more accurately the result of being "wiry." He was a nice-looking fellow with even features, but had small eyes that were more actually gray, though he insisted they were blue.

When the telephone rang, he was delighted because it took him away from the computer. He had learned that sometimes the only way to make progress on a stubborn book was a distraction. Leaving the story, leaving the article, and coming back later provided a fresh analysis that allowed him to break through. Sometimes it was so obvious that he wondered why he hadn't seen it earlier, without all the attending anxiety.

He put on his headset, which kept his hands free, punched the button at the top of the telephone, and said, "Yes?"

"Jason Parker for Jonathan Travis. Will you hold?"

Travis was tempted to hang up. He didn't like holding and didn't care for people who thought they were so important they couldn't place their own telephone calls. Had the writing been going well, he would have hung up. Instead, he said, "Yes."

A moment later the line clicked, and a voice said, "Mr. Travis, Jason Parker here."

"Yes."

There was a hesitation. Travis knew that Parker, whoever he was, now had to figure out what to say. He hoped that he had thrown him off-balance as repayment for making him hold, even for the ten seconds it had taken to transfer the call.

"You investigate UFOs?"

"I have."

"Yes, well, I have some questions, if you have a few minutes available."

Travis looked at the blank screen with its irritating, blinking cursor, and thought that he had a few hours, maybe a couple of days or weeks available. Instead, he said, "I have some time now."

"Well, good. Let me ask you a rather basic and maybe insulting question, but I need to get a serious answer."

"I'm always serious," said Travis.

"Yes. Are we being visited?"

"Simple, easy answer is, yes. I believe that the

evidence, when objectively examined, leads to that conclusion. The problem is that we have never had a real, ob-
jective investigation. All those mounted, whether by the
government, the military, or the civilian organizations have
always had a built-in bias and a desire to find a specific answer. Not surprisingly, they have all found the answer for
which they searched, which is not to say they found the
truth."

"Then you believe?"

"I'm uncomfortable with that term. The evidence leads
to a specific conclusion, and I accept that conclusion, and
will continue to accept it until I find additional evidence
that leads in a different direction."

"Okay," said Parker.

"Is that all?"

"No. I was just thinking. Let me ask you this. Do you
believe in alien abduction?"

"There is that word again. 'Believe.' My research indi-
cates that people reporting their abductions are sincere,
honest people who believe they have been abducted.
There are some problems with these reports, such as a
lack of credible physical evidence and little in the way of
corroborative testimony, but there is some substance to
the reports."

"What about SETI?"

"You are all over the map, aren't you?"

"I'm just trying to get a reading on this thing."

"Why?"

Now Parker hesitated. Finally, he said, "I'm just trying
to sort some things out in my own mind."

To Travis, that was fair enough. Someone with a strange
experience, trying to figure it out, might ask all sorts of
questions to make sure that he or she wouldn't be ridiculed.
Travis thought Parker might believe he had been abducted
and wanted to understand a little more before he told anyone about it or attempted to investigate it further.

"You asked about SETI. I think that it is a fine idea,
though I'm concerned because we are assuming that any

advanced civilization would be using radio, or rather electromagnetic radiation to communicate. That might not be the case and if that is true, then we're looking in the wrong place."

"SETI is wasted?"

"Oh, no. Anything that suggests there are others out there and has a real chance of providing that evidence is a good idea. Once one of those civilizations has been found, proving that other intelligent life inhabits the galaxy, then the idea of alien visitation becomes more palatable to the public. My job gets that much easier."

"Just what is your job?"

"I think of myself as a reporter," said Travis. "I follow the same dictates of my colleagues in the media, though I am sure they will all be angered that I have equated my reporting on UFOs, alien creatures, and space travel with the hard-hitting news they report."

"Maybe we should get together to talk," said Parker.

"For what purpose?"

"Well, I have an interest in this, and I have the ability to help take these investigations to the next level. To move it toward the respectable."

Travis laughed. "Haven't heard that one in a while."

"What do you mean?"

"Almost since the beginning of the modern era of UFO reporting, there have been those who were going to make UFO research respectable. They were going to accredit UFO researchers. They were going to establish a baseline for us all, and so far, we haven't made it. Too many out there without any training, any discipline, willing to accept every weird tale as the truth and screaming conspiracy at every turn."

"Maybe there is something that I can do."

"I try never to refuse help," said Travis.

"Good. If you don't mind, I'll have my secretary set up the appointment for the next day or two."

"Sure," said Travis. "Why not?" He couldn't help feeling that he had just made a mistake.

CHAPTER 4

[1]

SARAH BAKKER SAT AT THE HEAD TABLE AND wondered why the hell she had agreed to appear at the press conference. She had originally believed that the conference would help promote the work of astronomers, give the university some much-needed publicity, and show the world that American science was still far out in front of everyone else's.

She had arrived thirty minutes early, dressed not like she normally did but in her image of a modern, sophisticated scientist in a charcoal business suit with a knee-length skirt and a thigh-length jacket known as an abbreviated duster over a cream-colored blouse. She looked not like a scientist but like the public relations women who were hovering around, trying to get everything in place before the first of the reporters arrived. They had told her that the press would either be on time or a little late and that they wouldn't wait for those who couldn't get there on time. If the show was not on the road at the exact minute it was supposed to begin, the reporters already there would desert them.

A few of the crew arrived early to set up cameras or stake out the best place for the on-air "talent" to sit or stand. They strung cables, set up lights, and arranged the microphones carefully. In the old days the place would have looked like an electronics store had exploded. Now, the mics were small, almost invisible, the lights were just globes on poles with tiny reflectors, and the cables held a bundle of fiber optics rather than the bulky copper wire. They looked almost delicate.

Bakker, of course, sat watching quietly until the man who had called the press conference, State Senator Jason Parker, walked through the side door. He wore a suit but no tie. He moved toward Bakker, held out a hand, and said, "I'm Jason Parker. You must be Dr. Bakker."

"Yes."

"First, I want to thank you for participating in this press conference. We'll get started in a few minutes. I'll make a short announcement, then we'll take some questions. The others should be here in a few moments."

"Others?"

Parker grinned, showing his perfect teeth. "Yes. I have invited a few others, who bring another perspective to our announcement."

"But I thought you wanted to talk about the radio source and its implications."

"Of course. But that is all part of the package. Just relax. When we're through here, I'll bet that you can write your own ticket. The university will be falling all over itself to throw money at you for your research. Other universities will be bidding for your talent. And the government will be trucking the money in for you."

Bakker felt chills. Sweat popped out on her forehead; she was suddenly scared and slightly sick to her stomach. This wasn't going to be the closed, subdued event that she had envisioned but something a little bigger and certainly wilder. She wasn't sure that the university would be pleased.

Parker heard something and turned. He straightened and took a couple of steps forward. He held out his hand, and said, "Mr. Travis. How nice of you to come."

Bakker stood up and thought about retreating. There was a door to the right, and she was sure that it led out, into a hallway, then out, into the parking lot. She could escape before Parker dragged her into something she would later regret.

She heard her name called and turned. Rachel Davies stood on the other side of the table, a notebook in her hand, a small recorder piled on top, and a can of 7UP held in her other hand. Davies smiled broadly, and said, "I didn't really expect to see you."

Bakker shrugged. "I'm thinking that maybe the better part of valor is to escape right now. I think I might have been misled here."

And then, suddenly, she knew she had been set up. Across the room, being greeted by Parker, was Steven Weiss. He wasn't needed to talk about the radio source because she could do that with more authority. He wasn't needed to fill in the gaps in radio astronomy because she knew more about it than he did. All she could think of was that he was there to cause some kind of problem.

"You okay?" asked Davies.

Bakker looked at her as if she had spoken a foreign language. She stepped back and dropped into a chair.

"Just what in the hell is going on?" she asked.

Parker escorted Weiss, who was dressed in his vision of a scientist, wearing faded blue jeans, an old sweater that needed mending, and a day's growth of beard. He sat down, at the far end of the table, but then leaned forward and waved.

Bakker waited until Parker had taken his position at the center of the table, behind the short podium that stood there, and walked over to him. She asked, "Can we talk for a moment."

Parker looked at his watch and said, "Sorry, Dr. Bakker, but it's time to begin."

Bakker nodded and returned to her seat. She considered, again, just leaving, but decided she didn't want to leave the university's representation to Weiss. There was no telling what he might say, or what he might do. He had very little to lose if he antagonized the faculty.

Parker stood behind the podium, waited until the noise level dropped, the lights were turned on, and everyone had found a seat. When he was satisfied, he said, "Ladies and gentlemen, I am State Senator Jason Parker and over the last couple of days I have heard news that I find disturbing. Yes, it's exciting news, but it is also disturbing news."

He stopped, paused dramatically, then said, "Maybe the first thing I should do here is introduce the people with me. I think you will find that this is an excellent team and that they are all well trained and have reached their conclusions independently, in a proper scientific manner using the rules of science.

"At the far end, to my left, is Dr. Sarah Bakker, who is responsible for the discovery of the signal and for the verification of it's artificiality."

Bakker sat stone-faced, refusing to smile or acknowledge the reporters.

"Next to her is Jonathan Travis, a researcher and investigator into the paranormal."

Startled, Bakker glanced to the man sitting next to her. He looked average, looked to be sane, but she didn't like the description of a paranormal investigator. Suddenly the university was being associated, through her, with the belief in ESP, ghosts, and fringe phenomena. The administration wasn't going to be happy about that.

"To my immediate right," continued Parker, "is my administrative assistant, Susan Cairnes, who has helped coordinate this activity today and has conducted some of the investigation. And finally, at the far end is Steven Weiss, an astronomer who will be able to answer some of the technical questions."

With introductions completed, Bakker understood what was going to happen next. Weiss, the loose cannon, could say wild things and be believed because he was introduced as an astronomer and because, she, Bakker, with her degrees and teaching job with the university, added credibility to him and his opinions. That was needed because he didn't have a doctorate and the public didn't understand that a great deal of research, and many of the important discoveries, were made by those considered graduate students.

Travis was there to inject a supernatural air, and therefore a mystery into the press conference. It was the hook for the reporters that would allow them to get their minute thirty that night. He would tie the discovery of the signal together with some sort of supernatural horror that would propel Parker into the limelight, which is all he wanted in the first place. He wouldn't care if the information was accurate or not.

Parker reached into his inside jacket pocket and produced a sheet of paper folded the long way. He flattened it against the podium, glanced up, and said, "I have a brief prepared statement, then I'll entertain questions."

He paused dramatically, cleared his throat, and looked into the cameras one after another. He said, "Science has been both a blessing and a curse for the residents of planet Earth. It has brought us the wonders of modern life filled with computers and instantaneous transmission of our messages and colonies on the moon and Mars. But it has also brought the horrors of toxic poisoning and biological warfare. We, as laymen, are often confused by the various announcements of science, misunderstanding them, misinterpreting them, and often frightened by them."

He raised his voice, not unlike a tent revivalist moving to the meat of the message. "Sometimes we just don't understand the warnings because they are lost in the language of science. Today we have just such an announcement.

One that could mean an inconceivable leap in progress for the human race, but one that could mean the end of life as we know it."

"Senator Parker," shouted one of the reporters, "Senator, what sort of danger do we face?"

Another asked, "How can you be sure?"

Since Parker had said nothing about a danger, he wasn't sure what the reporter wanted to know. He said, calmly, pointedly, "Please, everything will become clear in a few moments. Then I'll be happy to take your questions."

He returned to his prepared statement. "In the last month, scientists here, around the United States, and overseas have reported signals from outer space. Dr. Sarah Bakker"—Parker waved a hand in her direction—"was the first to detect the signal and recognize its significance for the human race. Research has suggested that the signal is of an artificial nature and that it is coming from a point in space that is, galactically speaking, very close to Earth. Research continues as scientists try to decode the message embedded in the signal."

That couldn't pass without comment. The reporters were shouting questions, and Bakker was shaking her head, knowing that Parker had distorted the information on purpose and for his own benefit. She could only sit and answer the questions, trying to undo the damage when she had the opportunity.

Parker pointed to one man, who held a tiny tape recorder in his hand and was leaning forward, as if in a high wind. He was shouting the same thing over and over, and as the others fell silent, he asked, "Are you saying that we have found other intelligent life?"

"Yes," said Parker without qualification.

"Verification," shouted someone from the back. "There has been verification?"

Weiss reached out, as if to touch someone on the shoulder, and said, "We have, in the last month, worked with various observatories around the world. All have received the signal, verifying its existence. Consensus is that it is artificial, based on those observations."

"Consensus?" said someone, as if that removed the evidence or changed the meaning of the announcement.

Weiss said, "Maybe I should clarify. Every station that has listened has heard the signal. The variations in intensity, and the replicating nature of the signal suggests to us that it is artificial in nature."

Bakker suddenly said, "I think we are getting ahead of ourselves here. The distance between us and the source . . ."

"Is impossibly small," said Parker.

"I don't appreciate being interrupted," said Bakker.

"Sorry, Doctor," said Parker, "but I don't want to minimize the danger to the planet."

"Danger to the planet?" said Bakker, genuinely surprised. "There is no danger."

Weiss, seen as the other academic said, "Sarah, we shouldn't gloss over the danger here."

He didn't wait for a response, but looked back at the cameras and reporters. "The source of the signal is not a planetary system, nor is it star-based."

"What in the hell does that mean?" asked someone.

"It comes from a ship."

[2]

THOMAS HACKETT WAS HAVING A GOOD DAY. The quarterly reports were finished and in a form that could be transmitted, the semiannual reports were not due for a long time, and there was no one making demands on his time. His desk was clear, the changes to various Army publications had been made, the out-of-date classified had been properly destroyed, and all the ancillary training had been completed. Hackett was caught with no black clouds on the horizon and nothing to do. He considered taking the rest of the day off, to walk the campus, to catch a movie, or just to go home and sleep. It was a beautiful feeling that suddenly scared him. The gods were about to reach down and tap him on the shoulder, and that couldn't be good.

The telephone chirped, and Hackett touched the button to answer it.

"Captain, this is Colonel Ford. I want you up in my office right now."

Suddenly the sky had clouded up, and it was blacker than midnight in the jungle. It was darker than the inside of a terrorist's heart. Hackett knew from the tone of Ford's voice that something had gone terribly wrong and that he was somehow going to get splashed with the debris. The shit had hit the fan, but he didn't know which fan it had hit.

He hurried down the traditional Army hallway, with green tile on the floor that had been waxed to a high shine and a somewhat slippery finish, light green walls that looked as if they had been painted the day before, and lighting that chased away the gloom, making it brighter than the inside of an operating theater. It was brighter than the combined IQ of MIT and Stanford, and at the moment, to Hackett, it was just nothing more than a long run to impending doom.

He reached Ford's office, knocked on the door, and was told to enter. He walked in and sensed that something was wrong. He stopped in front of Ford's desk, saluted, and said, "Captain Hackett reporting as ordered, sir."

Ford returned the salute, and snapped, "Knock off the plebe nonsense and have a seat."

"I wasn't sure what to expect."

Ford pointed at the television, and said, "I got this about twenty minutes ago, and I believe the general will be calling shortly. You better, we better, have some answers for him, or our world will end in a flash of light and pain."

"What in the hell . . ."

"Just watch." Ford touched a button on his desk control and the screen brightened. Hackett saw a panel that included Bakker, who was the only person he recognized. He turned and looked at Ford. "I don't understand."

"Raw footage of a press conference held about two

hours ago. A reporter e-mailed me a copy and I downloaded it into the recorder so I could watch it. You're not going to be happy when you see what they say. You're not going to be overly happy with your girlfriend."

Hackett was about to protest the girlfriend remark when he heard a voice come from the television and turned to watch. He listened to the opening statement and the questions until one of the men said that they had a signal from a ship.

"No," said Hackett. "That's not quite right. I was given to understand that this signal is from a source fifty light-years away."

"Yes. Your Dr. Bakker tries to make that point, but all the reporters hear are the words about a ship in space and that the general direction of travel is toward the Earth. They see invasion fleets and burning cities."

"Crap."

"I haven't seen any of the cut-together reports, but this isn't going to look good."

"This really isn't our bailiwick," said Hackett. "Air Force and Navy."

Ford held up a hand to stop the protest. "In the final analysis, if there is an invasion fleet . . ."

"Invasion fleet? Where in the hell did that come from? We're talking about something fifty light-years from Earth, traveling, as I understand, under the speed of light, and now, suddenly, we're talking about an invasion fleet?"

"Ah, I haven't allowed you the opportunity to see Senator Parker's closing remarks as he demands that something be done to prepare us for the coming of the alien invaders. He seems to be of the opinion that they are on our doorstep. Of course, the reporters, seeing a good story, even if it is not quite as desperate as Parker has made it out to be, will get behind him on this."

"Senator Parker . . . I don't remember his name."

"*State* senator," said Ford.

Hackett fell back, relaxed. "Oh, he wants to add 'united' in front of the 'state'."

"Yeah, I think he has political ambitions, but that won't make any difference with the media. He has credibility, for the moment, and he's let the genie out of the bottle. We're not going to be able to stuff it back in. Not with him talking as if the enemy is about to arrive."

"So what are we, meaning the Army, supposed to do about this?" asked Hackett.

"I think we're going to have to prepare for that coming invasion."

"Crap."

[3]

BAKKER DIDN'T SUMMON WEISS TO HER OF-fice, nor did she suggest they meet in Avilson's office to discuss the breach of protocol. She stormed down the hall, and, without knocking, pushed open the door to his office, throwing it back. The knob struck the wall with a dull thud.

Weiss was sitting at his desk, looking smug. He grinned at her, and said, "Well, that ought to stir up the natives."

"Just what in the hell do you think you are doing?"

"Stirring the pot. Science doesn't advance when we sit on our discoveries."

"That was not your decision to make."

Weiss laughed. "Right. You looked so much better endorsing these alien abductions." His tone became mocking. "This ship is far away, so don't worry about it. Oh, by the way, we have aliens on our planet abducting people."

"That wasn't what I said, and you know it," said Bakker, her voice hard, cold.

"Well, my dad talked to Jason a few days ago, and Jason mentioned something about this and his plans. Maybe because they're old friends."

"Jason," she said, shaking her head. "Just who in the hell is Jason?"

"Senator Parker. Anyway, Jason called me and asked if

I could help him understand what we found, and I said that I could, of course."

"That an alien armada is on the way to Earth?"

Weiss shrugged. "That's not what I said, and you know it. I said that we found a signal, it wasn't associated with a planet, so the only conclusion that I could draw was that it came from a ship. Our figures suggested that it was heading toward Earth. That information is accurate."

Bakker felt the anger drain out of her. Not because Weiss was right, but because he was technically correct. His conclusion was that the source was a ship and it was heading, more or less, in the direction of Earth. She couldn't fight that. Anything she said would be drowned out in the stories told by the reporters, who would point out that the information supported what Weiss said. It would be arguing with a brick wall.

"You don't know the trouble you have caused," she said, her voice now flat.

Weiss grinned. "Sure I do." He turned and touched his monitor, almost caressing it. "I already have telephone calls from two major broadcast networks, three minor ones, a bunch of science shows, and even the National Geographic Channel. I know exactly what I have done."

"That's it? You wanted your face on TV?"

"Why not? I've already got money."

"You're finished here," she said flatly.

"Don't be too sure. Not that it matters. I've already heard from two universities offering teaching positions even without my doctorate. They also suggested they would fast-track me for my doctorate."

"You did this to advance yourself."

"Better than sleeping with the professor," said Weiss, grinning.

"I never . . ."

"Of course not. You are a superior intellect who used your talent to get through the program." He sounded sarcastic, as if he didn't believe it.

Bakker was suddenly coldly furious and about to respond, but she knew it would do no good. Weiss had made up his mind. He had decided that everyone planned and plotted to get to the top, and those who didn't were clustered at the bottom. He never believed that talent and ability could be enough. Maybe it was because he had so little of either.

"I suspect you'll be leaving soon," she said.

"Just as soon as I see the offer I want, and I don't think it will be long in coming."

"Don't wait too long," she said. She spun and walked down the hall.

[4]

SHE SAW HIM WHEN HE ENTERED THE BAR AND held up a hand as he surveyed the crowd. Tonight he was dressed in a blue shirt and blue jeans and looked for all the world like a corporate executive slumming with the hired help. Bakker didn't mind. She was wearing a tan blouse and a short black skirt. She looked like a junior executive who was mingling with the middle management.

Hackett finally spotted her and worked his way through the crowd. He leaned in close, and said, "Little noisy in here."

"It's a good meeting place. You have something else in mind?"

"Somewhere so that we can talk without shouting. My voice'll give out before long."

Without thinking, she grabbed his hand and pulled him toward the door. When they reached the sidewalk, she stopped and looked both ways, as if traffic would be a problem, but the street had been blocked years earlier for a pedestrian mall. Now grass grew where there had once been concrete.

"I think I know the place, if you don't mind not being able to drink the hard stuff."

Hackett shrugged, and said, "I don't need to drink."

She led him down the sidewalk and stopped in front of an iron gate. "This place is a little pricey, I think to keep the students out. It's quiet, we can get good food if we want, and we'll be able to talk."

Without a word, Hackett opened the gate and bowed slightly. "After you."

They found a table in the back, away from the traffic patterns, and sat down. Bakker had her back to the wall so that she could see into the room and watch the door. She thought that she had taken the seat almost as a guilty wife might take it so that she could see who was dining there in case her friends, or her husband's friends, might see her out with another man. Bakker felt that pang of guilt though she was neither married nor dating anyone seriously.

Hackett sat down, put the napkin in his lap, and shifted in his chair, looking nervous. He said, "I have my back to the door just as Wild Bill Hickok did."

"You think someone is going to sneak in and shoot you?" asked Bakker.

"No, but I've always been bothered by that since I read about Hickok."

"You want to switch seats?"

Hackett laughed. "No. I'll be fine here."

"So," said Bakker. "What'd you think of the press conference this afternoon."

"A little over the top, don't you think?"

"It wasn't what I expected. The chairman of the department was madder than hell and threatened to throw me and Weiss out of the university."

"But you didn't . . ."

"I was there," said Bakker quickly. "Once he calmed down, he realized that I had been ambushed, but he wanted to punch out Weiss. I think he would have tossed him, but Weiss has been getting telephone and e-mail offers from other places. I think Avilson thinks he might be able to exploit that sudden recognition for the good of the department."

"Is that a good idea?"

"Well, we tend to think that anything that puts us into the public forum is a good thing."

"Nope," said Hackett. "We look at it just the opposite. We don't want the publicity. Some of it can be very damaging even if it keeps the public interested. You just never know which way they are going to jump."

"Well, having talked to Weiss, I think he is enjoying all the notoriety. I think he's going to jump just as soon as he gets an offer that he believes is in keeping with his high opinion of himself."

"You know," said Hackett, "I'm not really interested in Weiss. This all going to cause you any trouble?"

"Nah. I've got it made. Anybody looking at the situation objectively is going to realize that this latest nonsense is not my fault. My mistake was talking to that reporter a couple of weeks ago. She took my comments about SETI and made it look as if I was endorsing this idea of alien abduction."

"So, you don't buy into that?"

"Not you too," said Bakker.

Hackett said, "Just asking. Don't bite my head off."

"Then don't ask those sorts of questions."

Hackett was saved by the appearance of the waiter. They ordered dinner, went to the salad bar, and returned to the table. For a moment they ate in silence. Bakker glanced up, saw that Hackett was concentrating on his food, and studied him. He was a good-looking man who didn't feel that he had to prove anything. He was intelligent, sharp, amusing, and considerate. It had been almost funny the first time they had gone out. Hackett had been so afraid of being labeled a male chauvinist pig that he had very nearly bolted from the scene.

He finally looked up, oblivious to everything around him except the food and Bakker. He asked, "What's on the agenda for this evening?"

"You mean after dinner?"

"Of course."

"Don't know," said Bakker. "We have quite a bit of work tomorrow, and it's going to be starting early."

"Well," said Hackett, "we don't have to stay out too late then. My mother always warned me against dates on a school night anyway."

Bakker grinned. "Let's not be too enthusiastic about calling it a night. Let's just keep things in perspective."

"I always do."

CHAPTER 5

[1]

MAJOR GENERAL GEORGE C. GREENSTEIN SAT behind a huge desk that was pushed into the corner of his big office. To his right and left were large windows that looked out on an expanse of lawn that sloped down to a slow-moving river. To the right and left of the windows were floor-to-ceiling bookcases that held volumes on military history, psychology, sociology, anthropology, astronomy, and a dozen other topics. Some visitors, who weren't the brightest bulbs in the display, asked if he had read them all. Greenstein, being a general, and a very smart man, always said, "Yes, except the ones I wrote."

He actually had written two books. One was about his adventures in Afghanistan so long ago that it seemed to be ancient history to him. The second suggested a better way to build an Army for the future based on the idea of what future wars would be like and how they would be fought.

Neither book sold well, which was fine with Greenstein. He was, after all, a general and not a writer.

Opposite him, in the office, were two chairs for his visitors, and off to the left was a large area that held a sofa, chairs, a coffee table, and two end tables. He thought of it as his conversation pit and when a meeting threatened to run long, he moved his visitors over to that area.

He studied his two visitors, Lieutenant Colonel Robert Ford and Captain Thomas Hackett. Both looked uneasy, and that was the way it should be. Lower-ranking officers should fear the generals because it made life simpler for the generals. It saved a lot of explanation, and it saved a lot of dialogue. The old expression, "Because I said to," worked very well for a general, especially one who had two stars.

Greenstein turned his attention to Ford, and said, "Why did I turn on my TV and see a bunch of people talking as if the aliens are inside the orbit of Pluto? Why did I get the feeling that invasion was imminent? Why did I not know that this was going to ruin my breakfast and the start of my day."

"I believe," said Ford, "that State Senator Parker is running for the United States Senate."

"And that is relevant, how?"

"He is looking for an issue."

"So he picked alien invaders?"

"General," said Ford, "I don't pretend to understand politicians. I do understand this. There is no threat. Parker invented the threat to get his face on television. Name recognition is the name of the game."

"People recognize the name Charles Manson, but nobody is going to vote for him."

Ford looked down, at the light green carpet. "People also recognize the name William Cody and people would vote for him unless they thought about it for too long."

"Point taken," said Greenstein. "Still, I would think that association with alien invaders and its relation with flying saucers would sink a politician."

"And it would except he has the scientific community behind him, at least on part of it. There is some kind of a signal and no one has been able to rule out an artificial source. Without that signal, Parker is dead on the lawn. With it, and with scientists saying that the ship is heading toward Earth, people are listening. He's getting the face time he wanted."

Hackett started to speak, but Greenstein cut him off. "Okay. I'll buy this running for higher office. Man has no principles, no ethics, but it seems to be a hell of a risk."

"Not unless they identify the signal as something natural, and I don't think that will happen in the next six months. After that, he won't care," said Ford. "He'll be in Washington, DC, which is the whole point."

"Well," said Greenstein, "all that is irrelevant now. He has stirred up the powers above me, and they have asked questions. I want answers, and I need to look as if I am doing something important here." He grinned, and said, "The third star is on the line, and I really would like to be a lieutenant general. Therefore, and in an attempt to expand my empire, which, gentlemen, is also the name of this game, I am creating the Galaxy Exploration Team."

"General," said Ford.

"Quiet, Colonel, I'm on a roll here. Captain Hackett, you'll be in charge of this team . . ."

"Excuse me for interrupting, General," said Hackett, "but shouldn't this assignment go to a field grade officer. Give it more prestige."

"Good point, Captain. I'll see about getting you bumped up to major, but don't hold your breath. And don't interrupt me again if you want to stay a captain and not sink lower."

"Yes, sir."

"Anyway, as I was saying before I was so rudely interrupted, this team will take, as its first mission, the identification of the signal as friend or foe."

"Sir," said Ford, "that is assuming that the signal is

artificial, and we really don't even know that at the moment."

"No, but with Parker getting his face on the TV with his talk of alien invasion, I must look as if I am responding to that threat. Therefore, for the sake of argument, I am assuming that it is artificial. If it turns out to be natural, which is the direction I'm betting, then I point to the composition of the team and say, see, we responded, but we didn't expend a great deal of our limited resources. Natural caution."

Ford just nodded.

"And if it turns out to be artificial, then we have the nucleus of our response formed." Greenstein grinned broadly. "I hope you understand the brilliance of this response. We look as if we are doing something when we are not, but if the situation changes, we seem to be prepared."

Hackett spoke up. "Then I'm to do nothing."

"Oh, no," said Greenstein. "I want you to form a team. A paper team. Get some of these scientists . . . this Bakker and that Travis on the team as consultants."

"Travis was the UFO guy," said Ford.

"So he knows about aliens," said Greenstein, grinning. "Make him understand that the makeup of the team is classified so we don't have to explain him."

"Why not just leave him off?" asked Hackett.

"Let's say," said Greenstein, "just for laughs, that this thing is artificial and it's coming at Earth. Wouldn't someone who has studied alien life, even in the context of UFOs, have some interesting things to say."

"Yes, sir, I suppose."

"Your enthusiasm, Captain, is overwhelming. Anyway, you have your orders. I want to see something inside of a week."

"Yes, sir."

"If you have no questions," said Greenstein, "I'll let you men get to work."

[2]

FRANK HALL DIDN'T LIKE GETTING TELEPHONE calls from the network news division, but only because it normally meant more work for him or that someone had screwed up on the local level. On a rare occasion there had been the recommendation to fire someone, even rarer, was corporate praise.

This time, he had been given instructions, and although it meant more work, it also meant that someone at the network had watched one of his broadcasts and found something useful in it. Hall was beginning to look like a smart man even though the report he had aired connecting UFOs and the alien signal had been a serendipitous accident. He hadn't planned it and didn't know that a state senator would suddenly find the information important.

He walked across the newsroom, which was quieter than he thought it should be. There was, of course, no clatter of typewriter keys. Hall couldn't remember the last time he had even seen a typewriter. But there was no clatter from keyboards either because those had been quieted. No ringing telephones, though they chirped occasionally. No excited shouts about the incoming teletype messages because there were no teletypes, just computers hooked into various news organizations through the Internet. And nothing seemed to excite the people working there. Hall missed the old days, when the reporters actually got excited about the news and it wasn't the prepackaged drivel handed out and aired by those afraid of offending anyone.

He looked into one of the editing bays and found Davies sitting quietly, eating a donut, and watching a soap opera. He knew that if he challenged her, suggested that she should be doing something constructive, she would say she had just completed an assignment and was taking the authorized, fifteen-minute morning break. Since there was no officially scheduled break time, he was forced to live with it.

When she looked up, not caring that she had been

caught watching television rather than working, he asked, "What do you have on the schedule?"

"This afternoon they're going to have the new methane car at the Ford place. Some kind of announcement about a national system that will now allow refueling in all fifty-four states except Hawaii."

"That can wait," said Hall.

"Seven and twelve will have it tonight. Be old news tomorrow," said Davies.

Hall ran a hand through his hair and dropped into the other chair. "Actually, it's not even news today. It's a commercial for the car company."

"We've got to do what we can for . . ."

"Please, I don't need to hear that today. If you feel the need to protect the environment, help Mother Nature, or have any other cause, find a new job."

"I just meant . . ."

Hall held up a hand. "I don't care. Network is interested in this guy Parker."

Davies sat up straighter and put her donut on the plate. "The network?"

"I'm not sure what they want, you can talk to the producer there so that you'll get the footage they need, but they liked that tie-in between the UFO guy and Parker and how it all relates to the signal."

"Yeah," said Davies, "I thought that people might find that interesting. I mean, it's not every day that we get some kind of message from space."

Hall looked at her closely, and asked, "Message?"

"Signal, message, the same thing."

Hall almost pointed out that it wasn't really the same thing and that a journalist ought to be more familiar with the exact meanings of words. Instead, not wanting to dampen her excitement, he said, "Get something new from that Weiss because he's a little less circumspect than Bakker and get some comments from the UFO guy. I don't think they're going to want the really weird stuff, but they'll let you know. I don't know what tone they're going to take with this."

"What do you mean?"

"I don't know if they're looking for a goofy filler or if they want to milk this for the little seriousness there is in it. You'll have to take the cue from them."

"Who do I call?"

"Get on the horn to Dennison at the network in Houston. He'll either know what they want or will be able to tell you who to talk to there. Let me know before you leave. You going to want a camera crew?"

"If I'm doing this for the network, maybe it would be best that way."

Hall shrugged. "Okay. If you need anything else, you let me know."

"When are they going to want this."

"I think just as soon as you can get it put together. Maybe tonight. Tomorrow for sure."

"Thanks for the chance," said Davies.

Ignoring her, Hall stood up and glanced up at the clock. He saw that it wasn't even ten in the morning. He wasn't sure if that was a good thing or not.

[3]

JONATHAN TRAVIS COULDN'T BELIEVE HIS luck. After years of laboring in obscurity, or trying to convince journalists and scientists that there was something to be learned from the study of UFOs, he found himself a hot property. People wanted to talk to him, journalists wanted to interview him, and he was invited to appear on some of the major television talk shows. His expertise, which some thought to have the same importance as knowing everything there was to know about *Gilligan's Island* or *Gomer Pyle, USMC*, was finally seen as having some significance. Aliens were heading toward the Earth, and the scientists had said so.

He sat in his home office. There were two chairs for visitors near his desk and these were now occupied by Rachel Davies and Jason Parker. Sitting in another chair, off to the right, one that Travis had brought down from the dining room, was Steven Weiss. Everyone had coffee except Davies, who was drinking a diet 7UP. Her camera was set up and pointed at the group, more or less, but at the moment it was not recording.

Parker stood up, walked to a point where he could see everyone's face, and said, "If you don't mind, John, I'll start off here."

Travis bowed his head, and said, "It's your show."

"Okay. I'm going to be frank here and assume that we are all adults. We all can stand a little criticism, and we're all smart enough to realize that what I say is meant as a way of introducing the topic and to get us all thinking."

He waited, letting his words sink in. When no one spoke and no one objected, he clapped his hands together once, loudly, as if signaling the start of the meeting.

"Okay. Here's my thinking. We are all"—and he gestured to indicate everyone—"we are all laboring at the lower end of the spectrum. I am a senator, yes, but a state senator who is involved in state politics for about half the year. I have another job to pay the rent and no one is overly impressed with a state senator, not to mention the fact that I'm not on any of the important committees and I'll need another decade to get into the big time. I need a cause that will propel me into, at the very least, the statewide limelight. National, of course, would be much better for me."

He looked from face to face and saw that he had their attention. "Rachel, if I might be so informal."

"Please."

"You're working at the number two station in a two-station city and what, the seventieth, eightieth market in the country. It'll be a couple of years before you can move up to the fiftieth and maybe ten before you can get into a large market, let alone attract the attention of a network."

"Well," she began.

"No, I'm not being critical. I'm giving you the facts of life. You need experience, or you need name recognition as much as I. Find the big story, and the networks will notice. Right?"

"Right," she agreed.

"On the other hand, you might just stay here, hoping each year for a break that never comes. In ten years, you'll be considered too old, though by then you'll have developed the very skills that would make you a top-notch reporter. Unfortunately, for you, that will be too late, unless you fall into something that gets you noticed at the other end. Well, I think that we can promote that break for you."

She didn't mention that the network had called, but that it was just for the little video that she could send them. She might not make it on the air in the national arena though the network now knew her name.

Travis broke in. "This is all well and good, but I don't see how this affects me."

"You write books . . ."

"And I've been on national television. I have even turned down opportunities to appear because the travel arrangements were annoying or it was just too inconvenient for me. Or I didn't like the forum."

"But how would you like an advance of a hundred thousand, two hundred thousand rather than what you get now. Write a book every other year rather than several in one year."

"Well . . ."

"Yeah, I thought so. Here's the deal, if you're on the inside with us, as we all come together, then the publishers will be coming to you to write the book. They'll be in a bidding war for it, and who knows how high that could go."

"Sounds good," said Travis, "but I'm not going to hold my breath."

"Just be patient," said Parker. He turned his attention to Weiss. "I know that you have all the money that you need, and that you can always find a teaching position, even if it isn't at a top-notch school. I think we can change all that."

Weiss said, simply, "I'm interested, but I must tell you, there have been offers already."

"You have just proven my point. This could be a break for all of us if we're willing to exploit it." He held up a hand to wave off the protests. "No, I'm not saying that we need to engage in anything illegal. We just have to be ready and willing to do what we have to do."

He waited for a moment, then said, "Then we're all agreed that we'll work together, we'll support one another and work the same side of the street."

Davies said, "What do you mean by that?"

"Simple enough. You need a quote about astronomy, you go to Weiss here first. You put him on the air first, and you mention his name every chance you get."

"I'm not sure about the ethics of this," she said.

"Nobody is talking about ethics. You need sources. You need good quotes. I'm not suggesting that you don't ask others for opinions, or that you go to him for quotes when his expertise is not relevant. I'm suggesting that you go there first and use the material first, if it fits in with what you need. You use his expertise rather than, say, that of Sarah Bakker. Call her for additional information, maybe get a quote from her, too, but go to Steven first."

She rubbed her forehead, looking as if she had a headache, but said, "I guess that's okay."

"And you go to Travis for the UFO stuff, and some of the space stuff, and you come to me for the political end of it. What is the state legislature going to do about this. That sort of thing."

"Okay."

Now he looked carefully at the others. "On the other hand, you don't talk to anyone but Rachel. You don't give a quote to someone until Rachel has a chance for it. The networks call, you talk to her about it first. Bring her in on it however possible so, at the very least, they know that she is out here. Make the networks realize that she's on top of the story, and they'll get their best stuff from her."

Travis said, "I don't get this."

"Let's say a network producer calls to ask questions. Tell them first that Rachel already has that information. See if they will contact her as well. Hell, the media are always ready to promote themselves into a position of authority. They're not going to object going to another media type for information. Sure, in the end answer them, and if you find yourself on one of their shows, mention her, mention me, mention Weiss. We all take care of one another."

Weiss said, "Okay. We're a mutual admiration society. But why are these people, these media people, going to be interested in anything we have to say?"

"Because we are the ones who hold all the information about the approaching spaceship. We have the answers, and we, and only we, are aware of the danger."

"That's not quite accurate," said Weiss.

"Christ with a Popsicle," said Parker. "Everyone else is going to be circumspect in what they say. They're going to be careful and guarded. What we have to do is hand them the quotes that are exciting. That's what's going to get on the air. A week later no one will remember what was said, only that one of us was the expert with the information, and they'll come back again because we gave them what they wanted."

Travis grinned, nodding. "Bad news is always good news for the media."

"Are you seriously suggesting that we create a panic in this country so that we can all advance our careers?" asked Davies quietly.

Parker stared at her, surprised by the question. Of all the people in the room, he had thought of her as the dimmest. He had thought of her as the most ambitious and the one who wouldn't understand what they were doing. He thought she would only see this as a way of advancing her career and be happy for all the help she could get. Now she had asked the one ethical question that had a pinpoint of thought in it.

"I am suggesting that in the next several weeks, possibly months, there is going to be interest in that radio source and that we, if we stick together, can exploit its existence for our own benefit. I'm not suggesting we create a panic or anything else. I'm not suggesting that we do anything illegal or that we lie to anyone. I'm suggesting that we, as the resident experts, can get our faces on the TV, we can be noticed, and that is all I'm suggesting."

Davies sat quietly for a moment, then nodded. "Okay. Given those caveats, I guess I'm in."

"Okay," said Parker. "Then we operate from these assumptions. One. There is intelligent life in our galaxy, some of it scientifically superior to us. Two. UFOs have visited Earth and the government has hidden part of the information. Three. We have detected an artificial radio source that proves number one and certainly increases the likelihood that number two is true. Four. The signal is coming from a ship in space and is not connected to a specific planet or star system. Five. That ship seems to be heading toward the Earth. Six, and most importantly, we don't know if they are friendly or hostile, but we must be prepared for the worst."

Weiss began to hold up his hand, then dropped it into his lap. He said, "I can think of another point. The craft is accelerating."

"Do we know that?" asked Parker.

Weiss shrugged. "We have no direct evidence, and, if it is pointed at Earth, more or less, it will be a long time before anyone can say anything with certainty. However, if this is a ship, then certainly it will either be accelerating or decelerating. I doubt that anyone will be able to provide proof positive that we're wrong for a long time."

Parker grinned, "And an alien ship accelerating toward the Earth is more threatening than one that is not. Very good. That's why you're here."

Weiss shrugged.

"Okay." He looked directly at Davies. "I think it is time for a feature about the danger this object represents to the people of Earth."

Weiss said, "You understand that even at light-speed this thing couldn't arrive for about fifty years."

"Doesn't matter. There is a threat out there, and I don't see the government doing a thing about it. When that happens, it is up to the public to make the government do its job."

Weiss chuckled. "So we create a threat."

"Don't you remember the big smallpox scare after the World Trade Center was attacked? Someone thought that terrorists might use smallpox as a biological weapon and the next thing you know the government is ordering nearly 300 million doses of the vaccine. All because the news media needed something to fill that twenty-four-hour-a-day news hole."

"Now wait a minute," snapped Davies. "We don't make the news. We report it."

"Oh, grow up," said Travis. "Of course you make the news. It isn't news until you say it is and report it. What about the millennium bug? There was a nonstory if I ever heard of one, but companies and governmental agencies spent hundreds of millions of dollars to combat it because the news media stepped in and ran with it."

Before Davies could respond, Parker said, "No one is suggesting that your job is any less important than any other. We need to work together here or none of us is going to get very far."

Davies looked at him, then back at Travis. "Well, at least I'm not chasing flying saucers."

Travis grinned, and said, "Neither am I. I chase UFOs."

Parker said, "If you two don't mind, let's plan a little strategy here."

Travis nodded, and Davies said, "Okay. Strategy."

CHAPTER 6

[1]

SARAH BAKKER WASN'T SURE WHY SHE HAD
been flown to Albuquerque and then driven south along Interstate 25 until they had reached the small, sun-baked dis-
aster that was called Socorro. Once there, they had turned
off the interstate and driven to the west along a two-lane
highway that, at first, crawled through some shallow
canyons and over some short hills until they had burst out
into the desert. The highway stretched out in front of them
like an endless gray ribbon that faded into the distance.
Heat was radiating from the concrete and the compacted
ground on both sides of the road. There seemed to be little
break in the landscape except for the promise of distant
mountains.

They rode along quietly, the radio filled with the buzz
and chirps of a late-afternoon thunderstorm somewhere
within a hundred miles, though the sky over them was

nearly cloudless, the blue so deep that it hurt. There was nothing to see other than the cobalt of the sky and the brown of the desert landscape.

Bakker sat silently, not listening to the radio, thinking instead of Hackett. He hadn't been happy that she was about to disappear into the wilds of New Mexico, and she wasn't thrilled about it either. Hackett seemed to be an interesting man, for an Army officer. He was educated, articulate, and clever. He didn't seem caught up in the macho image of an Army officer but seemed to be comfortable with who he was. She decided that she liked him and wished that he had been able to come to New Mexico with her. For a day or so it had seemed he would be given orders to accompany her, but, in the end, it hadn't worked out.

Finally, in the distance was a shimmer of white. The driver pointed off to the right and up ahead she spotted the first of the antenna that made up the Very Large Array. She asked, "How much longer?"

"Maybe fifteen minutes," said the driver, Caleb Castelton. He was a graduate student who probably would never get his Ph.D. Though a nice young man who was fairly bright, he just didn't have a flair for physics or astronomy. He could do the work, he could understand the concepts, he just couldn't think in an original direction. Brilliant when given instructions or told what to look for, he just couldn't originate ideas.

He wasn't particularly good-looking, though he wasn't bad-looking either. He was . . . nondescript. Light hair that might have been blond or perhaps brown, hazel eyes that reflected the color of his clothes, light skin, and fine features. He blended perfectly into the crowd, and people failed to recognize him. Had he been a bank robber or an assassin, he would have been described as average, and only the most careful observer would have been able to pick him out of a lineup.

But he was a nice man, who rarely said anything negative about anyone, worked hard and competently, and was regarded by nearly everyone as a friend. They all wanted him to achieve his degree, but they just didn't think he would be able to do it without a great deal of help. Of course each of them was prepared to offer that help, but he never asked.

Bakker rolled down the window and stuck a hand into the slipstream. "It feels awfully hot out there."

Castelton glanced at the temperature gauge mounted on the dash, and said, "It's pushing 115." He grinned. "But it's a dry heat."

"That dry heat will roast the hell out of my turkey," said Bakker.

"Sure will."

He slowed as they approached a sign that told them the turnoff was just ahead. They found it and headed to the south, now bouncing over a road that was little more than a graded track through desert. Behind them a cloud of dust rose, almost as if marking their progress along the road.

"You know," said Castelton, "this was a shallow lake a few thousand years ago."

Bakker smiled at that, and said, "You know, I don't really care."

A short, single-story building loomed up, and they pulled into the parking lot near it. There weren't many cars, and all of them had cardboard signs that filled the windshields, reflecting the bright afternoon sun. The theory was that it would keep it cooler in the car, but all the cardboard did was protect the interior from the direct rays of the sun.

As Bakker climbed stiffly from her car and arched her back to stretch the muscles, Castelton shut down the engine. A side door opened, and two people, a young man and a tall woman, exited. They walked over, and the man asked, without preamble or greeting, "Are you Bakker?"

The two new people were dressed about the same, wearing khaki-colored shorts and T-shirts. They had sandals on their feet, but they looked clean, well-groomed, and fairly cool. Bakker wasn't sure what she expected of those left out there, isolated for weeks or months on end, but these people looked a little too casual for her taste, though she too wore shorts.

She said, "Yeah. Who's Gibson and who's Taylor?"

The woman, taller than Bakker and taller than her companion, said, "I'm Taylor. Call me Liz."

Bakker couldn't help smiling. "Elizabeth Taylor?"

"My real name is Sally, but everyone calls me Liz."

"Okay."

"And this is Gene Gibson. He's in charge of our project out here."

Gibson, a fireplug of a man, held out a hand, and said, "I was in charge. I guess you take over now."

Bakker shrugged. "I'm not sure that take over is the right word here. I've got an agenda handed to me by Dr. Avilson, so I guess that would take precedence over everything else, but I'm not taking over."

"Don't misunderstand," said Gibson, "I'm not complaining. Hell, most of the work we do can be put on hold. Nothing moves very fast, relatively speaking."

"Anyone think maybe we could get out of this heat?" asked Castelton.

"Where are our manners?" asked Taylor. "Please. We're set up in the conference room, though I'm afraid it's rather crowded."

Gibson opened the door and gestured. Bakker stepped through, followed by Taylor. When he reached the door, Castelton asked, "Will the car be safe out here?"

Gibson gestured at the wide-open space around them that looked deserted, other than the buildings associated with the radio telescopes and the telescopes themselves. The plains looked as they had a hundred, two hundred, ten thousand years earlier.

"Nothing around but the rattlesnakes and the scorpions. It might melt, but no one is going to bother it."

As Castelton stepped through the door, he said, "I was going to ask about that. You see many scorpions?"

"Nope. They don't want to be inside here, and they usually hunt at night. Wear heavy shoes at night, and shake them out before you stuff your feet into them in the morning, and you'll be fine."

They reached the conference room, which had a door with a hole punched in it about chest high showing that it was a hollow door made of pressed particle board. Inside the conference room was a long thin table, the center of which held piles of paper, disks, books, pens, and several empty soda cans. At one end was a computer terminal that looked as old as the desert outside. There was no sign of a keyboard or voice input. The screen was flashing through displays that Bakker couldn't recognize.

Taylor gestured at one of the empty chairs, and said, "Have a seat."

As Bakker sat, Taylor walked to the bank of windows that opened on a view of the outside that could only be considered panoramic. They could see across the plains, to a low rim of mountains that had to be fifty miles away. Taylor closed the blinds and sat down close to the monitor. From somewhere she pulled a wireless keyboard and set it on her lap.

"Okay," she said, as both Castelton and Gibson sat down. Gibson lifted a pile of debris, papers, books, disks, files, and charts from one of the chairs and set it all on the table.

"Okay," repeated Taylor, "what do you know?"

Bakker said, "Well, we found the damned signal, so I guess we know as much as anyone."

"Of course," she said, "then you know it's faded."

Bakker raised an eyebrow, but asked, "Just when did it finally fade?"

"We lost it all about twelve hours ago."

"You find anything embedded in it?" asked Bakker. "We hadn't had much luck."

Now Gibson took over. "Well, as you know, it was a very weak signal. Even with our capability, it was hard to hold it. Drifted all over the map."

"Yes," said Bakker.

"And we couldn't find a code embedded in it."

"There has to be something," said Bakker. "No reason to send a signal if you have no way to communicate."

"Well, we thought about that," said Taylor, "and our conclusion is that it is not a signal meant for interstellar communication."

"Meaning?" asked Bakker, though she knew what the answer was going to be.

"Meaning that the signal was not meant for us, or any other terrestrial civilization. It was meant only as a means for them to communicate with their home," said Taylor.

"Or another ship," added Gibson. "If that's the case, there would be no embedded message just as your cell calls have no embedded message. It was straight-up communication with others of their own kind."

"Still," said Bakker, "there must be something that we could learn from this."

Taylor shrugged. "I don't know what it would be. We can tell you everything about the signal you'd want to know from the frequency to the precise location, until it faded. But if you want me to tell you anything specific about the message, then I have to say we haven't gotten very far."

Bakker fell back, in her chair, raised her arms, and locked her fingers behind her head. "Well, crap, this is useful."

[2]

SOMETIMES IT WAS JUST NECESSARY TO CHANGE the immediate environment to think. The change of scenery, no matter how small, provided the inspiration for thought, but as Bakker wandered through the building, looking at the computer screens, at the various displays, at the star charts and the list of natural radio sources scattered throughout the galaxy and universe, she found no inspiration.

She returned to the conference room, where microwave-heated pizza was sitting on top of stacks of computer print-outs. She dropped into one of the chairs and turned so that she could look up at the monitor in the corner. At the moment it showed nothing other than the desert near one of the array antennae. She saw a shadow and thought it might be a coyote.

Taylor said, almost as if reading her mind, "There are wild dogs out there."

Bakker shrugged, then turned, picking up a piece of pizza, holding the back in one hand, and supporting the cheese-dripping point in her fingers.

Gibson said, "We tried to decipher the signal."

Taking a bite of pizza, Bakker nodded, and finally said, "So did we."

"What'd you get?"

Bakker set the pizza on a plate and took a diet 7UP. She drank, then said, "Nothing. We tried the Drake idea using prime numbers as the frame but all we got was what looked to be a random scattering of dots and dashes. Tried that using a variety of bases, but it just never resolved itself."

Now Gibson grinned. "You were looking for the embedded message, assuming that the signal was meant for us. We decided that we were eavesdropping, so we tried to decipher it on the basis that we should have already known the language."

Bakker, now very interested, leaned forward. "Yes?"

"We assumed, first," said Taylor, taking over, "that we would probably see what we wanted to see. I was afraid that we would create a message, or image, based more on faces in the clouds than in what the message might really be."

Bakker, still eating her pizza, nodded.

"Then we assumed that what we had was not radio, but television. That changed the dimensions of our search."

"Of course," said Bakker.

"Now we're dealing with something that is at the very

limits of our ability to detect, so whatever we found was
going to be filled with our interpretation."

"So," said Gibson, "we separated into different rooms,
didn't communicate with one another, and tried to refine
the signal so that we could see what it was."

"You thought of it as a television signal?"

"Yes. And we assumed that it was a signal that we intercepted although it was not for us. We broke it down with
those thoughts in mind."

"Did you get anything?" asked Bakker.

"Watch the monitor. The results were less than spectacular, which is why we haven't said anything to anyone yet.
We thought we could refine it."

"Let me have a look."

Taylor turned and touched a keyboard. "It'll appear on
the monitor."

Bakker, for some reason, had no sense of what was
about to happen. She was thinking in terms of Earth-based
television and of typical television programming. She
wasn't thinking in terms of the first glimpse of an alien life
because the people in the room with her had not been overwhelmed by what they had discovered and hadn't excit-
edly pushed her in that direction. Their announcement had
been more of a "by the way" suggestion rather than any
kind of leap forward in cosmic knowledge. They had even
waited for her to get settled in, get a look at the facility, and
get a feel for the equipment before they mentioned anything.

She picked up her pizza, took a bite, and turned to
glance at the monitor. There were shadows there. Dim
grays and flat blacks, stirring. Something that might have
been human-shaped, moved from right to left, and something that might have been a stunted tree, with few
branches and leaves, was standing in the background.
There was a hint of something on the screen, almost as if
obscured in fog, but nothing that could be resolved or
clearly seen.

"Not much, is it?" said Gibson.

Bakker leaned forward, put her pizza slice on a plate, then stood up. She took a step toward the monitor. She rubbed her chin, smearing a bit of grease there, and said, "This is the best?"

"Well, this is the version that seems to be the most consistent with the data. We have speculated and allowed various programs to run. We'll give you a look at some of the other theories, but remember, it is all highly speculative, and so far beyond the data that I hesitate even to let you see any of it."

Bakker stood quietly and waited while the image on the screen faded, then came back.

There was still almost no color, but the images were sharper, though not well-defined. The moving object had two appendages that seemed to branch off a thick neck that supported a head that was of basketball proportions. There were no facial features except for a thick ridge above where the eyes would be.

The other object now looked like a pole with four or five branches pointing upward. It had a yellowish cast. There was no background detail and nothing else of interest.

"We have, of course, attempted to convert more of the signal, but the frequency seems to drift, and we can get nothing that is consistent. This is really all we have."

Bakker asked, "Can I see it again?"

"Sure. Which version?"

"The gray one, then this."

They ran the videos again, then the screen darkened. Bakker looked at the people in the conference room, and said, "I'm at a loss for words."

"Why?" asked Taylor. "This is more of an exercise with the computer than anything we think has relevance. We could be so far off."

"Yes, but think about it. If this is the right track and we let others work on it—maybe someone with a little better computer available or a few different skills—we might be able to refine it some more."

Taylor reached for the pizza, took a bite, then set it on her plate. "But we really don't have anything that isn't open to various interpretations, nor have we been able to refine any more of the signal. It might be said that we took random bits of information, combined them in a way that fit our needs but that had no relation to the way they should have been combined, and found what we were looking for."

"Okay," said Bakker. "But my point is that this line of inquiry, while dead-ended here, might suggest something to someone else. Sharing the information might open it up further and give us a real look at the aliens."

Gibson said, "But you misunderstand. This was more of an exercise to please us than actual scientific research. We just don't have anything here that I would feel comfortable sharing with others. It's a cartoon doodle."

Bakker understood that. Scientists were sometimes unforgiving when it came to the scientific process. Looked as if you took science lightly, and they would turn on you. From that moment on everything became a fight, with others sniping from far off. Those who were building careers had to be careful about choosing which fights were important and which were not. Gibson and Taylor seemed to have decided that this was not an important fight.

Bakker asked to have the video run again and studied both versions. In the first there wasn't much other than shadows and motion. In the second, highly speculative video, there were images that looked almost as if they could be refined and understood. They were just beyond perception.

The thing to do, thought Bakker, was to alert her colleagues to the possibility of a video stream inside the signal and see if they could pull anything from it. Just suggest to them that it might be there and find out if they could detect it.

[3]

AFTER TEN DAYS OR SO, JASON PARKER real-
ized that his take on the alien signal was wearing a bit thin.
At first the news media had been excited by his sugges-
tions, based as they were on scientific fact. But now there
was nothing new to report. The signal, as far as he knew,
had not been deciphered. There was nothing new to it, and
the threat seemed too far removed to excite the media,
which sometimes grew excited when an asteroid was
going to pass close to Earth and at other times found nothing of interest in a murder investigation.

But now Weiss had handed him the exciting news.
Weiss, still being courted by several universities, including his own, had seen the note sent by Bakker from New
Mexico and had downloaded the file. There he had found
the still of the alien creatures. He knew that it was just the
sort of thing that Parker would want and that could be
used to get them all back on the television.

He had driven to Parker's office, unannounced, but got
right into the main building. Parker, who was typing at his
computer, saved his work and sat back in his chair.

Weiss stood in front of the desk, almost like a kid ordered to the principal's office. Without preamble, he said,
"This is the latest. Came to me from New Mexico." He
handed the photograph across the desk.

Parker propped a foot on the bottom desk drawer and
studied the photograph. "This is really pretty crappy," he
said. "What's it supposed to be?"

Weiss laughed, and said, "I've just handed you what
might be the very first pictures ever from an alien civilization and all you can say is that it is pretty crappy? How
about a little praise for those of us who managed to do
this, remembering that the signal is extremely weak and
has traveled through fifty light-years of space being subjected to various types of radiation, gravitational effects,
and who knows what else. The fact that anyone managed

to translate the signal into a picture ought to be worth a little bit of astonishment."

"Point taken," said Parker. "It's just that this isn't going to frighten very many people."

"Is that your mission?" asked Weiss. "To frighten people?"

"My mission," said Parker, his voice frosty, "is to let the people know what they need to know to protect themselves and their families from this onrushing alien menace. I find that the message sometimes gets lost unless we have a bit of drama to inject into it."

"Well, then," said Weiss, "this might help. This is a computer-enhanced version of the same thing."

Parker took the photograph and glanced at it. Vague shapes that seemed more real, more human, but still nothing that could be considered frightening.

Weiss said, "I don't think you understand what you're holding there. This is a photograph, such as it is, from an alien source. The human race had nothing to do with this. You are holding the first glimpse into an alien civilization."

Parker nodded but still seemed to misunderstand. "This the best you have?"

"That is the best that we got from New Mexico."

"But you have something more."

Weiss shrugged, and said, "Let's just say that I was able to gather a little additional information from the signal once I knew what to look for." He lowered his voice. "This is, of course, highly speculative."

"Let me see what you've got."

Before Weiss handed over the last of the photographs, he said, "The beauty of this is that the basis for it is scientifically sound. They can complain about this interpretation, but when we ask if it is completely without foundation, they're going to have to admit that it is not. They're going to have to admit that the first two versions came, not from us, but from their own people in New Mexico."

"Give."

Weiss handed it across the desk and finally Parker was stunned. The gray blobs of the first and the indistinct, slightly colored shapes of the second had been refined. The humanoid-like blob had been changed into a creature that was only vaguely human-looking, meaning that it had a single head, two eyes, and a mouth, but that was about all. The head was round without sign of hair or ears. The eyes, hidden under the brow ridges, were small and might have been about anything including some sort of weird nostril. The skin was a slight, pale blue that somehow just didn't look right.

Parker was almost speechless. He stared into what might be the face of an intelligent, alien creature, seen for the first time by members of the human race. Without looking up, he asked, "Just how accurate is this?"

"Probably not very," said Weiss. "It is an extrapolation based on some very sketchy evidence."

"Still, this is dynamite. We get that woman who said she was abducted on the air, talking of alien invasion, maybe add another drawing based on what she says they look like, and compare the two. We do that, and we're going to own prime time tonight."

"You're going to run with this?" asked Weiss.

"You said that it is an extrapolation based on some very solid science. You said that two-thirds of the steps to get to this"—Parker waved the photograph like it was banner—"are solid science. Yes, I'm going to run with this."

Weiss just nodded. "Excellent."

[4]

THE PRESS CONFERENCE, HELD IN FRONT OF two radio reporters, a newsgroup reporter, and Rachel Davies, didn't provide the coverage that Parker had hoped to gain. As he walked into the room, he grinned because he knew, after the information was printed, aired, and uploaded, his press conferences would always be well attended.

He walked to the podium, pulled the photographs from the inside pocket of his suit, and laid them down. He glanced back to the rear of the room, where the projector had been set up next to the computer display. He turned and looked up at the screen that was blank, and then out at the few journalists present. Finally, he turned toward the table set to his left, where Weiss and Bachmann sat waiting to answer questions. He hoped that Bachmann would play her part as well as Weiss had played his earlier. Her tentative identification of the aliens as those who had abducted her would be the frosting on the cake.

He glanced out over the thin audience, thought about getting a drink of water but decided that he would keep the reporters waiting no longer. He said, "Ladies and gentlemen, you have made the right decision by covering this press conference. In years to come, your colleagues will suggest that they were here, with you, but we all will know exactly who was here. In the next weeks they will comment, they will define, and they will pontificate, but the truth is, they will know less than you or I, and they will be scrambling to look as if they were in on this from the very beginning."

He gestured toward the table, and said, "When I have completed my remarks, I, along with Steven Weiss, an astronomer, and Susan Bachmann, who has interacted with alien creatures, will answer any questions you might have."

One of the radio reporters leaned over and turned off his tape recorder. It was a sign of contempt, and Parker knew that the man was actually thinking of walking out. He didn't want to sit in a room with an abductee and listen to tales of alien creatures, but Parker knew that once he began presenting the evidence, the reporter would quickly turn the recorder back on.

"As you know, and as we have discussed over the last several weeks, we have received a signal from a radio source that the scientific community has labeled as artificial. They had determined, to a reasonable degree of accuracy, where the source is. They have spent time trying to decipher the signal, and today I want to announce they have had limited success."

He pointed at Weiss, and said, "Steven Weiss will be able to provide information on exactly how the signal was deciphered."

Weiss stood and moved to the podium. He nodded, and the first of the pictures appeared on the screen. The reporters seemed unimpressed with what they were seeing.

"This is the first pass at the signal. Now, according to what I have been told, there was not a message hidden in the signal. You might think of it as a communication between those aliens on their ship and their home world, or with creatures on another ship. It is a sort of internal communication that we are not meant to hear or understand. There is nothing nefarious in this. It's just a communication between two points in their civilization."

One of the reporters, Parker didn't know which one, said, "This is a load."

Weiss continued. "The second picture is a computer refinement of the first. Now we begin to resolve the shapes a little bit. We begin to get some idea of what we are looking at."

Parker now moved back to center stage, standing near Weiss. Parker gestured, and the last of the pictures came up, in full color, giving them a good look. He hesitated, waiting for the gasp he knew would come. He waited as they processed the information and understood what they were looking at. He waited as they slowly began to form questions and comments. Then, finally, Parker said, "This is the enemy. This is what they look like."

The man who had turned off his recorder reached over, his eyes still on the screen, and turned it back on. Davies stood up, as if that would help her see the picture better, but, of course, she had already seen it and her report was already in the can. They would break into the regular programming with the announcement as soon as they were finished here.

"You said 'enemy.' Why 'enemy'?" asked one of the radiomen.

Parker said, "Because they have attempted to conceal themselves from us. Because they are heading in our general direction. And because Ms. Bachmann believes that the being we see in that picture might be from the race that has been abducting her on a regular basis. Their very actions, both in space and here on Earth suggest that they are an enemy."

"Abducting her? We're supposed to buy that?"

Parker stared down at the man, and said, "Why not? We have evidence, scientific evidence, that an intelligent life is out there, very close to Earth, relatively speaking. We have evidence that they are a spacefaring race whose biggest ship is now heading toward our planet. It seems to me that the possibility that Ms. Bachmann is being abducted by these creatures has just increased significantly. We have gone from a position of questioning the possibilities of other intelligent life in the universe to one in which we know that intelligent life exists."

"But that would mean the aliens could be here, well, now," said the reporter.

Weiss leaned forward and pulled the microphone closer. He said, "If I might?"

"Go ahead."

"Overlooking Ms. Bachmann's report of interaction with the alien creatures, the thing that no one seems to have understood, the thing that we have all overlooked, is that we are dealing with a spaceship. Under the circumstances that we had originally believed existed, we would have been dealing with a signal that came from a star system, and that system wouldn't be traveling through space. The signal we detected came from a ship, and we are looking at the position of that ship as it stood fifty years ago. If they have been traveling all that time and depending on their capabilities, they certainly could be here right now."

"My God," said Davies.

The two radio reporters looked at one another, then sprinted from the room.

CHAPTER 7

[1]

THE NEWS WAS STUNNING. FIRST RACHEL Davies told the local audience what had been discussed at the press conference, providing a feed to the network headquarters. They broke into the programming nationally, letting everyone in the United States know what had been reported.

Within minutes, the local radio reporters, including the one who had turned off his recorder so that he missed some of the announcement, were on the air with what they had heard. Davies, the network, and the radio stations put information onto the Internet, prominently featuring their stations' logos and the word, "Exclusive." Finally, the rest of the television stations and the other networks, both broadcast and cable, told of the alien creatures that had been seen in the signal.

Radio couldn't show the pictures and made up for that

by focusing on the story told by Bachmann, and making it clear that hundreds, if not thousands, had been reporting alien abduction for more than seventy years. The slant the radio reporters used was that alien creatures were taking sleeping humans from their beds for experiments designed to provide information about human frailty and vulnerability. They hinted broadly, just as Parker had, that the invasion fleet was on the way.

For those who had missed the first reports, or who were caught in the vacuum between one rundown and the next, the Internet supplied the three photographs. These, according to the various websites, were the first pictures of alien creatures that were not in complete dispute as hoaxes. There was a provenance for them and even if there was some computer manipulation, it wasn't much and it was clear that another of the human race's questions had been answered. Intelligent life was humanoid in form. The new problem was that no one knew how dangerous the aliens were.

As the afternoon progressed, Davies and her television station stayed far ahead of the competition with the most complete, and the most frightening, of the reports because she had an interview with Weiss. She had recut the interview with Bakker to add additional credibility for her reports. She had the first interview with Bachmann, and now she had the pictures that Parker had given her before the news conference.

The only way to make the story better was for her to use the video that gave motion to the aliens. That ploy they were holding back until they had gotten everyone's attention. Then they would broadcast the short clip that showed some motion. For some strange reason, even though the shapes were vague, nearly unrecognizable, they were much more frightening when they moved. Still photographs of gray shapes were not nearly as frightening as ghostlike pictures that moved.

Hall, once he understood what they had, told Davies she had five or six minutes, in fact, she had all the time she needed, and that she needed to be ready in an hour. They didn't want to miss this. She had been the only television reporter in that room, she had a unique perspective, and the network would be eating it up as soon as they could air it. Hall knew that this was his shot at moving to the network if Davies said nice things about him, and the network understood that the story would not have existed without his insight and intelligence. Davies didn't tell him that she had everything he wanted ready because she had been working on the inside. Some aspects of her news gathering were best left unmentioned.

The immediate reaction, outside the newsroom, outside the station, outside the inner world of journalism, was one of stunned silence. People sat staring at the flashing television screen and just didn't know what to think. This wasn't the tongue-in-cheek UFO reports that had been aired so often by the media. There had been no comic byplay between the anchors when the story ended. There had been a serious tone that added to the credibility of what had been shown.

There had been a few telephone calls to the station to make sure that some kind of joke was not being played. All callers were assured that the story was real and that it hadn't come from UFO investigators but from scientists working in various parts of the country and the world.

Others turned to their computers and found the same information. They could sit and stare at the screen and see and hear whatever they wanted. They could replay video, listen to the audio, or just manipulate images until they had sucked every bit of information from the Internet. It all added a note of credibility to an incredible situation.

More people, suddenly faced with the unknown and who didn't fully understand the implications, found themselves in the streets, in the malls, on the university campus, anyplace that people gathered. They stood, stunned and nearly silent, mentioning only how unbelievable the whole thing was but drawing comfort in the mass of humanity around them. They commented on the tone of the story and the implications in it for them. Alien creatures were not only deep in space, they were not only on a ship, but they could be here, at Earth, now. That woman had said just that after the scientific evidence had been presented.

There was also an anger bubbling through the crowds. It was about the only emotion that allowed them to deal with the information without falling victim to fear. They were angry at the government for not knowing, though many claimed the government did know but hadn't told them.

They were angry at the aliens for upsetting their lives. They didn't know what the aliens thought or believed, but they had been conditioned by more than a hundred years of movies, television, videos, and DVDs to believe that aliens were more than likely invaders who wanted Earth's resources, or water, or air. They came to kill and plunder but not to assist.

They were angry at the university because it was the scientists there who had brought this information to them. Had the eggheads not been snooping where they had been snooping, no one would know about the aliens and everyone could go back to his or her mundane and mostly unexciting life. It was their fault that the world had been turned upside down.

And that might be where the spark was lit. They couldn't attack the government and they couldn't kill the aliens, but the university was right there, not a hundred feet away. One man, standing on a short wall that enclosed the reflecting pool of an old fountain, pointed at the physics building, and yelled, "It's their fault. They told these creatures where we live."

It made no difference that Earth radio and television broadcasts had been sent into space for more than a century, suddenly there was someone to blame. It made no difference that those signals probably had nothing to do with the alien ship and that the university was not responsible for the situation. It was there, and it could be attacked.

"They're sitting in there, having betrayed us, and no

one gives a damn," yelled the man, wearing a T-shirt that held the university's crest.

Someone in the back of the crowd screamed, "Maybe we should burn them out."

"Let's get them."

The man on the short wall and the university T-shirt said, "They have brought this down on us. They didn't ask what we thought. They didn't care what might happen. They were just interested in getting information and seeing their names in the history books."

A rock flew from the rear of the crowd and shattered a window of an administration building. Someone else ran across the street and threw a brick into the glass doors of the physics building. They starred, then frosted and collapsed.

"Let's go," yelled a male voice.

The crowd, as one, moved toward the physics building. There was shouting. Someone dropped out of the crowd and began probing around the bushes. He began to hand rocks to those hurrying past him.

One of the rocks arched forward and struck a window. The glass shattered. There was a spark, a flash, and then flames. Someone had found a newspaper and set it on fire. He tossed it through the broken window.

They reached the doors and kicked in those that hadn't been broken. They surged through, smashing anything that would break, pulling at the television monitors hanging from the ceiling, kicking in doors, and ripping apart books. They pushed computers to the floor and turned over furniture. They broke anything they could, smashed glass and windows. They set more fires. Bells began to ring and the sprinklers activated but people began to grab at the sprinkler heads, pulling them down, destroying their effectiveness.

They climbed the stairs, chased people from offices, and then destroyed everything they could find. When they reached the top floor, they started down again, spreading out from the stairwells, looking for anything that had survived the first surge. Back on the street they could see fires burning in a dozen windows, saw smoke pouring from more, and heard the approach of the fire department. Even with police cars following closely, the crowd refused to break up. They stayed to fight the fire department.

[2]

RACHEL DAVIES STOOD NEAR THE WINDOW ON the second floor of a housewares store, looking down at the swirling mob in the street. She had retreated, camera in hand, when the first empty beer bottle had been thrown an hour earlier. The crowd had become too angry, and its violence was directed at anything and anyone who might have told the story. Davies got out before someone blamed her for broadcasting the report.

Now, with the window open and the camera mounted on a tripod, she had an unobstructed view of the situation on the street. She could video the riot without having to be down there where she could get hurt.

Standing on the hood of a car was a man in faded khaki pants and a light blue shirt. He held papers in his uplifted hand and he was shouting at the crowd. Davies could hear the sound of his voice but could not understand the words. There was too much noise and too much wind.

Whatever he was saying resonated with the crowd. They screamed their approval. Some of them held up lighters, or rolled up newspapers that were blazing. It looked like a scene from a Frankenstein movie, where the townspeople were about to storm the castle. Those at the end of the mob peeled off and ran toward the display windows of the shops. They smashed the windows. A few grabbed the merchandise and tried to run off. Others swarmed through the broken windows or demolished the doors to gain access. Moments later they appeared carrying computers or televisions or DVD recorders or anything else they could find.

Davies had been on the street long enough to know that people had been angry, had been upset, because of the discovery of the alien ship. She knew that they all felt betrayed, as if the scientists and the government had lied about the danger posed by the ship. Others believed that they now had proof that the government was working with and had signed treaties with the aliens. Life as they knew it was about to end. Before it did, they were going to register their outrage by stealing everything that wasn't nailed down.

She didn't understand how stealing a computer was going to make everything right again. The riot she was watching was an excuse to destroy and steal and, if anyone thought about it, they would realize that. At the moment, though, they wanted to smash and destroy.

She kept her eye on the view plate, slowly moving the camera to take in the whole street. She watched as cars were overturned and set on fire. She watched as one looter tackled another, grabbed the booty, and ran off with it. She saw police attempt to disperse the mob, then retreat under a hail of rocks and beer bottles. She saw a fire truck, surrounded by people, unable to move toward one of the burning cars. She watched the crowd as it flooded into the buildings, stole everything they could carry, and fled into the night. She watched fights and she saw one woman, her shirt ripped away, run into a lamppost at full speed and collapse into the street. No one stopped to help.

The police finally formed a line at one end of the street and slowly began to march forward, pushing the people along. They let some of them dodge down side streets or escape into open restaurants or shops. Their mission wasn't to catch looters or arsonists, but to break the crowd up into smaller and smaller parts until the people either went home or were arrested. They didn't bother with tear gas or rubber bullets. They just marched along forcing the crowd to move in some direction, taking control away from the mob's leaders.

When the street was cleared, except for the smoking

remains of some of the cars, the debris from the looting, and the police officers, Davies shut off her camera. She stayed where she was for a few minutes, watching the flames flicker, watching the cops circulate as they searched for looters and stragglers, and watching as the business owners arrived to assess the damage. She knew that a good reporter would go down and ask the cops some questions and interview the store owners, but she didn't have the heart. She believed, at that moment, that her report had been responsible for what had happened.

[3]

WHEN THE IMMEDIATE, LIVE, UP-TO-THE-MINUTE coverage of the riot ended, Parker pushed himself out of his chair and walked over to the television. He turned it off, then looked back at the end table, where the remote was half-hidden by the newspaper. Parker believed that all exercise, even if it was no more than walking across the room to turn off the television, was good. He made a virtue of walking to the television set.

"Christ," said Weiss. "We cause that?"

"No, we didn't cause it. But I think the reactions of the public were completely predictable."

Weiss swirled the liquor in his glass, listening to the ice clink. "You expected this and went ahead with that press conference anyway?"

"There are fundamental truths to politics, and one of those is that controversy gets your face on the screen. If I want to launch a run for national office, the people of the state must know who I am. This controversy is one way of ensuring that. Portions of the press conference have already been shown on every television in the state and will continue to air for the next day or two. The same is probably true around the country."

Weiss shook his head in disbelief. "You caused a riot for personal gain?"

"Climb down off your high horse, Steve. You were sitting right there, hogging the camera at every turn. Don't tell me that this wasn't a boost for your career."

"I didn't know people would riot."

"Then you're an idiot. Of course they're going to riot. We just told them that aliens from space are on the way, that the ship everyone talked about being fifty light-years away hadn't been in that position for fifty years and then we trot out the lady who claims she has been abducted by the aliens saying that some of them are here already. Just what the hell did you think the people would do?"

"I hadn't thought about it."

"Then you're an idiot. You must always think of the consequences and how they are going to impact you. In this case, I'm not going to be blamed because I made no discovery, but I am going to be hailed as the savior because I warned them about the danger. I told the people the truth. I warned them of the possible consequences."

Parker walked across the room to the wet bar. He poured himself another bourbon and held up a glass.

"Nah, I'm good," said Weiss.

Parker walked over and sat down on the couch. He took a sip, then said, "Look, anyone with half a brain knows that we're in no more danger today than we were six months, a year ago. The only thing that has changed is that you found that signal. Had you not found it and we didn't know there were other intelligent creatures out there, we wouldn't be sitting here now and you would be toiling away in some obscure position at the university."

"What about that woman? That Bachmann?"

"What about her? The story she tells does not alter the equation, nor does it alter reality. She believes that she has been abducted by aliens, but her story is the same as those told for more than fifty years. There is no physical evidence and nothing to prove the case. Maybe she's right, maybe she's deluded. Doesn't matter to us. Doesn't matter to the vast majority of people because even if she's right, it only affects a very small number of people and not the rest of us. Nobody cares until the numbers are in the thousands and they can see the reality of the situation themselves."

Weiss took a pull at his drink, swallowed, then said, "Shit."

"Listen. The name of the game is to get noticed, and now I'm noticed. I'm the expert on this, and I'm going to call for us to repel the aliens. We must put picket ships at the far ends of the Solar System and we must build, at a minimum, one ship that can attack the approaching aliens. Something with sufficient firepower that it will stand a chance of destroying the enemy if they actually get close to us."

"There go weapons into space."

"Oh, grow up. What makes you think there aren't weapons in space already? They've been there for over half a century. Now we have a reason to use them."

"Okay," said Weiss, draining the last of the alcohol. "All this is fine for you, but what about me? How is this going to help me?"

Parker grinned broadly, and said, "I thought you'd never ask."

CHAPTER 8

[1]

THOMAS HACKETT SAT WATCHING THE VIDEO replay of the news programs that morning and thought about how some things just seemed to resonate with the public consciousness. What had started as a local story about a UFO abduction and combined with the information that SETI had succeeded had become a national hot potato. Many, if not most, in the general public now believed that the radio source was not only artificial but was on some kind of a ship and jumped to the conclusion that the ship was hostile and heading to Earth. A reporter asked, not without some justification at least to Hackett's way of thinking, where else the ship might be heading? Clearly the Earth had the only technologically advanced civilization in this part of the galaxy and, if we could detect their radio signals, why would we think they couldn't detect ours?

And, of course, everyone was frightened because the aliens had a ship in deep space. Hackett, like everyone else, assumed that there was a crew on it. They were traveling in deep space.

Almost as if reading his thoughts, Colonel Ford asked, "Could we do that?" He looked first at General Greenstein, who sat at his huge desk, then at Bakker, whose attendence was via a television monitor. She was still in New Mexico, trying to wring the last little bit of information out of the radio telemetry.

"Technically," said Bakker, "the problem isn't all that difficult. We need a large ship, a way of tapping into fuel sources in space, assuming that we have a human crew, and then, of course we need to create the life support. The ship would not be able to travel the speed of light or anywhere close to it under current technology."

"Didn't we launch a probe into deep space, what seventy-five, a hundred years ago?" asked Greenstein.

Bakker grinned. "Well, sort of. We had designed an explorer probe that was to tour the outer planets, sending back telemetry. Once it crossed the orbit of Pluto, it entered deep space, heading, if I remember, in the direction of Alpha Centauri, about four light-years away."

"When did it get there?" asked Greenstein.

"Get there? It won't arrive for another seventy, eighty thousand years."

"Eighty thousand?" said Greenstein.

"It's traveling at sub light-speeds and not all that fast," said Bakker.

"Then this thing," said Greenstein, pointing at the television screen though Bakker couldn't see the other set, "might be tens of thousands of years from reaching Earth."

"That's kind of the way we see it, General," said Bakker, "Though I suspect it is continuing to accelerate. Even so, it should be decades before it could arrive."

"Then what in the hell is going on?" he asked. "How come you haven't made that comment to the media?"

Bakker shrugged, and said, "I have, but they're not

interested in my wait-and-see attitude. They have visions of aliens invading, which makes for great television and raises the ratings, while me saying nothing is going to happen makes for dull television and loses ratings. Besides, they had that picture pirated from us here in New Mexico."

"We need to get this information out. To tell people that nothing is going to happen for a long time, if ever."

Hackett leaned forward and turned up the volume on the set. "You might want to watch this." He looked at Bakker on her television, "This is one of your colleagues."

"I wouldn't describe him as such," said Bakker dryly.

Weiss, looking for all the world like the calm, rational scientist, told the television reporter, "Well, we can only speculate about the appearance of the enemy, but there are some solid assumptions we can make based on what we have been able to develop based on our research of the alien signal . . ."

"Did you hear that," said Greenstein, "the dumb son of a bitch called them 'the enemy.' He actually said that in a room full of reporters."

". . . two eyes, because they would need stereoscopic vision and depth perception to survive the prehistory phase of their evolution," said Weiss. "A third or fourth eye doesn't do much to increase the survival potential, and we see a symmetry in the face though it isn't well resolved. And we can assume a hand with an opposable thumb for grasping and later for tool manipulation. Bipedal, I would think, though I suppose they could have four legs and two arms. And a symmetrical body, again based on the limited information we have based on our observations on both the video stream and from our own evolution. I wouldn't be at all surprised if they were humanoid, though not necessarily human, in shape and form."

"That's end of the twentieth century, or earlier, thinking," said Bakker. "We don't know what environmental dangers an alien race would endure that would impact on their evolution. We can't make these sorts of assumptions."

"He certainly does like to hear the sound of his own voice, doesn't he," said Ford.

Hackett spoke for the first time. "You have to admire this. They're pushing all the right buttons. Enemy. Humanoid. Coming at us. Forget that they're decades away. Forget that they might not even be coming here."

"Are we in danger from these creatures?" asked the reporter on the television.

Weiss tented his fingers under his chin as if thinking about the question, then said, "Let me put it this way. Here, on Earth, anytime that a technologically superior civilization has come in contact with a technologically inferior civilization, that inferior civilization has ceased to exist. Just ask the Aztecs, Incas, or the Plains Indians."

"That's a little simplistic," said the reporter. "The Vandals sacked Rome."

"Somebody fed her that question," said Bakker. "She would never have thought of it."

Weiss, without missing a beat, said, "Yes, but the Romans were not technologically superior to the Vandals. True, they had a highly developed civilization, but their weapons and their armies were no better equipped or trained than the Vandals'. You can't stop an arrow with a book."

"Crap," said Ford.

Greenstein hit the mute button, and said, "I really don't want to listen to any more of this. I have already been called by a senator, two congressmen, one congresswoman, and four governors. They are all responding to calls, e-mails, faxes, and other communications from their constituents. They want action, and they want it now."

"What action?" asked Bakker.

Greenstein stared at her, then realized that she was not military and that he had invited her to participate for her expertise. "More than one suggested that we launch a counterattack."

[2]

SITTING BEHIND HIS DESK, JASON PARKER looked at the blinking lights on the telephone and knew that each light represented a reporter who wanted a quote from him. The value of the publicity was incalculable. It was hundreds of thousands of dollars in the local races and millions of dollars if he decided he wanted an even higher office. Name recognition would come with all those reporters talking about him in the media.

He leaned forward and touched the intercom. "Susan, who's next on the Hit Parade?"

"You didn't tell me that half the planet's population was going to call you. I'm not paid enough for all of this. I want a raise."

"You'll get it just as soon as the election is over. Who's next?"

"You want national or local?"

"National."

"Print or electronic."

"Something that will get my face on the airwaves. Electronic, please."

A moment later a new voice said, "Mr. Parker, my name is Harrison B. Smith."

"Yes, Mr. Smith."

"If you have a moment, I have some questions that I would like to ask, and then maybe issue an invitation for our nightly program, *Probe*."

"Ask away."

"How do you know that the space ship is hostile?"

"An old fighter pilot's logic. If it is pointed at you, then it is hostile. You assume hostility until you learn otherwise, and you stay alive."

"Isn't that a bad attitude to use when meeting an alien race for the first time?"

Parker chuckled. "I'm not suggesting we meet them with guns blazing, but I think due caution is necessary. We don't know anything about these creatures other than they are intelligent and they are traveling toward us. It seems to me that a prudent course is to prepare for the worst and hope for the best."

"Just what do you advocate?"

"That we build an interstellar ship and meet the aliens halfway. We confront them, if that is the proper attitude, beyond the confines of the Solar System. That way, if they turn out to be hostile, we won't suddenly be fighting for our lives in our own backyard."

"Can we do that?" asked the reporter.

"Of course we can. We have the technology now. The cost of a proper ship, designed to operate within a light-year or two of Earth, is well within our technological capabilities. To this point, we haven't had the incentive to build such a ship."

"An armed ship?" asked the reporter. "A battleship?"

"Let's not assign a pejorative here. Let's have a ship that can meet and greet the aliens, but one that is not without the capability to defend itself."

"Such an undertaking could expend our national wealth and that of the majority of the world . . ."

"No. No. No," said Parker. "We have some of the structure already constructed. We have ships working the asteroid belt, the moon, and even Mars. A diversion of just a few of those resources and a little new design so that the ship could defend itself would be all we need. The technology needed to outfit such a ship would be off the shelf. We tie it all together in space, outfit it for a year's patrol, and we're set."

"Okay," said the reporter as if he hadn't been listening to a word Parker said. "Let's do this. I'll have my producer call you this afternoon and we'll arrange for your appearance tonight. We'll have the same discussion."

"Sounds good," said Parker.

[3]

PRESIDENT WINSTON BUSKIRK SAT IN A CHAIR, near a couch, in his office at the White House. Not the Oval Office, where he sometimes spoke to the nation, or where he sometimes met the heads of state who assumed the Oval Office was where he worked, but a square room, that had a desk in the corner, floor-to-ceiling bookcases that held every book ever written by a president, many of those written by members of the government, and quite a few that told the history of the United States. There were a couple of large, leather-covered chairs, a credenza that held an assortment of alcoholic beverages, and a television set tuned to one of the news channels.

Buskirk was a man in his middle sixties, who had a full head of long, white hair that he darkened slightly, bright blue eyes, and a heavy, round face. He was a rotund man who was somewhat reminiscent of William Howard Taft, though he didn't have the same massive bulk.

Today he was in shirtsleeves because no one outside the government was scheduled to see him until later. At the moment, he, and four of his advisors were sitting, watching the smoking ruin that had been the heart of Paris. It looked as if someone had carpet bombed the downtown, but the damage was from a riot started by those who were afraid of the coming aliens. They had turned down the volume so that they didn't have to listen to the breathless reporting.

Buskirk had summoned his top advisors, then had sat among them saying nothing. He wanted them to become uncomfortable with his silence. He was waiting for one of them to say something, anything, that would get the meeting started. Buskirk was there to listen to them talk, toss around ideas, to brainstorm, because there were people in the street who believed that the alien menace could be stopped by throwing a brick through the window of a store and grabbing as much loot as could be carried away.

Finally, Norman Lowe said, "Mr. President, if I might suggest, we need to take a proactive initiative here."

"And that would be?" asked Buskirk.

Lowe, the youngest of the aides invited, but who was on the far side of fifty, shrugged. "I think we need to do something about this situation."

"Yes, you said that. You state the obvious. What would you have me do?"

"Obviously," said William Devine Ward, the oldest of the aides. He was still serving because he could stand neither sitting around the house in retirement nor his wife. "You must use the media to announce that we have nothing to fear."

"Is that correct?" asked Buskirk.

"Well, Mr. President," said Ruth Campbell, the science advisor, "it is correct for the next fifty years. That ship—if there is a ship—is that far away even if they can travel at the speed of light."

"Do we know there is a ship?" asked the president, quietly, looking from face to face.

"That, I think, we have already established. We know nothing about the ship, including the size. All we know for certain is that the source of these signals is an artificial platform among the stars with no evidence that it is on a planetary surface or associated with any of the stars in that vicinity of space. It must be some sort of ship."

Buskirk finally waved a hand to stop the debate. He realized that this group of advisors had no idea what to do about the alien ship. They hadn't looked at the historical perspective, nor had they looked at the pop cultural history. They had little or no idea what a presidential statement would do, or for that matter, should do. They didn't understand that anything he said on the topic would underscore the credibility of the situation and that either he had to say nothing at all or say something that could not be misconstrued and taken out of context by even the dumbest reporter. He had to be very careful.

Tired of the group, he stood up abruptly, and said, "Thank you all for coming."

[4]

THEY HAD CAPTURED A CORNER BOOTH, AWAY from the noisy businessmen who were laughing about how they had avoided the latest round of layoffs. They sat, with their drinks in front of them, leaning forward so that they could speak in quiet tones and not be overheard by anyone who might be interested in hearing what they had to say.

Rachel Davies sat next to Travis and across from Weiss. She didn't know that both of the men were hoping that the other would leave so that he could have a few minutes alone with her. Both were willing to wait hours for the opportunity and both realized that she might decide, at any moment, that it was time for her to go home without either of them. The two men were walking a thin line between getting what they wanted and seeing it disappear out the door.

Davies, glancing first at Travis, then at Weiss, and without meaning to, attacked at the point that was most likely to irritate both of them at once. She said, "I would have thought that a UFO guy and an astronomy guy wouldn't have much to say to one another."

Weiss started to speak, but Travis cut him off. "We both deal in evidence. It's just that astronomers sometimes ignore solid physical evidence of UFO visitation and pretend that it doesn't exist. This from a science that basically takes place on another planet and whose evidence takes the same form as mine but is out of reach of nearly everyone."

"Except," said Weiss, "that if I tell you I see something on one of those planets, you can look through your telescope and see it too. Not like UFOs, which have all the substance of, oh, I don't know. Swamp gas?"

"Yeah, tell me again about the canals on Mars and how the vegetation expands with the changing of the seasons and the shrinking of the polar caps."

"Legitimate conclusions drawn from the data at hand, and later reevaluated when the data were improved."

Davies interrupted to say, "But doesn't this ship mean that John might be right?"

"Well," said Weiss, not wanting to offend her, "it certainly changes the equation substantially."

Travis glimpsed a waitress and signaled for another round. He leaned back and put his arm up, on the rear of the booth so that it almost looked as if he was embracing Davies. He decided that a fight over the reality of UFOs was useless and that the alien ship, even if it never made it to Earth, did mean that some of the tales of alien visitation could now be proven. As he said, the equation had been changed.

"What do you think will happen?" she asked. "When it gets here, I mean."

"I would guess," said Travis, "based on past experience, nothing. Lots of talk and lots of ideas and maybe even a call for some kind of congressional investigation, but in the end, nothing will happen."

Weiss smiled, and said, "I don't agree. We now have the evidence of the ship, and we have the news media"—he stopped and nodded at Davies—"present company excluded, in the palm of our hand. They'll report whatever we say, find others to back us up and others still to debate. This will go on for months. There will be some kind of official investigation."

"Okay," said Travis. "I'll concede the point, but in the end, they'll ignore the data that we, meaning those of us in the UFO community, have collected."

"Don't need it now," said Weiss. "We have a real alien ship out there."

"What about the signal?" asked Davies. "Will we ever understand it?"

"I don't know," said Weiss. "We have to remember that whatever it is, it's in a foreign language. Unless they are attempting to communicate with us, meaning trying to set it up so that we can understand more of it, we'll be totally lost. We won't be able to understand it."

"That tells us nothing," said Travis. "At least with the UFOs we get some kind of communication."

"You get what you want there. We're dealing with science."

Davies interrupted again. "Then we don't know what they're saying."

"And I don't think we'll figure that out," said Weiss, "which means we won't be in communication with them."

"Then this is useless," she said.

Weiss grinned and said, "This is a situation that we all created. People upset with the aliens, suddenly afraid. There is no reason to feel that way. We just don't know anything about these aliens. Parker created this whole crisis to move his career forward, and we went along with it."

The waitress brought the drinks, set them in front of each person, and asked, "Anything else?"

"Nah. We're fine now. Thank you."

As she disappeared, Weiss said, "But it's not useless because it tells us we're not alone."

"Hell, I could have told you that," snapped Travis, "if you scientists had ever bothered to listen."

"Yeah, but you couldn't prove it."

"If you would have paid some attention to what we had in the way of evidence, I think we could. I think the evidence was there for all to see."

"Anecdotal testimony, fuzzy pictures, and burned areas on the ground that suggested a chemical engine for an interstellar craft. What crap."

"One man's anecdotal testimony is another's empirical evidence. It all comes down to what you want to accept and what you want to reject and sometimes that is a personal opinion not based on science at all. And, I say again, the point is moot because the ship is out there."

"If you boys are going to argue," said Davies, "I'm going home."

"Rather than go home," said Travis, "let's get something to eat."

"I thought you would never ask."

Weiss sat there for a moment, unsure of what to do. Travis hadn't looked at him, and Davies didn't seem to care if he accompanied them or not.

Finally, Davies looked at him. She didn't know which of these men could advance her career the most or the fastest. She smiled, and said, "You going to dinner with us or not?"

Weiss nodded, and Travis groaned.

CHAPTER 9

[1]

"THE IMMEDIATE SOLUTION, AS I SEE IT," SAID
the president, "is the creation of an office to take charge of
this situation. An agency that would have the responsibility for coordinating the information and overseeing our
response to it. An office that would command our assets
and direct their distribution so that we are not caught off
guard."

Major General George Greenstein had a sinking feeling
in the pit of his stomach. He sat opposite the president, in
the informal office with a cup of coffee in his hand. He had
met the president twice before, and each time the news had
been good. This time, the third time, he felt that his luck
would run out. He knew what was coming.

"This new agency would report directly to the secretary
of defense, and the officer in command would have access
to me as the need arose. It would be a job of great respon-

sibility because we would want to keep the panic from spreading." He waved a hand, indicating the windows and the world beyond that.

Greenstein knew that protocol demanded that he say nothing about this and not question the president, but his mouth ran away with him. "Wouldn't the science advisor, or any of the hundreds of scientists on the government payroll, be better at handling something like this?"

"Well, General, we thought about that and realized that, basically, this isn't a science question. Yes, you'll have scientists to assist you, but, in reality, we're talking about a military response here. And, as I understand it, you actually initiated some of the anticipated protocols a number of weeks ago, which puts you way ahead of the man in second place."

"Yes, Mr. President." His own forward thinking had finally come back to bite him in the butt.

Buskirk grinned broadly, and said, "There is a promotion to lieutenant general in this. Your name could be sent to the senate for confirmation by four this afternoon."

"Of course, Mr. President, I will take any assignment that I'm given, even without a promotion."

Buskirk laughed. "Now that I have promised the promotion, you suggest that the bribe was unnecessary."

"I didn't mean . . ."

"Of course, you didn't, General, and I didn't mean to imply that you did. Now, here's what I think we need. First, we have to quiet the population. They are . . . concerned that there is an alien ship out there. Overly concerned based on what has been reported in the last forty-eight hours."

"Yes, sir, I noticed that."

"And our creation, at this level, of an agency to deal with it is only the first step. What will happen next is that you will establish a headquarters and assemble a list of needs and priorities," said Buskirk, "but then, I'm sure you're aware of what needs to be done here."

"This strikes me as a little premature, Mr. President,"

said Greenstein. "I mean, the aliens are more than fifty light-years from Earth."

"But the people are uncomfortable right now. They want to see a government response to the implied threat. I am required to provide that response."

"Yes, sir, but if I might be so bold, isn't this just another example of creating a committee to examine a problem so that it looks as if something is being done?" As soon as he said it, Greenstein wanted to bite his tongue. The proper response was to say, "Yes, Mr. President." It was not to question the president's political motives.

Buskirk leaned forward and put his coffee cup on the table in front of him. "We're not creating a committee here to study the problem, but an agency to respond to it. We are taking a proactive stance and moving forward."

"Yes, sir."

"At the moment," said the president, "you have the bureaucrat's dream. You are not to worry about budget, equipment, or personnel. You can have whatever you feel you need and Congress will undoubtedly give it to you."

"Yes, sir."

"I want temporary offices set up at the White Sands Spaceport, but later I think we might want to move the operation into space, with headquarters either on the moon or Mars." Buskirk waved a hand to stave off protest. "No, we'll think about all this later, it's just something for you to keep in mind as we get this thing rolling."

The president stood up, signaling the end of the meeting. "I'll want you to brief the secretary of defense, and I'll want you to keep my science advisor informed. Other than that, you're free to roam far and wide."

Greenstein had stood when the president did. He asked, "Just what is the mission, Mr. President?"

"I thought that was obvious. To prepare to meet with the aliens."

[2]

THOMAS HACKETT WAS NOT HAPPY. HE HAD learned that Greenstein would be promoted to lieutenant general, and he was happy about that. He had learned that Greenstein would command a unit whose mission was vague, meaning that they would have a great deal of leeway in accomplishing it, and he was happy about that. But he had just learned that Greenstein had tapped him for his new aide, and Hackett wasn't happy about that. He was as unhappy as the kid locked outside of the toy store while his friends ran wild inside eating chocolate and drinking Coke without any adult supervision at all.

Now he was going to be an aide-de-camp and hadn't yet realized the power that trickled from the throne. When he made a suggestion, even those who outranked him would assume that he was speaking with the authority of the general. They would accomplish their assignments, not because Hackett had give them, but because they would assume that Greenstein would give them. If he was careful, Hackett could exercise his power and accomplish a great deal. If he was not, he would find himself back on the outside with a number of high-ranking officers angry with him. He would find his career dead with no chance of resurrection.

So he now walked around the temporary headquarters in New Mexico, literally a hundred miles from anywhere, and that anywhere was either El Paso, Texas, or Albuquerque, New Mexico. There wasn't much to do at White Sands except go somewhere else or watch the occasional launch of a rocket or missile. But he was one of the most important people there, and as soon as he drove through the front gate, he noticed the shift in power. There had been a lieutenant colonel waiting for him so that they could begin to prepare for the arrival of the general. The ranking officer at White Sands was only a major general, so Greenstein outranked him. Everyone at White Sands was well aware of that fact though Hackett had yet to fully understand the consequences of it.

The colonel, a fairly young man who had a receding hairline and the beginnings of a potbelly, looked like he had been a technician rather than a warrior. He didn't have a robust, strong look, but more of that of the intellectual. The black, horn-rimmed glasses seemed to cement the image.

As Hackett was attempting to convince the MP that he was neither a Chinese spy nor some lowlife civilian without insurance for his car, the colonel stepped forward, and asked, "Are you Captain Hackett?"

"Yes. I'm Major-designee Hackett," he said with a grin.

"Will the general be here shortly?"

"The general, wise person that he is," said Hackett, "is remaining in Washington for a few more days. I am the advance party."

"We have the guesthouse prepared," said the colonel.

"Yes, sir. You are?"

"Forgive me. My name is Clarke. I'm the adjutant."

"Well, Colonel, this wasn't really necessary. I can find the VOQ and get settled in. I will need to meet with the commander because there are a couple of things that we'll need, which is to say that the general will need, when he arrives. I require almost nothing."

The MP finished with the documentation that Hackett had given him. He said, "Everything appears to be in order, sir."

Clarke said, "I'll take care of it all. We'll go on base." He stopped near the door, and added, "I'm not sure where to put you. I could give you the guesthouse, which is much nicer than the VOQ, and I suppose you could make sure everything is ready for the general."

"As long as it's not a tent out on the desert," said Hackett, "I'll be happy."

"Even our tents are air-conditioned, and when we go to the field, our satellite tracking will pull in HBO. We are not Marines. We understand comfort."

"Isn't that scrambled? HBO, I mean."

"Not when we're through with it," said Clarke.

They walked out of the guard building, and Clarke asked, "Mind if I ride with you?"

"Nope. Aren't you leaving your car?"

"MPs'll bring it around when I want it. It's a staff car, so someone will take care of it."

They climbed into the sun-hot car. Hackett cranked the air conditioner up to max power and turned down the radio. As he pulled out of the parking lot, he asked with a grin, "Where am I taking me?"

"Let's swing by the guesthouse, and we'll work it out from there." Clarke gave instructions.

The guesthouse was a new building, erected because the spaceport, which had originally been an emergency landing strip for the old space shuttle, had been enlarged and turned into more of an actual port facility. Now there were ships that could be launched into orbit, modified from the original shuttle design that allowed them to take off like an airplane, gain the upper atmosphere using their wings, then turn into rockets as the atmosphere thinned and disappeared. They could dock with the space station or go on to the moon, where they docked with other orbital craft so passengers and cargo could be taken down to the surface.

White Sands had turned, slowly, from a missile-testing range hidden in the desert of New Mexico into a port facility. It might not have the glamour of Houston or Kennedy, but it was functional, it was far from prying eyes, and could be the perfect staging area for any military force launched to meet the alien ship.

All this explained why there was a new guesthouse on the range, for the dignitaries who often stayed inside the White Sands fences when there was an important launch. There was a large, long building that looked more like a motel than a VOQ, that held "minisuites," which meant they were larger than a motel room, had small refrigerators and microwaves, and even a parlor area away from the bed. Those were for the less-important dignitaries, though there was always a fight over who would get the big house and who would be relegated to the "motel."

Clarke pointed at the parking lot, and Hackett pulled in. For a moment Clarke sat. Then he said, "I really don't like getting out into this heat."

"But the building is air-conditioned," said Hackett.

"Of course. If you have a United States senator in residence, you would never put him or her into an environment that might be considered uncomfortable."

"Then I say we make a run for it."

"Okay," said Clarke, "but if you have heat stroke, it's your fault and not mine."

[3]

SARAH BAKKER WASN'T SURE WHAT HAD HAPpened. One minute she was a tenured professor at a fairly prestigious university and the next she was being dragged into government service against her wishes and desires. She was told that her job would be waiting when she finished her government service, but at the moment they needed her expertise more than a bunch of undergraduates who didn't seem to understand that astronomy was not astrology nor that they weren't going to learn how to predict the events of their lives by studying astronomy.

She stood in her apartment, books piled everywhere except where she had put her clothes. Every flat surface had been covered save in narrow walkways between the piles of clothes and books and the places she needed to get to. The air-conditioning was rattling, adding to the pounding in her head. She just wasn't happy and knew no way of changing the situation short of bolting out the door and disappearing into the night.

She finally realized that someone was knocking on the door. She opened it and found Avilson standing there. He was dressed for the weather in jeans and a T-shirt but looked as if he had spent too much time outside. He didn't look much like the department chair.

She backed up, let him in, and closed the door. She asked, "Can I get you something?"

"No. I just dropped by to give you the tickets and the travel arrangements."

"Why do you have them?"

"For some reason they sent them to the university. I guess they thought you'd be in your office."

"You know, this isn't really fair. I just got back from New Mexico, and now you're sending me there again."

"Well, I'm not sending you and, at least, you know what to pack."

Bakker moved deeper into the apartment, pulled the books off one of the chairs, and offered it to Avilson. She pushed some clothes aside and sat on the couch.

"How are you at spaceflight?" he asked.

"I don't like it. I get sick and stay sick for two or three days."

"Happens to a lot of people."

Bakker shook her head. "Surely there must be someone else who would be better qualified than I."

"Possibly, but you have been requested by name. The university will grant you a leave, and you'll be welcomed back when your assignment has been completed."

"Weiss is in on this."

"Steven Weiss is not going to represent this university in any matter of importance. He operates only in his own self-interest, and everyone and everything else be damned."

Bakker sat back and scrubbed at her face with both hands. "I can't see this as a boost to my career, speaking from a self-interested point of view."

Now Avilson grinned. "Government service at the request of the government because of your unique qualifications. We'll be hard-pressed to retain you as the other offers come in."

"I think this assignment might last a year or more," said Bakker. "I think they're going out to meet the aliens."

Avilson raised an eyebrow, and said, "Listen, anything you do in the next year is going to be important. The prestige will be of great value to the university."

Bakker closed her eyes for a moment, then opened them, looking around the apartment. She said, "But I live here. I don't want to move to New Mexico, even for a year. I want to stay here, in my house, living among my friends."

"You agreed to this," said Avilson.

"Yes, I did. I wish now that I hadn't."

[4]

FRANK HALL STOOD AT THE DOOR TO THE ED-iting bay, watching as Davies selected some of the equipment that she was going to take with her. He said, "You know what we want?"

She looked up, surprised, and said, "You want me to slip some exclusive stuff to you as I give my feeds into the network."

"Well, yes. You owe us."

Davies turned and sat down. She slowly crossed her legs, letting her skirt ride up as she watched Hall's eyes slip down to look. She said, "I don't owe you much of anything. I have this assignment not because of anything you did or any recommendation you made. I have it because I was on the story from the very beginning, and I happen to know some of the people."

"You forget that I assigned this story."

"You're beginning to sound like the man who sold Mark Twain his ink and paper. That has little or nothing to do with the situation as it exists today."

"I think you should remember that a year ago you were lucky to get any airtime."

Davies rubbed her eyes, almost in disbelief. "Just what is it you're after here, Frank?"

He stepped into the editing bay and slid the door closed. He looked down at her face, and said, "I understand the power has shifted here. I understand that the odds of your coming back to the station when this is over are very small. But I also understand that others can benefit from the situation. There are going to be people here, at the university, who can get in the way of your reporting. We can make sure that everything goes smoothly so that you can move up to the big time. But a little side reporting here and there, a couple of bones that we can exploit might help us all get out of here and move into a larger market. All I'm asking is that you keep that in mind. Help us out. We did help you."

Davies grinned broadly and nodded. "Of course, Frank. I'm sure there'll be lots of sidebar issues that you can exploit here. You need something from me, or I find something that can be of value to you, of course I'll keep you in mind." She tugged at the hem of her skirt. "Anything else?"

Hall realized that he was being dismissed by his employee. He could get angry and tell her off, but that would gain him nothing at all. She could make a single phone call and move up. The network was picking up the expenses, including Davies' salary. He could only ignore the nasty comments, pretend he didn't hear them or understand them, and move on.

"When you're ready to leave, meet me in the conference room for a few minutes."

"Of course."

[5]

STEVEN WEISS, AS HE HAD DONE ALL TOO often in the recent past, sat on the leather couch in Jason Parker's home office, watching the television. He held a drink in one hand and a cigar in the other. He looked as if he was celebrating, but that was the farthest thing from his mind.

Parker, who had just muted the TV, looked at Weiss, and asked, "Why is Bakker going to New Mexico and you're remaining here?"

"Well, I could be flip and blame you, but the truth of the matter is, she found the signal, and the government requested her help. I'm just the guy who sat on the sidelines and made trouble with talk of enemy aliens."

"I want you in New Mexico. I need a pipeline into what they are doing there."

Weiss took a drink of the bourbon, then set the glass on the end table. "That might not be all that easy. White Sands is a government installation."

"It is a public installation built with public funds being used as a public port facility. You have as much right to be there as Dr. Bakker. I know a couple of people in New Mexico who could arrange for you to get onto the base and observe what they're doing there."

"If I might make a suggestion," said Weiss, "maybe it would be better for me to go to the VLA. I could coordinate the search there, and I certainly would be in a position to let you know what has been heard or found. The board of regents here, interested in keeping the endowment of the university secure, would certainly listen to someone of your stature."

Parker laughed. "Not to mention the strings your father could pull."

"Well, there is that," said Weiss.

"So, maybe you base yourself at the VLA. It's not much of a trip down to White Sands from there."

"I've been thinking," said Weiss. "I'm not sure that the academic environment is the arena in which I want to play. I might be interested in something in the political field."

"You want what?"

Weiss picked up the glass, studying the liquid as he swirled it around. "If you are successful in your bid for the

Senate, you're going to need a staff. I would think that a position on that staff that could lead me into bigger and better things might be something of interest."

Parker couldn't help but grin. Weiss was so transparent that even a child could see through him. He nodded, and said, "Providing I win the election, you'll be the first on my staff."

"So, I guess I better go pack. I have to make a trip to New Mexico."

[6]

IT HAD BEGUN TO LOOK AS IF NO ONE WAS IN-terested in what a UFO researcher had to say about the on-coming alien ship. The telephone calls had dried up, a couple of producers who had said to call at any time seemed to have forgotten his name in recent days, and even his editor had brushed him off. Travis thought that it had been nice to be in the spotlight, and it certainly had diverted his attention, but now that was over. All that was left was the completion of his book, which would probably sell well enough that he could write others, but not well enough that he would have the money he wanted.

The ringing phone caught his attention. He reached over for the headset, punched the button, and said, "Yes?"

"Hello, Jonathan. This is Rachel."

Travis laughed because he thought she would be another of those who never bothered him again. "Well, hello."

"I've just got a few minutes," she said. "I'm on my way to White Sands. I wondered if you were going to be there."

"I have no plans at the moment."

Davies said, "I was thinking that your expertise would be of great help to me in New Mexico."

"Given the direction of this situation," said Travis carefully, "I'm not sure just what I might be able to provide or what expertise I bring to the table."

"We're going to be taking Susan Bachmann with us," said Davies. "But her knowledge is limited to what she has experienced herself. You, on the other hand, have a wide body of information that could be useful."

"Then you'll be picking up the expenses?"

"Well, no. But if you go to New Mexico, I'm sure that we can pay you something for your trouble and hire you as an expert consultant. It wouldn't be much, but it would be something."

"You said that you are on the way out. How soon do you leave?"

"Later this afternoon, but I'll be staying at the Holiday Inn in Alamogordo, at least for a few days. You can reach me there if you need to."

Without much conviction, Travis said, "I do have the book to finish."

"Go ahead," said Davies. "I'm going to New Mexico. I was hoping that you could make it, too."

CHAPTER 10

[1]

THE CONFERENCE ROOM WAS BIGGER AND BETter than anything that newly promoted Lieutenant General George Greenstein had seen in quite a while. It was paneled with dark woods but had an all-glass west wall that provided a magnificent view of the Organ Mountains. Naturally the glass was tinted, and as the sun tracked across the sky, the tint seemed to thicken so that the sun's rays did not completely penetrate to annoy those in the room, or to overheat the interior.

The conference table was more or less diamond-shaped, so that someone sitting at one of the points of the diamond would be able to see everyone else. The table was made of dark wood and held a silver water service with a pitcher beaded with moisture.

The chairs were high-backed and well padded. In front of each were a notepad and a pen. The preprinted conference agenda was sitting on top of the notepads. There were also keyboards that could be shared by three people. They had used keyboards rather than voice input so that there would be no interruption to those speaking if someone wanted to access the mainframe.

Greenstein sat at one of the points with newly promoted Major Thomas Hackett sitting beside him. Sarah Bakker was in the room, as were Robert Ford and Rachel Davies. Greenstein had reluctantly agreed to the presence of the reporter because he planned to discuss nothing of a classified nature.

Steven Weiss, who had traveled down from the VLA, was also there, though Bakker had protested. She didn't believe that he would have anything to say that anyone would want to hear. She believed that Gibson and Taylor, who had remained at the VLA, had provided her with everything known to Weiss. She had told all this to the general, but Greenstein had allowed Weiss to stay.

The rest of the positions were filled with men and women appointed for various staff functions, some of whom had arrived in New Mexico only in the last forty-eight hours. The single and most notable exception was Captain Ray Lewis, a naval officer who would command the ship once construction was finished and it had been outfitted.

Greenstein sat quietly for a moment, then nodded slightly. Hackett touched a button and an LCD screen slowly descended, locking into place. The tint on the windows darkened at the same time, throwing the room into gloom.

There was a slight flickering and the images on the screen coalesced into a color picture of rioting in the downtown area of an American city. Without commentary, the scene switched, first to Paris, then to London. Each showed burning cars, broken plate-glass windows, hundreds—maybe thousands—of people running, some of them covered in their own blood. Each was a scene of chaos as the world reacted to the information about the alien ship and the pictures reported to have come from it.

The scene changed to a news anchor standing near a podium, looking sincerely into the camera, with the most dramatic and most highly speculative of the pictures over her shoulder as she read the TelePrompTer. She didn't bother to mention that the picture was an extrapolation from a computer model and could be horribly wrong. The impression she gave, as did all the others who reported on the story, was that the audience was seeing, for the first time in human history, a being from another planet.

When the segment ended, the screen went dark, and the windows brightened. Greenstein looked from face to face, then said, simply, "Comments?"

"The rioting is all out of proportion to the information that we have," said one of the military men.

Greenstein glared at him, and said, "What would you have us do to stop it?"

Bakker said, "Better information distribution."

"Not going to happen," said Greenstein. "The press is in business to make money and gather viewers. Sexy and exciting win over a gray-toned splotch that could be almost anything. What broadcaster is going to want to show the splotches when they have the color picture in which the shapes are resolved to a point that looks as if we have something real."

Bakker nodded, and said, "Point taken."

Greenstein waited, but there was no more commentary. Finally, shrugging, he said, "Okay, I'll tell you what we'll do. It is simple, but it is expensive, and it is the reason that we're all here. We go meet the alien ship."

"But we don't know that it's coming here," said Bakker. "All we have is a general track toward us."

"Granted," said Greenstein, "and irrelevant for two reasons. First, we must prepare just in case the ship is headed to us. And second, the president said that we were to prepare. Therefore, we will."

Hackett touched the buttons again, the windows darkened further, and the screen brightened. Now there was a science piece on one of the orbiting space stations. It was a large, cumbersome craft fitted with dozens of gigantic solar panels to gather energy from the sun, and twenty or more silver pods connected to a long, cylindrical center structure that housed the main crew quarters and most of the electronic equipment. The whole structure was twenty years old and had been used as a backup system for the last five. A smaller, but more efficient station, had finally been built and was in use.

Greenstein said, "This is going to be the core of our ship. It will be retrofitted with weapons systems, redesigned for a larger crew, and made somewhat self-sufficient. I don't want to get into design specifics here and now, but each of you will find the technical details published on the local web, with access restricted by code word and specific networking. In other words, it is a closed system."

Lewis, who would captain the new ship, stared for a moment, then asked, "We're supposed to fly this relic into deep space, meet the aliens, and convince them not to invade?"

Greenstein stared at Lewis long and hard. It seemed as if hours passed, as if the seasons changed, and decades slipped away. Finally, he said, "I thought you understood. Our real mission is to convince the public that we're doing something about the alien menace. Our mission is to look good, provide comfort, and, in the end, if necessary, launch our ship into deep space. Everything so that the people feel safe."

"Time frame?" asked someone.

"We work at a frantic pace," said Greenstein, "until the public loses interest in this, then slow down. We have plenty of time. Decades, actually."

Bakker looked uncomfortable, and said, "Well, that's not quite accurate. We know where the ship was fifty years ago, but it has been traveling. We need to find it again so that we have a clue about how long it will take to get here."

Greenstein didn't appear surprised by Bakker's revelation. He smiled slyly, and repeated, "We work frantically until the people move on to the next fad, then we slow down. But make no mistake, we will launch, and we will travel out beyond Pluto."

[2]

WHEN THE MEETING BROKE UP, AND WITH Greenstein stuck in conversation with both Lewis and Ford, Hackett hurried from the room, following Bakker. He caught her near the door that led outside.

"You don't want to go out there. It's hotter than hell at this time of day. I wouldn't be surprised to learn that the cars had melted in the parking lot."

She turned and smiled. "I thought you'd be busy with the general."

"Normally," said Hackett. "But he can spare me for a few minutes. He needs to talk to Lewis about taking command of the starship."

Bakker couldn't help herself. She laughed out loud. "That what you're calling it. A starship?"

"Yes."

"You know, technically, it isn't. As I understand it, the ship will never really get out of the Solar System."

"We're going beyond Pluto in it."

"Yes, beyond Pluto you have the Oort Cloud. Cometary material that is still in the Solar System. It's about a light-year or so out, but is still part of the Solar System."

Grinning, Hackett said, "It's the best we can do on such short notice."

Bakker was tired of waiting. She asked, "You taking me to dinner tonight or not?"

"Where did you want to go?"

"Las Cruces isn't all that far from here."

"I'm not sure that I can get that much time off. The general has an awful full plate here, with the rush to get something visible accomplished."

"Then take me to dinner at the officers' club if that's all

the time you've got. I'll plan on Las Cruces but won't be too disappointed."

"Don't you need to go back to the VLA?"

"Not for a couple of days," said Bakker. "I've got people there who are watching the system."

Hackett looked around, saw that the hallway was vacant. Not a sign of anyone. Just the quiet background hum of the air-conditioning and the buzz of the overhead lighting. He stepped closer to Bakker.

"I thought the military frowned on public displays of affection."

"They do . . ."

A voice seemed to fill the hallway. "Hackett, where in the hell did you get to?"

Bakker laughed again. "Wonderful intercom system you have here."

"I'll call you," said Hackett as he turned and dashed up the hallway.

[3]

GIBSON WAS QUIETLY EATING PIZZA AND watching a DVD on his laptop. The movie was twenty years old, but the special effects were still spectacular. It looked as if the war had been fought in space. Even the science seemed to be on the beam, without noisy explosions, just flares of bright light that flashed as a ship's oxygen fueled a fire for a few moments. It was a dazzling dance of momentarily bright colors, flashes, then blackness.

With the earphones on so that he bothered no one else, he didn't hear Taylor speak to him. He didn't see her glance at him, annoyed, but he did hear her shout. He pulled the earphones from his head, and said, "What?"

"We got it."

"We got what?"

"Signal. Found it again. About five minutes ago."

Forgetting the DVD, Gibson stood up. He tossed his half-eaten pizza slice onto a plate, and said, "Show me."

Taylor stood to one side, away from the monitor. She pointed at the screen. "About here."

"Hell, that can't be it. It's not in the same place."

"Of course not. A ship moves. But the signal matches what we got before."

"Same message?"

"No. It's the same sort of signal."

"How far away?"

Taylor stared at him and said, "Still preliminary. Don't have much data with which to work . . ."

"You know, don't you?"

Taylor nodded. "Yeah. We make it about thirty light-years."

"Christ, they've traveled twenty light-years in a matter of weeks."

"Well, we don't know that," said Taylor. "I mean, the signal we're getting is thirty light-years away and the last was fifty, but we don't know how long it took them to get there. Maybe weeks, maybe years."

Gibson wiped his mouth with his fingers as he thought about all of this. With a ship, they didn't know how fast it could travel. All they knew was that one signal was fifty light-years away and the next closer. The only thing they could say was that the first signal had to travel fifty years and the second thirty years to get to Earth. It really gave them no clue about the location of the ship now.

"Get Bakker on the phone. We've got to tell her we got the signal again."

"Already done."

[4]

WEISS LEARNED OF THE NEW SIGNAL ABOUT the same time that Bakker did. He was sitting in the cool, darkened room of the VOQ, working at his computer, an-

swering some of the mail that had accumulated since he
had left the university. He found two new job proposals
and one of them actually looked as if it would be worth
chasing.

But then he found the e-mail that had been sent to
Bakker with a copy to him and a copy to Avilson. He
scanned it quickly, grinned to himself, and stood up. Suddenly he was excited. He felt full of energy. He had to
move around, though what he wanted to do was run. He
felt an almost physical need to run, but there was nowhere
to go, and the things that he had to do required he sit still.

He walked to the window and pulled apart the curtains
so that he could look out on the sun brown landscape. It
was obvious that some deluded soul had believed that
there should be a lawn around the building and had tried to
get it to grow. The expenditure of funds on a lawn had been
cut, at some point, because there was little left except the
brown remnants. Near a couple of trees, near a flower bed
that held cactus was the last little bit of pale green. The
lawn was going into hibernation and would probably die
from a lack of water.

He took a deep breath and then another and finally a
third. He walked slowly across the room and broke the seal
on a bottle of bourbon. His father drank Scotch, so he
would drink bourbon. It annoyed the old man.

He poured two fingers, sucked it down in one burning
gulp, then poured again, nearly filling the glass. He knew
he should, at the very least, drop a couple of ice cubes in
the bourbon, but he didn't want to cut its power.

Finally, he sat down at the telephone, got an outside
line, and dialed. He took another long pull of the booze as
he listened to the phone ring at the other end.

"Parker."

Weiss grinned to himself. Well, at least the private line
was a private line that Parker answered himself. Without
identifying himself, believing that Parker would recognize
his voice, Weiss said, "I have the next big announcement
for you."

There was a slight hesitation, then Parker said, "And what would that be."

"The ship is closer."

"You sure?"

"Christ, Parker, I'm not the idiot that you think me to be. Of course I'm sure."

"How close?"

"Thirty light-years."

There was a snort, and then, "That's still decades away."

"Not if you package it right. Two months ago we're worried about a ship that is fifty light-years from Earth. Now that same ship has traveled twenty light-years and is much closer. Just in a matter of months, weeks really."

"They've got faster-than-light drive," said Parker.

Weiss laughed. "Hell, I don't know. This really doesn't mean that, but everyone is going to jump to that conclusion. It could have taken them twenty years to travel that distance. It could be a different ship, responding to the first. Could be lots of things, but everyone is going to believe that it has faster-than-light drive. That the aliens have faster-than-light drive."

"They know this in New Mexico."

"Of course."

"What's the reaction there?"

"Hell, I don't know. I just found out about it myself. I'm sure they just found out. No time for any sort of a reaction."

"How did the big meeting go today?"

"Just about what you'd expect from any major bureaucracy. Nothing was really accomplished other than the general suggested that we're moving ahead full speed until the people lose interest. Then they'll fall back to regroup."

"He said that?" asked Parker.

Weiss picked up the bourbon and took a strong pull at it. He felt it burn down his throat and pool in his stomach. "Not in so many words, but that was the drift."

"Okay. Listen, I'm not going to quote you. I don't want them to think you're feeding me information."

"They're not stupid. Where else could you have learned that the ship is closer and that the general here doesn't take the threat all that seriously?"

"You just watch the news broadcasts. There will be some fireworks today, and you won't get burned."

[5]

WHEN THEY WERE IN THE CAR AND OUT THE gate, driving along the road that led up, into the Organ Mountains, Bakker said, "So, the general didn't need you tonight."

"I told him that I needed some time off. I wanted to go into Las Cruces for dinner," said Hackett. "I needed something other than mess hall food no matter how good that food might be."

"And he assumed that you would be taking this trip all by yourself?"

"He said, and I quote, 'I hope that Doctor Bakker has some fun, too.' End quote."

They came down out of the mountain pass, and the land around them opened up. The highway became wider, and there were hints of civilization. They came to a stoplight, slowed, but the light changed and they accelerated. From somewhere came the wail of a siren. Hackett wondered where it was. The sound seemed to bounce around the landscape, confusing him. He couldn't figure out the direction to it.

They slowed for another light, and Hackett saw a fire truck to the right. The air horn sounded as it approached the intersection, and although the light for Hackett was green, he pulled to the side of the road and stopped. The fire truck turned and began to race down, into Las Cruces.

"Wonder what that is all about," said Bakker.

There was another siren, and a police car followed the

path of the fire truck. More sirens, these from behind them, sounded. Hackett glanced up, into the rearview mirror and saw two police cars and a highway patrol car. A fire truck followed them.

"Something big," said Hackett. "Turn on the radio and see if you can find out anything."

Bakker scanned through rock and roll, jazz, all-sports, talk radio, and country and western. She found an all-news station, but it was in El Paso, and kept trying. She could find nothing that would provide local news.

Hackett kept driving south, into the more built-up areas of Las Cruces. Then, in the distance, in what would have been the downtown area, he spotted a black cloud growing. He pointed it out to Bakker.

"What do you think?" he asked.

"Riots?" said Bakker, then something on the radio caught her attention. "Listen."

Hackett recognized the voice. It was Jason Parker telling a reporter that he believed the alien's signal had been found again. The enemy ship had moved and was now much closer to Earth.

"The danger has increased dramatically," said Parker. "Yet the government, the military, our authorities are doing nothing about it. Instead they insist there is no real danger. But ask yourself, just why haven't they bothered to tell us they have reestablished contact with the aliens. What are they hiding?"

"Contact?" asked the reporter.

"We know where that ship is, and they haven't bothered to tell us that," said Parker.

"Shit," said Hackett. "We're going to have to go back to White Sands."

"Yeah."

"How in the hell did he find this out so fast?"

"Weiss told him. Had to be Weiss," said Bakker. "He's still on the university e-mail, so he was copied with the message to me."

"I can have him thrown into jail," said Hackett.

"What good would that do? The report has already been made. You heard it yourself."

"We could keep him from making any more."

"We can do that by cutting off his flow of information," said Bakker. "The university isn't going to be happy that he has, once again, gone public with no authority."

"Shit, if we were in a state of war, waiting for the enemy invasion, we could have him shot as a spy. I could have him shot so full of holes that he would whistle when he walked."

Bakker grinned, but said, "And make him a martyr, not to mention putting Parker into the Senate."

"Still, it has a nice ring to it. And, it has the added benefit that we wouldn't have to hear from him again."

Hackett pulled into the turn lane, waited for the traffic to get out of his way, and then made a U-turn. They were now headed back up the long, gentle slope to the Organ Mountains.

"The general is going to be pissed," said Hackett.

"A lot of people are already pissed."

CHAPTER 11

[1]

THERE WAS A SUDDEN DEMAND, COMING FROM senators, from politicians, from the public, to put someone in space, to get something done and to do it immediately. The radio was telling Hackett and Bakker that. Even as some of the cities burned and the people were in the streets stealing everything that wasn't nailed down, the politicians were trying to find the best way to exploit the situation for their own benefit.

Hackett raced up the Organ Mountain highway. They reached the top, and the valley beyond was spread out in front of them. In the semidarkness of the twilight, he could see the lights of White Sands and the dark smear in the desert that was the spaceport. The lights along its runways and around its hangars had yet to come on. Or someone had turned them out.

The access road that led from the main highway down

to the base looked as if it was outlined by lights. There was a double-wide white line that didn't move. At first Hackett was puzzled, then realized the line was made of cars, all heading in, toward the base.

"We've got trouble," he said.

Bakker, who had been sitting quietly, her face a mask, nodded. She hadn't spoken, except to answer a question or two, since they had turned around to return.

"Can we get onto the base?"

"I think the access road is going to be blocked. I think the people are going to throw rocks at anyone who looks as if they're assigned to the base."

"So how do we get back?"

Hackett pulled the car to the side of the road. He sat there, studying the situation below him almost as if it were a military problem drawn up on a sand table at West Point. He leaned over across Bakker and opened the glove box, taking out a pair of binoculars.

"I'll see if I can spot anything," he said as he opened the driver's door.

As he got out, he heard more traffic and turned in time to see a line of cars coming down out of the mountains. Clearly some of the citizens of Las Cruces had decided to see if there was anything they could destroy at White Sands. There was a bright glow behind them that suggested hundreds of people were leaving Las Cruces.

Hackett jumped back into the car and jammed it into gear. He spun the wheels and didn't bother looking back. He just wanted to beat the oncoming traffic before it boxed him in, leaving no way to get back on the base. He wanted to be at the head of the line.

"What in the hell are you doing?"

"We've got to get down there before all those people behind us block the way completely."

Bakker turned in her seat. "Where the hell did they all come from?"

"Don't know and don't care," Hackett said as he slowly

increased his speed until they were traveling over a hundred miles an hour.

"How we going to get onto the base."

"I figure that they have the road going in blocked, but not that coming out. I'm going to drive up the wrong way."

"Isn't that dangerous?"

Hackett, his eyes on the road, said, "Everyone on the base is going to be locked in. No one is going to leave. We'll be fine if we're careful."

They rode in silence for a few minutes, but then, as they neared the turnoff, they found a line of cars backed up along the access ramp and out onto the shoulder of the highway. Hackett slowed and pulled in behind the last car in line.

"We could walk," said Bakker.

Hackett grinned. "I learned long ago that you never walk when you can ride. We have wheels, so, we just have to think about this for a moment and get a good view of the lay of the land."

"Then we're not blocked?"

"Of course not." He pointed out the windshield. "You'll notice that everyone has done exactly what he or she is supposed to have done and pulled to the shoulder. Ever wonder why the majority of the people in a mall or airport concourse walk down the right side? We unconsciously obey the rules of the road. Aliens are in space, coming here for who the hell knows what, but people automatically obey the rules of the road."

"And this is an important psychological observation because?" asked Bakker.

Without answering, Hackett pulled out of the line and began passing the cars. He drove up, on the opposite shoulder of the access ramp to avoid those cars still sitting on the main part of the roadway. He came down off the ramp, pulled around another car, and without worrying about the stop sign, began driving down the left-hand side of the highway. Any cars on that part of the road would be met head-on.

Just as he suspected, once he had introduced the idea, others followed suit. There were cars pulling out of the line and joining in a column behind him. He began to speed up, hoping that no one in front would pull out.

As he approached the guardhouse and main gate he saw that the roads had been blocked by two big trucks pulled sideways across the road. One held a spotlight and the other a machine gun pointed at the cars.

"Okay, here's where it gets a little dicey."

"It gets dicey here?" asked Bakker.

Hackett pulled to the side of the road and parked. "Get out slowly, hold up your hands so they can see we're unarmed, and walk forward. They'll tell us to stop before they begin shooting."

"You're sure?"

"Nope."

Hackett pushed open his door and got out. He stood, his hands in the air, waiting until Bakker was out on the other side. Once she had closed her door, Hackett began to walk forward slowly. Out of the corner of his eye, he saw people, on the other side of the road getting out of their cars. Most were just watching him, to see what happened.

A small spotlight focused on him and he noticed a bright red point of light on Bakker's chest. He looked down and saw one on his. Snipers had illuminated their targets in case they were ordered to shoot.

"Tom, I don't like this."

"It's okay. They're just being careful."

"Halt," ordered a deep male voice. "This is a closed installation, and any attempts to penetrate the perimeter will be met with deadly force."

"I'm Major Thomas Hackett. This is Dr. Sarah Bakker. We are assigned to this facility and request that we be allowed to enter."

Bakker leaned closer and whispered, "Was that a good idea?"

For an instant he didn't understand, and then heard a murmur run through the crowd. They now had the identities of Hackett and Bakker and there were some who found that troubling.

"Advance," said the voice.

Hackett and Bakker began to walk forward. There was a shout from the crowd then. Someone yelled, "Get them!"

Something landed at Hackett's feet. He turned and saw a man throw a rock. He jerked Bakker to the left and sent her sprawling. He ducked and heard the rock bounce off the pavement.

There was a burst of machine-gun fire and the shattering of glass. The gunner had fired into the radiators of the nearest cars, smashing them and breaking the headlights. Radiator fluid gurgled on the ground.

Lights all along the perimeter came on. Some flashed on the people standing on the highway. Everyone was momentarily stunned by the shooting and the new lights. Hackett reached down, grabbed Bakker's hand, and jerked her to her feet. They ran toward the closest of the trucks.

A uniformed man appeared, a weapon held in his hand. "Identify yourself."

Hackett began to reach for his ID card, but a voice from behind the truck said, "They're okay. I recognize them."

"I'm passing them on your authority, Colonel."

Hackett and Bakker squeezed between the front of one truck and the rear of the other. One man approached, and Hackett recognized Ford. He said, "Good evening, Colonel."

"You picked a hell of a night to leave the post."

"Yes, sir. That I did."

Ford glanced at Bakker. "Are you all right?"

Bakker looked down. She had torn her skirt and scraped and bloodied her knee. She said, "This is the last time I allow him to take me to dinner." She smiled as she said it.

[2]

LIEUTENANT GENERAL GEORGE GREENSTEIN
sat in the White Sands communications center, looking at
a black box that held a single, cyclopean eye. There had
been a cameraman behind the box, but once he had everything in place and locked down, he left the communications room. He was not cleared to listen to the discussion
that Greenstein would hold with the president.

Slightly lower and to the right were three small television monitors. On two of the screens were other military
officers, including the chairman of the Joint Chiefs of
Staff, Marine general Norman Valance, and the other was
the chief of Naval Operations, Admiral Edward P. Reese
who had the current responsibility for the space station that
would be used to meet the alien ship.

The center screen showed an empty desk that had the
presidential seal on the front. There was an American flag
to one side and the president's flag on the other.

Greenstein watched as the president entered the room
and sat down behind his desk. "All right, gentleman, I
think that we can get started."

Valance said, "I am required to remind all that this is a
closed circuit signal that is shielded, but that we have not
had time to make sure that the signal is completely secure.
We must be circumspect in what we say because there is a
chance, however minuscule it might be, that our signal is
compromised."

"That's understood, General," said the president. He
shuffled a couple of papers on his desk, then turned to the
right so that he could look at a computer screen. He used a
mouse to scroll down, found what he wanted, and stopped.

"According to the latest reports," said the president,
"there are riots in fifty-two cities. There have been, so far
this evening, twelve deaths and countless people injured.
We won't have any idea of the damage until tomorrow.
This situation cannot be allowed to continue."

"Mr. President," said Greenstein, "the problem, at the

moment, is that we've had a leak to a relatively unknown politician who desires higher office and is using this information to . . ."

"General, I am uninterested how this information got out."

"Yes, sir. I merely pointed out that we have identified the source and that it is plugged. No more information will be leaked."

"You have failed to grasp the point here, General," said the president. "The real point is that the people are frightened, and they are reacting to that fright. They see some obscure politician telling them about an alien ship coming toward the Earth, and hours later, we're required to confirm the information is accurate. It makes us look as if we're hiding something."

"The information was preliminary . . ."

"That's not the point," snapped the president. "The point is, the people are afraid of this ship and what it represents. They want us to take action."

Greenstein nodded but said nothing more.

"Mr. President," said Reese, "the Navy is ready to act whenever we have the orders."

"And what would you do?" asked the president.

"Move up the launch dates. Put some people onto the space station immediately. We can always send up more matériel. We've got enough ships that we can ferry matériel to it, even if we've already launched it."

Valance said, "Might be interesting to move the headquarters to Mars. That would certainly limit communications and therefore limit the leaks. Worst case, we would have a couple of weeks to make a decision about what to say."

Now Greenstein interrupted. "Mr. President, it's bad enough being in New Mexico. Now you want me on Mars?"

Valance laughed.

The president grinned. "General, you screw up, and you go to Mars. Screw up again and I think we have an outpost on Titan that could use a commander. Screw up a third time and I'm thinking Pluto."

"I didn't screw up," said Greenstein, but the moment the words were out of his mouth he was sorry he said them.

"General," said the president, "I understand that. But we do have a crisis situation developing here, and I believe that positive action is the only way that we're going to bring this thing under control."

"Yes, sir."

"How soon can you put some of your people onto the space station?"

Greenstein sat quietly for a moment, then said, "If it is operational, I know of no reason that some of them couldn't go up within forty-eight hours. We have a launch vehicle here that is nearly ready. They couldn't do much for a couple of days, but I can get them there quickly."

"Then I'm going to announce tomorrow that we'll be sending up the first contingent in a few days. Let it be known that we plan to meet the threat, whatever it might be, head-on."

"That's fine Mr. President," said Greenstein. "There are some issues we must iron out before that happens. Issues that might be better discussed in person."

"General, why don't you plan to come to Washington on Friday, providing the launch has gone well and some of your people are on the space station. I have some time for you then."

"Yes, sir."

"If there are no other comments about this," said the president.

Valance said, "Do you wish to use federal troops to end the riots?"

"No, General, I thought I had made that clear earlier. If the governors wish to use the National Guard, that will be their decisions. If they request federal aid, we will provide what we can within the limits of posse comitatus. Federal troops will not be used for law enforcement activities. They can have equipment if it will not damage our various military commitments."

"Yes, sir."

"Anything else?"

Each of the officers could see that the president was interested in ending the discussion. Each of them said, "No, sir."

There was a moment of silence, then a voice somewhere said over the system, "Breaking down." Each of the pictures faded, and Greenstein was left staring at the camera, all alone in the communications room.

[3]

HACKETT HAD BEEN UP ALL NIGHT AND FELT like it. In his younger days he sometimes designed his work, whether in college or in the Army, so that he was awake all night. There was something exciting about having managed to resist bed, to complete a task, and find the morning sun there to greet you. Now, he felt tired, dirty, old, and annoyed. He could have used a shower, a breakfast of steak and eggs, and a nap. Instead he sat in the conference room, looking at a number of other men and women who looked as if they'd had little sleep, could use a good breakfast and a shower, and who were now feeling the strain. They looked like those who had been given the impossible but attempted to do it anyway. But they were more tired than the mountains, hungrier than a football team, and dirtier than Redd Foxx.

Bakker, dressed in khakis, her hair pulled back from her face, was drinking water constantly. She seemed to be dehydrated, though Hackett could think of no reason for her to feel that way other than they were on a desert.

Weiss was the only one who looked as if he had gotten any sleep. He seemed refreshed and happy. He wouldn't be once he found out the direction the meeting was going to take. Then he would be as annoyed as most of the others in the room and angrier than the Palestinians.

Hackett was surprised to see Davies sitting at the table, a small video camera in front of her. She was dressed fashionably, wearing a mock–suit jacket that had a masculine look to it, a silk shirt with a man's tie. Like Weiss, she looked as if she had gotten a full night's sleep.

Greenstein appeared at the door, wearing a clean class-A uniform complete with all his awards and decorations. He was freshly shaved, and his hair was neatly, and recently, trimmed. He looked as if he had just stepped from his quarters, where he had been waited on by his staff and that he had no cares or worries.

"Ladies, gentlemen, the commanding general," said Hackett as he climbed to his feet.

When Greenstein reached his chair, followed by two others, a man and a woman, he said, "Take your seats."

There was a rustling as everyone complied. Davies reached for her camera and took a panning shot of the room, starting at one point of the table and working her way around it. Hackett was surprised when Greenstein said nothing to her as she focused the camera on the general.

"I'll open this meeting," said Greenstein, "by mentioning that Mr. Travis here, and Ms. Davies there, are invited guests. Travis for his expertise with UFOs and Ms. Davies as the pool representative of the various media outlets." For the moment he didn't introduce the woman with him.

He waited as that sank in, then added, "All aspects of the mission will be discussed in this room and nothing held back, even if you believe there are security considerations." He turned his attention to the reporter. "You'll have to clear your reports with me before you'll be allowed to transmit them, but that is only to prevent the accidental compromise of classified material."

With her camera pointed at Greenstein, she said, "That is unacceptable, General. I will report what I believe is important, without restrictions."

Greenstein's facial expression didn't change. His voice deepened slightly, and there was a hard edge to it. "Well, then, why don't you pack up your camera, and I'll have the military police escort you from this facility immediately. I'm sure that one of your fellows out there will understand the need to protect materials that are lawfully classified."

"You can't do that. There are open meeting laws, and I am here as a properly credentialed member of the media."

"And this is a military installation, and the meeting is of national security importance. Therefore, my authority supersedes your sunshine law. Either abide by my decision here or get out now. There is no middle ground."

She got to her feet, picked up her notebook, but kept the camera trained on the general. And then she thought better of it, and realized that outside she would be just another reporter, but in here she was an observer to history. There was no graceful way for her to retreat now. She had begun to make her stand, and if she surrendered, the fight was over. Finally, realizing she had no real choice, she dropped back into the seat without acknowledging her capitulation.

Greenstein then turned his attention to the others in the room. He said, "I have been advised by the president that we are to begin our mission within twenty-four hours. What this means is that, Captain Lewis, you are going to be lifted to the space station either late this afternoon, or just after dawn tomorrow morning."

There was a buzz in the room, but only Lewis spoke out loud. "I can't be ready then. The station can't be ready that quickly."

"Work crews were dispatched from the moon about six hours ago. They are powering up the main fuselage, checking for micrometeorite damage, flawed lines, radiation leaks. I should have a report inside an hour about the condition. All things being equal, and with an adequate oxygen supply, you and several members of the team will lift off tomorrow."

Davies couldn't contain herself. "I'll be on the flight." She said it as a statement, but it was a question.

Greenstein said, "I'm not sure that space, or weight considerations, will allow us a reporter."

"The network will insist, and I'm sure that someone there will call a senator, or a friend at the FCC, who will be able to pose a question to the president. Maybe our representative in the press corps will be able to ask it of the press secretary at the afternoon briefing."

"Ms. Davies, I am not your enemy here. Let us finish constructing the mission package and once we have a feel for that, we can make a proper determination. I would think that you'd be delayed no more than a day or two at most."

"Thank you, General."

Greenstein nodded at Hackett, who touched a button so the screen would descend. The windows darkened again, just as the screen was locked into place.

Images of riots appeared, showing cities in flames. There was a gruesome shot of a European street, several buildings burning and others looking like piles of rubble reminiscent of the worst pictures of World War II. Lying in the street were twenty or thirty bodies. It wasn't clear who had killed the people, only that they were dead, and a few of them were children.

"This," said Greenstein, "is our motivation. Every time there is another announcement, every time someone produces a new theory about the aliens, every time the media"—and here he looked directly at Davies—"reports on another aspect of this story, the public goes nuts."

He waited for comment, and when there was none, he turned to his left. "This is Dr. Jessica Johnson, a psychologist who specializes in panic. I'm going to give her a minute or two so that she can explain what is happening out there. Dr. Johnson."

Johnson pushed her chair back and stood up. She moved to the podium set in one corner, but stopped next to it rather than behind it. She was a young woman, maybe thirty-five or forty, trim, with long brown hair and large, wide-set eyes.

She wore a brown suit with a cream-colored blouse. The bottom of the jacket ended about midthigh, and her skirt was only about an inch or so longer. She looked comfortable, professional, and confident.

Her voice was quiet and throaty. She grinned often, showing perfect teeth. She said, "What we are witnessing here, nightly, is probably not unlike what the Aztecs felt when Cortez appeared at their city gates. True, he seemed to be fulfilling an ancient prophesy, but they eventually realized that he was an unknown invader coming in the guise of one of their gods. He was a threat to them and their way of life, though they didn't understand the nature of that threat."

She smiled at them, and continued. "We have no similar myth, but we do have a rich cultural history of alien invasions, beginning with H.G. Wells, so many years ago. That has been translated, meaning the idea of alien invasion, into other books, movies, plays, documentaries, and television. The difference today is that we know the aliens are actually out there. Dr. Bakker and her team have done extraordinary work discovering this alien ship."

"But," said Bakker, somewhat annoyed.

"The release of the information has been poorly handled." Johnson held up a hand to stop the protests. "I understand that no one was attempting to create panic and that the information was released as it was obtained . . ."

"This guy Parker," said Greenstein, "he was certainly exploiting the information for his own benefit."

"And that is the wild card in the equation here. But, as I was saying, we're dealing with an unknown here, one that could wipe out the human race, and I think everyone understands that. It's not the alien that is feared, but the unknown alien that is feared."

"So why are people in the streets burning and looting?" asked Ford.

"Because that's what they always do when confronted with a mob situation. People celebrate a victory on the football field by destroying part of the city. They react to government dictates with a riot and by destroying part of the city. How many court verdicts have been met with rioting by the portion of the population that was dissatisfied with the verdict or outcome."

"We don't have those elements here," said Greenstein.

"No, we have a fear of the unknown as the precipitating event. People come out of their homes, their caves, if you will, and see the reaction of others. But they are frightened people, and sometimes the only emotion that can overwhelm the fear is anger. When they are angry they are no longer afraid. And when they are in a group of people, all with similar fears and similar anger, they begin to think and act as one. Their motivation is destroy that which makes them afraid, but since the aliens are in deep space and out of their reach, they attack the universities where the eggheads who found this threat live. And they attack the government, which seems to do nothing about it. They do so because there is nothing else they can do."

"It would seem to me," said Bakker, "that they would attack the messenger as well. The media brought all of this into their homes. and yet they aren't burning the television stations."

"Yes, but in this situation they see the media as helpless as themselves. The media doesn't have any answers for them, only a few facts that have trickled out from the government and the universities, and nothing more."

Johnson moved to the rear of the podium and leaned forward on it. She continued to smile, and said, "That is why this mission today is so important. It is a response to the alien invaders. Yes, I know there are no alien invaders, but at the moment, that simply doesn't matter. It is the public belief that matters, and that must be countered."

Davies, who had been taping the whole lecture, asked, "You believe that the mere launch of our craft will be enough to end the rioting and the chaos?"

"Coupled with evidence that the alien presence is still far from Earth, in deep space, yes. People will see that the government is doing something positive, will see that we are going to meet the aliens, if not in very deep space, certainly far enough from Earth that our planet will be safe. They will take comfort in those facts."

"And that's enough?" asked Davies.

Johnson shrugged and continued to smile. "What will be important is that we can meet the aliens in space away from the Earth. Period."

Before Davies could ask another question, Greenstein said, "Thank you, Doctor."

Johnson returned to her chair, nodded at Davies, then sat down.

Greenstein looked at the man, Travis. He asked, "Did you have something that you wanted to say about your function?"

Travis stood up and moved only to a position behind his chair. He was unconsciously erecting a barrier between himself and those at the table. It meant that he was uncomfortable with being in the room, in front of a crowd that he viewed as mainly skeptical and probably a little hostile.

He looked down, at a point on the table about three feet in front of his chair. "I confess that I feel that I am flying under false colors here. My expertise is in UFOs. I have studied them for most of my adult life. I have interviewed hundreds of witnesses who have seen them, I have worked with those who analyzed photographs and other physical evidence. I have spoken with those who believe they have been abducted. I suppose, on one level, if we're talking of an extraterrestrial presence, I have as much expertise as anyone else you could name."

Ford said, "If we accept the premise that there has been alien visitation."

Travis's finger shot out, pointing at Ford, and he said, "Exactly. If I have been dealing with alien visitation, I know more about it than anyone in this room. If, on the other hand, as some claim, I'm dealing with delusion, hallucination, fabrication, hoax, and a host of other mental instabilities, then I know nothing that will be of particular use here and now."

"Except," said Greenstein, "a mind-set that is somewhat different than that of anyone else in this room. You are experienced in attempting to understand an alien mind."

"Which makes me realize," countered Travis, "that an alien mind is, by definition, alien. We have nothing in common with them except self-awareness and intelligence. We have no common history, ancestry, evolution, or ways of thinking."

"So you have considered that," said Greenstein, "and that puts you in front of my officers, who have never even considered this situation. The mind-set might be of greatest use here."

Travis nodded, and said, "At any rate, that gives you an idea about me. I just hope that you don't think of me as van Helsing from the old vampire movies. I do not have a vast wealth of hidden knowledge that will answer the esoteric questions. I don't have a magic talisman that will deflect the alien technology. And even if I am right about alien visitation, there is nothing to suggest that the aliens who have visited Earth in the past are the same ones in that ship heading our way."

Someone, it might have been Lewis, said, "Well, that certainly sets my mind at ease."

Travis looked around the table, at all those studying him, some believing that he should not be in the room. He said, "But I have been studying this question for quite a few years, and even if there has not been alien visitation, I might have some insights that wouldn't occur to those of you here, in this room. My contribution will be a way of thinking that might not fit the molds of those trained in more conventional arenas. In that way, I believe I will be helpful."

As Travis sat down, Greenstein said, "I have prepared a roster of those who will transfer to the space station just as soon as I have been assured that all the critical systems there are up and functioning. That information will be available at the completion of this briefing. Is there anything else that we need to talk about here?"

Hackett looked from face to face, trying to read them in light of the general's announcement. Clearly Davies was excited. She wanted to fly off into space because it would advance her career as nothing else could. If she wasn't allowed to go, there would be no reporter there at all, which, of course, didn't bother him.

Lewis, of course, would want to go, simply because he would be in command, and he was an experienced space traveler. Bakker might want to go. Hackett had never talked to her about it, but she'd want to see the aliens from as close a vantage point as possible. She would want to be there for the first official contact between Earth and the beings of another world.

Some of the others probably wouldn't want to go simply because space travel was often cold, especially as they traveled away from the sun. It was as dangerous as crossing the Atlantic in a steamship had been about the beginning of the twentieth century. There were lots of things that could go wrong, but there were safeguards and possible rescue when there were problems. At least that was true until they got out beyond Pluto. Then they'd be days, if not weeks, from help, and that could be disastrous.

Greenstein nodded at him, and Hackett used the keyboard to put up the roster. He hadn't seen it until that moment. He scanned the names and didn't see his. He was both relieved and a little annoyed. Apparently he wasn't important enough to go up on the first flight.

He saw Bakker's name and glanced at her, but could read nothing in her face. She was just staring up at the list, as was everyone else in the room.

Davies giggled once when she saw that she would be going. Her career had just been made. She would always be the only journalist on the historic first meeting. And from that point, the networks would be competing for her work, no matter how bad it might become. She could cruise on her reputation.

Travis seemed resigned to his fate, almost like a soldier about to hit an enemy-held beach. He believed that things would turn out fine, but he just wasn't positive. Given a choice, he'd probably prefer to remain at White Sands, listening to the reports from space and offering what advice he could from afar. It didn't look like he was happy about traveling into space.

Weiss was annoyed because he was going along with Bakker. It meant he would be subordinate to her, but more importantly, it cut his lines of communication to Parker and others. The role he had played in getting the mission started was now over. His name would always be in the footnotes as an "also there."

Ford, of course, wasn't on the list. He would be remaining at White Sands, but no one expected anything else. He would be of more value on the ground.

Hackett leaned back, in his chair, first looking at Bakker, who had not taken her eyes off the list, then up at the list himself. He scanned it again, didn't see his name until he looked right at the top. Under Lewis, listed as the overall mission, as well as ship commander, Hackett was listed as the contact commander. He wasn't sure what it meant, only that he was about to take off into space.

CHAPTER 12

[1]

BAKKER HAD LEFT THE MEETING, TALKED briefly with Avilson via Internet hookup, then visited with Weiss, who was in his room jamming clothing into a bag. She stood in the open door, leaning against the jamb, waiting for him to say something.

"You know, they're going to supply clothes for us on the station. You just need your own toothbrush."

"This is a load," said Weiss. "I have no function to perform that can't be handled by someone else."

Bakker stepped into the room and closed the door. She said, "We going to call a truce, or are we going to continue this fight into space."

He stopped packing, and said, "I don't know what you're talking about."

"Of course you do. I'm not stupid, and neither are you."

He walked over to the small table, poured a splash of

whiskey into a glass, and drank it straight. He offered her nothing. Finally, he turned and sat down.

"What's the deal?"

"I'll sponsor you for your doctorate. I'll chair the committee and see that you get a fair shake. We won't take crap for work. You won't be able to buy us or charm us, but I'll make sure that no one sabotages you just because it is you."

"Why?"

"Because we're about to go into space, and that's dangerous enough. I don't want to be looking over my shoulder all the time, worrying about you or what you might be doing."

"I'm not going to do anything that will harm the ship or the mission. I'll be on it too."

"Okay," said Bakker. "I just wanted to be sure that we could work together. None of this going behind my back to announce, prematurely, our discoveries."

Weiss hesitated, then grinned. "Okay. We'll be friends for the flight."

"It strikes me," said Bakker, "that a dissertation on the first alien race to be contacted, the first crewed trip beyond Pluto, the first personal examination of the Oort Cloud, or any of a dozen other topics might be of great interest at the university. The observations made, along with access to the ship's library, ought to provide a solid base for that dissertation."

Weiss picked up the bottle again, held it up, and asked, "A drink to celebrate . . . what? A drink to new relations."

Bakker walked deeper into the room and picked up one of the glasses. She held it out, and said, "Not much. We'll be flying this afternoon."

As he poured, he said, "Parker isn't going to like this."

"Parker isn't here, and once we've taken off, there really isn't any way for you to contact him. Besides, he's done enough damage already."

"The man is going to be a senator."

"So was Joe McCarthy. Getting elected to an office doesn't automatically bestow wisdom."

Weiss poured the drinks, held his glass up, and said, "Bygones."

"Okay," said Bakker. "Bygones."

[2]

SUSAN CAIRNES SAT IN THE OUTER OFFICE and tapped the phone pad again. She heard a momentary ringing, then a click, and a fast busy signal. The connection broke after a moment, and the line was again dead. She didn't understand what was happening, and she knew that Parker wasn't going to be happy.

"Senator, I have been unable to reach Mr. Weiss, the base operator, or anyone else at White Sands."

"Is the problem our line?"

"No, sir. I can get anyone else on it I want. Service to New Mexico, or rather White Sands, is interrupted."

Parker appeared at the door, and said, "Just to White Sands."

"Yes, sir. I guess there is a problem with the wire."

"Oh for Christ's sake, Susan, they haven't used wires for twenty years. There's no wire to be down and if there was a problem with the satellite relay, they'd just transfer everything to another satellite. This is crap."

"Yes, sir."

He stood for a moment, studying her, staring down at her, almost as if he was looking through her blouse. She became uncomfortable with his stare and turned slightly so that she couldn't see him as easily.

"Okay," he said finally, "try to get the governor."

"Ours?"

"No, New Mexico. And see if you can find a number for the *Albuquerque Journal*. I want to get some answers."

"Yes, sir."

Cairnes returned to the telephone, trying one last time

to reach Weiss in New Mexico. When that failed, she tried the governor's office, but the secretary there had nothing to say and suggested they contact either the public affairs office at White Sands or one of the newspapers in the area. If that failed, maybe she should report the trouble to the telephone company.

Cairnes was surprised by the attitude in the New Mexico governor's office. She had found, in the last several weeks, that everyone wanted to talk to Parker. He was getting his face on the television, and if anyone annoyed him, he might say something rude about that person or organization to the press. Now the governor of New Mexico didn't want to talk to Parker, and Cairnes found that just a little strange.

She found the same thing at the Albuquerque newspaper office. The reporter seemed to know who Parker was but had no information that would be of interest to Parker and declined the opportunity to conduct an interview with him. Parker's stock had fallen through the floor in the last twenty-four hours.

She rocked back in her chair and looked at the telephone as if it had turned into something evil. It was no longer an instrument of communication, at least for Parker. No one wanted to talk to him.

The last poll, taken a week earlier, had showed Parker running way out in front in the Senate race. In an election held on that day, Parker would be sitting in the United States Senate with a fairly substantial political base. Everyone wanted to talk to him, interview him, or return his telephone calls as quickly as possible. He was important. Very important.

And now, a week later, Weiss was unavailable, which could be the result of some kind of problem with the communications net in New Mexico or at White Sands. But the New Mexico governor had avoided the telephone call, and the newspaper reporter didn't have time for Parker. Something had shifted. Something was different.

Suddenly, Cairnes was afraid for her job. It had paid

well, the work was pleasant, and there had been a chance
that she would be moving to Washington, DC. The secretary or receptionist for a United States senator paid a lot
more and there was greater prestige there than for a state
senator here. Now she wondered if the job would last
much longer. She wasn't sure that Parker could get re-
elected as a state senator even if he had time to run for that
office. Somehow the situation had changed, and she was
becoming aware of it.

The intercom buzzed. "You get any of those calls?"
asked Parker.

"Still having some trouble."

[3]

THE GOLD-COLORED ORBITAL VEHICLE SAT ON
the runway like a pregnant airliner awaiting clearance for
takeoff. It was a triangular craft with a sharp, needle nose
that slowly fanned out into flat wings. The center fuselage
was a rounded hump that had stealth capabilities simply
because it had no shape angles or edges to reflect old-
fashioned radar waves. Eight rocket engines powered it
and could lift it straight up, even fully loaded. The design
allowed for aerodynamic lift until it reached the upper limits of the atmosphere, where brute rocket power took over,
boosting the craft into orbit or pushing it on toward the
moon.

At the moment, the engines weren't functioning, and
the electrical system was energized by an auxiliary power
unit plugged into a recessed port aft of the passenger and
cargo compartments. That solar-powered unit generated
enough energy that all the electrical systems were on-line
and the air-conditioning was humming. Without it, even
with the craft painted a bright white-gold to reflect the
sun's energy and the outer skin's capability of dispersing
the heat, it would soon have been unbearable inside the
ship.

Hackett sat in one of the five seats in the cockpit, but back, away from the controls. He could see the panel, see the CPUs and instruments, but didn't understand much of what was there. He could only tell that the instruments were in the green and that the craft seemed to be in working order, even though the engines had yet to be powered up.

Lewis sat in the captain's chair, on the left side of the cockpit, in a silver flight suit and white-topped helmet. He sat quietly, watching the panel and occasionally looking out the windshield at the shimmering heat reflecting from the silver ribbon of a runway that stretched across the desert into the area of white sand dunes.

The copilot—Hackett hadn't caught his name—was dressed the same way, but the rest of the passengers, all arranged in airline-type seating behind the bulkhead that separated the cockpit from the passenger compartment, were in regular clothes. They wore no special suits, had no special protective gear, and if there was an accident, they were basically on their own. Hackett couldn't think of an accident, either on the ground or once they had taken off, that wouldn't be fatal regardless of what they wore.

Lewis turned in his seat, and said, "We've got clearance. We'll be starting the engines."

"You want me out of the way?"

"Nah, sit right there and enjoy the show. Just buckle up."

Hackett reached back and pulled the shoulder straps down, grabbed the strap that came up between his legs, and hooked them all into the seat belt. He jerked them as tight as he could wondering if the restraints had ever saved the life of anyone when a spacecraft began to break up. As far as he could tell, all of this would only make sure that his body didn't leave the seat, though the seat could be tumbling through the air for a long way. He felt as safe as the passengers on the *Titanic*.

Lewis looked back over his shoulder, and said, "Today it'll take us about two hours to reach our max altitude, when we kick in the rockets and really begin to fly this baby."

"Why so long?"

"Weather here and there getting into the way, and we want to take some advantage of the jet stream. We'll be maneuvering for the conservation of fuel."

"When do we leave?"

"Just as soon as they disconnect the auxiliary power . . ." There was a dimming in the lights, the air-conditioning cut out for an instant, then everything was up and running again.

"Well, now that we're independent of the ground power to the auxiliary units," said Lewis, "we can fire this up."

Hackett watched as Lewis and his copilot worked through the checklists, first making sure that everything was turned off and then slowly, carefully, turning it all back on. After five minutes, there came a slight buzzing and just the hint of a vibration as the first of the jet engines was started. The noise increased slightly as each of the other engines was brought on-line. Lewis's head swiveled back and forth as he kept his eyes moving from one instrument to the next.

To Hackett he said, "We're about ready to go." Then, over the intercom system, he said, "Attention back there. We're about to move out, onto the active runway. Everyone should be seated and strapped in. If there are any problems, someone alert us. I'm going to move in ten seconds."

When there was no comment from the rear, Lewis reached down, released a lever that might have held a parking brake if they had been in a car—Hackett didn't know for sure—and the craft began to creep forward. The speed increased for a moment, then they stopped. An instant later they moved and began to turn.

To everyone, Lewis said, "Takeoff roll."

The buzz at the rear of the craft increased to a roar, and the vibration became uncomfortable. Hackett was worried that the craft would shake itself apart, when, suddenly, the nose came up and they lifted from the New Mexican landscape. The roar died away, and the vibration dissipated. A moment later there was a thud, and the sound of the en-

gines was lost, so that it seemed they had all quit at once.
Outside, the sky color changed slightly so that it seemed to
be a darker blue that bordered on purple.

Lewis seemed visibly to relax. He looked back over his
shoulder at Hackett, and said, "We're off and running. In
ten minutes or so, you can unfasten your belt if you want
and move around a little."

"How long to the space station?"

"ETA in twenty hours or so."

"You going to feed us?" asked Hackett.

"Me? No. There are some lunches that have been
packed, and there are some mild sleeping pills for those of
you who would rather pass the time sleeping."

"I think, for the moment," said Hackett, "I'll stay awake
and watch the world shrink."

[4]

TAYLOR WAS BEGINNING TO FEEL UNLOVED.
All the high-powered university people, all the press, and
even the military liaison officers, had left. The scene of the
story had switched out of the Very Large Array and down
the highway to White Sands. The alien signals were being
tracked by others, in Puerto Rico, Russia, and Australia.
The work to understand the signal was being done at a
number of private facilities and by the CIA and several
other intelligence organizations that had broken sophisticated codes in other environments.

With the world watching those others, with some of the
people lifting off into space to meet the aliens, there just
wasn't time for the VLA and those working there. Anything they learned at the VLA would probably be learned
sooner somewhere else. The routine had returned, and Taylor wasn't all that unhappy with the situation. She could
again work in peace, without the artificial pressure to find
something immediately.

She was sitting in the conference room with her feet up,

looking into the dung-colored desert as the sun faded. She held a slice of pizza, hot from the microwave, in her left hand as she periodically studied one of the computer monitors mounted on the wall. She was watching the parading of the numbers for a search of part of the sky for new radio sources. Others, both at the VLA and at other radio astronomy facilities, were still trying to figure out what the alien signal meant.

Gibson pushed open the door, grinned, and said, "Are you lonesome?"

"Grab a hunk of pizza and stop with the tired sexual come-ons," she said.

"I meant, do you miss the limelight. Do you wish the reporters would return?"

She sat up, putting her feet flat on the floor. She dropped her pizza to the plate and wiped her fingers on a napkin. "What have you got?"

Gibson pulled out a chair, sat down, and leaned forward so that he was no more than two feet from her. "We found it again. One signal is still about thirty light-years out, but the new one is somewhat closer."

"Faster-than-light drive?"

"Don't know. Could be a second ship. We do have two signals out there."

"Yeah," said Taylor thinking fast, "but we're looking at the ship where it was thirty years ago."

"And now we see it within a dozen light-years."

Taylor waved her hands as her mind raced. "You got a plot? With three plots we can deduce where it might be going." She closed her eyes momentarily, then asked, "It is the same ship?"

"First things first," said Gibson. "Yeah, I'm fairly certain it is the same sort of signal. I mean, if you can build one starship, surely you could build a second. So, I would say the signal is from the same civilization but not necessarily the same spaceship."

Taylor waved a hand. "Wait. Wait. If they have more

than one ship, then why haven't they gotten here before. I mean, they just didn't learn how to navigate space."

Now Gibson grinned. "Who's to say that they haven't been here already."

Taylor ignored that. "And if it is the same ship, then it clearly is traveling faster than light. That's the only way to explain the signal from two parts of the sky at once."

Gibson reached over and picked up the pizza. He took a bite, looked disgusted, then put it back. "What I want to know is whether we alert the university or just call Dr. Bakker?"

"Bakker is at White Sands."

"So she could be here in a couple of hours. Let her answer the hard questions."

Gibson rocked back and laced his fingers behind his head. "You know, we're becoming a little cavalier about all this. I mean, we have detected, for the third time, a signal that is clearly intelligent and one that is suggestive of a second ship, yet here we sit calmly discussing it while eating some really bad pizza."

"And look how happy the world has become now that we have found this signal."

"Not my point and not really relevant. I'm merely suggesting that another intelligent signal has not induced any awe in any of us. We're damned calm."

Taylor stood up. "Let's go look at this new and miraculous signal."

"It's just more of the same."

Taylor laughed as she pulled the door open. "It strikes me that we might be getting all excited over something as simple as someone's laundry list."

"Even if true, it is a laundry list that belongs to an alien creature."

"Well, there is that."

CHAPTER 13

[1]

ALTHOUGH HACKETT HAD NOT TAKEN THE
sleeping pill, he found that he slept for long periods during
the trip. He would awaken, circulate, sit down next to
Bakker and talk to her for half an hour or so, but soon
either he, or she, would be yawning. They would decide to
catch a little more sleep, so he would walk back up to the
cockpit and strap himself in.

Or he would stand between the two seats for the pilot
and copilot, looking into the velvet blackness of space,
wondering what had happened to all the stars. Out the side
windows he would see the glowing sphere of the Earth,
sometimes a bright blue as they flew over an ocean and
other times a brilliant white as the sun reflected from the
cloud cover. Some of the clouds turned dark and ominous,
with flashes of lightning tracking through them.

He retreated to his seat, dropped into it, and buckled

himself in, loosely. He pushed the button that lowered the back to about a forty-five-degree angle and brought up the footrest. While not the horizontal surface of a bed, it was certainly comfortable enough to sleep. He would drop off quickly, often surprised at falling asleep again.

When he woke up, he felt himself drifting upward, against the straps of the seat-belt and shoulder harness. He glanced forward and saw, in the distance, the sun-bright space station looking like a toy stuck together by a kid with way too much imagination and no sense of engineering. There seemed to be pieces, pods, antennae, and solar panels stuck on at various angles; but Hackett could see that everything faced the sun that needed to—suggesting that someone had actually thought about it before sticking the pieces together.

"How far out are we?" asked Hackett, his mouth tasting like the bottom of yesterday's birdcage and his head aching from too much sleep at the wrong angle.

"We'll start docking maneuvers in about an hour," said Lewis.

"Then I have time to stand up, find a way to brush my teeth, and maybe a cup of coffee."

Lewis turned slightly, looking over his shoulder at Hackett. "We're in zero gee now. Unless you've got on your Velcro slippers, I would be careful about standing up, let alone walking about. I wouldn't worry about brushing your teeth because water rusts and, unless you're used to spaceflight, I'd be careful about drinking anything at the moment."

"You're just a bundle of helpful information."

"There are some mints in the head, and you can drink the coffee if you want, but I don't want to deal with vomit as I'm trying to dock with the station."

"Okay. Mints and a little water," said Hackett.

"You are free to move into the back," said Lewis. "Then I don't care what you do, as long as you do it back there. Drink all the coffee you want and have a ball."

Hackett thought of Bakker, sitting in the back, but he

had the best passenger seat from which to watch the docking. In the back he would be able to look out the side windows, but he wouldn't be able to see forward. Staying where he was seemed like the best idea, and he would be with Bakker in a couple hours. No, he would stay put.

"Anything from the ground?"

"Routine traffic. The general is getting a little antsy for us to dock, though. I don't know why. He knows the schedule as well as any of us."

Hackett stood up for a moment, stretched, then sat back down. He pulled a mint from his pocket and popped it into his mouth, sucking on it quietly. He watched as Lewis and the copilot worked their controls, and the station grew larger as they approached it.

He had expected to see some activity on the parts of either Lewis or the copilot, but the closer they came to the station, the less either of them did. They punched a couple of buttons and moved a switch once or twice, but they didn't seem to be controlling the ship at all. Computers were maneuvering them toward the docking bay.

Hackett finally said, "You guys look a little useless up there."

Lewis decided not to take offense. He said, "If something goes suddenly wrong, we can abort. We can take manual control and save the situation." Now he laughed. "We're the backup system in case all the high-priced electronics fail."

"And do they?"

"Fail? Sure, and then the backup system takes over and if that fails, then I might get to touch the controls and save the day. But no, they never really fail."

Hackett could hear, or maybe feel, the slight pulse of the navigational rockets as they fired in some ill-defined sequence, pushing the craft ever closer to the station. It looked as if they were speeding toward it, then it looked as if they had stopped, not moving at all.

Eventually there was a dull clang that seemed to transmit itself through the craft, and Lewis leaned back in his seat. "That's it. We're there."

"Now what?"

"We wait to see that everything is locked down properly and that the air supply is safe."

"I thought there were already people in the station," said Hackett.

"There are. This is known as redundancy. We're making sure that everything is set before we open the hatch and expose ourselves to the air from the station."

"Board's green," said the copilot.

Lewis unfastened his shoulder harness and seat belt, tossed them aside, and stood up. He floated away from the deck, hovering a couple of inches above it.

"This is the best part," he said. "Makes me feel as if I'm supernatural."

"Right until you float into a bulkhead," said the copilot.

Lewis ignored him, and said, "Come on. Let's go see what they have for us."

[2]

BAKKER HAD WATCHED THE STATION AP-proach during the docking. It looked to her as if they had slipped sideways, close to the metallic frame of the station, until they stopped, hovering fifteen or twenty feet away. She knew, having seen video of other dockings, that the nose of the craft had pushed through some sort of large ring and was held there magnetically. Something like an old-fashioned jetway would connect the craft to the station for them to float through. Unlike the jetway, this was sealed to keep the air in.

When word was passed that it was safe to exit, Bakker carefully unfastened herself from the harness and sat holding on to the arms of the seat. She put her feet onto the floor, then lifted one, hearing the satisfying ripping sound that told her the Velcro sole had gripped the matting on the deck. She stood up and waited as the line in the aisle slowly moved forward, joining it when she could.

At the hatch, which was circular and had irised open, she bent at the waist and pulled her feet up. She reached through the hatch, into the tube that connected them to the station and grabbed the first set of handholds.

As she emerged at the other end, she saw Davies, small camera in hand, attempting to video those coming out. Davies lowered her camera, and said, "Dr. Bakker, back up and come out again. I want to get a shot of that."

"There are people behind me," Bakker said as she put her feet on the Velcro strip. "I don't have time for this sort of nonsense anyway."

She moved to the right and looked down what she thought of as a corridor. The walls were dull and metallic, and at the point where the walls, or bulkheads, met the ceiling or overhead, there was a cluster of pipes and wires.

Others were slowly walking down the corridor with a shuffling step that kept one foot in contact with the Velcro at all times. There was a constant ripping sound as they walked, but no one was floating around.

A young man dressed in white shorts and a white T-shirt—the standard uniform—stood there, directing the people down the corridor. To Bakker, he said, "Just follow those people into the main pod for the orientation lecture. We'll get you all settled."

Bakker stepped aside and watched as the others crawled out of the tube until Hackett finally emerged. He turned, grabbed the handle over the top of the tube, and pulled his feet out and put them down.

"Thought you got lost," said Bakker.

"Stayed up in the cockpit to watch them shut the thing down, then came out."

The man in shorts came forward, and asked, "Are you Major Hackett?"

"Yes."

"Please come with me, you have a communication from White Sands."

"Already? I just got here."

"Yes, sir."

Bakker hesitated, then said, "You go on, and I'll get settled. There's some sort of meeting pod, and I'll see you there when you've finished."

"Sure. Sounds like a plan to me."

[3]

THE FIRST THING THAT HACKETT NOTICED WAS that the station wasn't warm. He had wondered about that, but every time they had shown pictures of crews in any of the space stations or in the old shuttle, or on the moon base, they were in abbreviated costumes of shorts and T-shirts. That suggested to him that those environments were warm, but he could feel the cold around him. It was uncomfortable, and he didn't like it.

They passed some of the others who had flown up in the craft, then turned down another, narrow corridor that had handholds welded above his head, suggesting they could just move down it without having to walk along the deck. The motion, using the handholds, wasn't much different than a monkey swinging through the branches of a tree.

The man looked back over his shoulder, and said, "We're going to the communications room. There you can make a scrambled call to the general."

"Why is that necessary now?"

"No one has condescended to provide that information to me. All I know is that I'm to take you down there for a scrambled communication."

They reached the room, which had a circular door that was not unlike the hatch that had led from the craft into the station. Beyond it was a pod that curved in on itself. Directly in front of the hatch were two chairs on swivels, and just beyond them were the communications control panels. He had expected more lights and dials, but the equipment had moved beyond that long ago. Printed circuits, bubble memory, and self-diagnosis had taken care of the need for warning lights and illuminated dials.

Hackett followed the man through the hatch and stepped to the right, out of the way.

"Take a chair," said the man. "I'll get the equipment set, and once the general comes on the line, flip this switch. That'll automatically start the encryption. Be advised there will be a time delay caused by our distance from the general's transmitter and by the necessary encryption work."

Hackett sat down and leaned his elbows on the small table in front of him. He felt as if he was in a giant lighted egg that had too many computers and televisions in it for any one human to appreciate.

The man tuned the equipment, watched as a picture coalesced on the center flat screen, then said, "When you're finished, touch this button. That will break the connection. You know how to cycle the hatch?"

"Just push the green button on the side."

"Right. I'll wait outside. When you're ready, hit the transmit button to open the connection. Everything should work automatically from there."

When the man was gone, Hackett took a deep breath of the cold, metallic-tasting air, then scrubbed at his face with both hands. What he really needed was a shower, some hot food, and about eight hours of uninterrupted sleep in a real bed, or—now that he was on the station—the netting that kept the inert body from drifting down the hallway. He needed some relaxing, REM-inducing sleep and not the catnaps he'd taken on the craft.

Satisfied that he was as ready as he would ever be, he touched the button. A moment later, only three or four seconds though it seemed longer, a feminine face appeared.

"General Greenstein, please."

"The general will be right with you, Major. How was the flight?"

"Long and boring."

The screen flickered, and Greenstein appeared. He was seated, wearing his khaki uniform, complete with all his awards and decorations, which could only mean that he had been recently interviewed by the press.

"I see you have arrived, Major."

"Yes, sir. About fifteen minutes ago."

"Sorry about this, but there has been another development. Please only convey this to Lewis and Bakker. I don't want to see any more headlines."

"Yes, sir."

"We have a new signal, this one no more than ten light-years out. Plotting of the course, if it is the same craft, shows it is coming toward our solar system. We have no ETA."

"Same craft, sir?"

"The signal from thirty light-years away has not faded, giving rise to speculation that there is a second craft that is substantially closer. Our schedule must be advanced."

"General, I have no idea what shape we're in. I just got here, and, frankly, it's cold."

"What's that supposed to mean?"

"That things, and I haven't seen many of them, are just getting wound up here. They haven't gotten the station up to speed."

"There is nothing I can do about that," said Greenstein. "We have got to move if we're going to prove to the world that we are ready for whatever might come."

"Yes, sir."

"I want, within twenty-four hours, an assessment of what you need and how soon you can begin to move that thing out of orbit. I want us going, moving along, as quickly as possible. You understand?"

"Yes, sir."

[4]

"THIS ISN'T GOING TO BE MUCH OF AN ORIENTATION lecture," said the young woman wearing brief white shorts and a white, form-fitting T-shirt, "because there isn't

much that we can tell you. We don't know much of anything."

Bakker grinned at that and looked around the center
room of the main pod. It was, maybe, a hundred feet long
and about half that wide. The walls, or as they were called
by everyone on the station, the bulkheads, were unpainted
metal. There was a deck with Velcro strips and lights overhead that seemed to hint at a spacial orientation, but it was
confusing because there were Velcro strips on the walls as
well. Then Bakker realized that the orientation of floor and
ceiling were meaningless in space. The floor, or deck, was
whatever they decided it was. With no gravity, they could
just as easily walk on the walls.

"What we need to do is go over the emergency procedures," said the woman. "They are simple. If there is a hull
breach, the hatches will automatically seal off the various
sections of the station. Stay where you are and you should
be fine. If you are in the section breached, then find the
nearest emergency suit and don it as quickly as possible.
You'll have ten to fifteen minutes . . ."

Bakker tuned her out because she knew the emergency
instructions for those in the area of the breach were crap.
There simply wouldn't be enough suits available, and if
the breach was large enough, there wouldn't be the ten or
fifteen minutes needed to climb into a suit anyway.

She saw Hackett appear, walking down the corridor,
and half lifted her hand. He saw her and, ducking down, as
if that would avoid interrupting the lecture, tried to sneak
over to where she waited.

When he was close, she whispered, "What was that all
about?"

"Some last-minute news from the general. I'll tell you
about it later."

"Pod assignments . . . and I guess you can think of them
as room assignments, have been made according to rank,
position, job, and gender. Commander Lewis and Major
Hackett have been assigned personal space. Everyone else
gets a roommate."

Bakker leaned close, and whispered, "I guess that means that my roommate will be someone else."

"Just as long as it's not Weiss, I'll be happy."

"Me too."

"Our galley has a limited capacity," said the woman, "so that we'll have to stagger the meal times. You'll find a schedule in your pods."

She grinned broadly, and said, "We have a limited water supply, though it isn't as critical as it will be once we move out of orbit. We encourage you to shower together to conserve water. It will be our most precious commodity."

She looked from face to face, then said, "I know that you have just arrived, and I know that I've given you very little information, but if there are any questions, now is the time to ask them."

"Communications with Earth," said Weiss.

"Will, of necessity, be limited and must be approved by either Lewis or Hackett. That includes both official and personal communications. There will be some opportunities for everyone to call home.

"While in orbit here, and during the first part of the journey, we'll have access to the satellite feeds, so there will be no interruption in the programming. As we get deeper into space, we may have trouble with interference, and we'll be able to begin to pull programming from the Martian satellites. If nothing else, it'll be an interesting diversion."

"When is the next shuttle scheduled?"

"I don't have the information, but I understand that the schedule has been pushed forward."

"How many people are going to be assigned."

"In the end, I think there will be fifty people who will make the whole trip."

She held up a hand, and said, "There is a short welcome speech on the main computer system, along with a great deal of information about this station and the coming trip. I think that it will answer all the questions you have. Might I suggest that those interested in that read it. That way we can break here and give everyone a chance to get oriented. Thank you."

Bakker stood up, but Hackett didn't move. She said, "What's your problem?"

"I just got here, and already I have had a coded conversation with the general, and now, suddenly, everyone wants me to move somewhere else and I don't know where I'm supposed to go."

"Why don't you come with me? That way you'll know where I am so you won't get lost," said Bakker.

Hackett stood up. "Okay. I'll follow you."

"And remember, I will have a roommate, so you'll just have to behave yourself."

"Great. Just what I wanted to hear."

CHAPTER 14

[1]

STEVEN WEISS, BECAUSE HE WAS AN AS-
tronomer and because he was assigned to work on the station, had access to all the messages that had come in that
dealt with astronomical matters, which included the reports on the alien ship. Reading through that material, he
learned, to his surprise, that another signal had been detected and that it was no more than ten light-years away.
There was some speculation that it might be as close as
eight. It meant that the fifty-year window they believed
they had when the first signal was detected had evaporated
in a matter of months. Now, at best, they had maybe ten
years.

Weiss sat in the molded plastic-and-composite carbon
chair that was bolted to a swivel stand bolted, in turn, to
the deck. He leaned his elbows on the narrow table that
could be used as a desk. It was barely wide enough for a

keyboard, though he preferred the voice input since he was alone in the pod.

At the moment he had no roommate, though there was a second bunk welded to the bulkhead. They were stacked like bunk beds, but the distance between them was barely two feet. Opposite the bunks was a metallic locker that held two shelves and a short rod for hanging clothes. To Weiss, it was reminiscent of those tiny boxes the Japanese thought of as businessmen's hotel rooms. A place to sleep, store a few clothes, and little else. At least the pod had a flat screen that doubled as the computer monitor and the entertainment center.

His only thoughts at the moment were how he could get the latest information to State Senator Parker so that he could continue his run for national office. Parker could turn the latest into another news story that would capture headlines and keep his face in front of the public. Weiss knew that others, such as Bakker, would prefer the information suppressed, but he didn't care about that. His future rested with Parker, not Bakker or academia, no matter what deal he had made with her.

After he read the whole report, available to anyone who wanted it in the station's computer library, and probably on CD for those who needed their own copy of the data, he stood up, stretched, and wondered how easy it was going to be to call down to Earth. The welcoming committee had suggested it was fairly easy but strictly controlled. He didn't like having to go through a public satellite system.

He opened the hatch and stepped into the narrow corridor. He noticed that there were handholds along what he thought of as the walls, a wide Velcro strip on the floor, and a blank, plain metal surface along the ceiling. He began to walk, carefully, down the corridor until he came into the main room of the central pod. Others were sitting around, talking, one or two held drinks in capped cups with straws, and one man, sitting alone, was eating a sandwich, his head surrounded by a thin cloud of crumbs. Air filters would eventually capture the debris and recycle it, but Weiss thought the man rude.

The people in the pod were the same ones who had ridden to the station with him and, therefore, would be of no help in finding the communications center. True, he had looked at the station maps on the computer, but the moment he had stepped through the hatch of his pod, he was lost. He wasn't sure how to find anything.

He wandered across the pod, to the hatch on the opposite side, and stopped. A voice spoke behind him. "May I help you?"

Weiss turned and saw the woman who had welcomed them. He said, "Yes, I think you can. I'm sorry, but I didn't catch your name earlier."

She held out her hand formally and said, "I'm Diane Stanley and when you think about it, confuses a lot of people wondering if I'm male or female, based solely on my name, especially when it is written as Stanley, Diane."

Weiss shook her hand and thought of a number of comments, but decided that the proper thing was to keep them to himself. Instead, he said, "Nice to meet you. I'm Steven Weiss."

"Steven or Steve?"

"Steve, please."

"Now, how might I help you?"

"Communications center. I need to send a message."

"You have clearance from Commander Lewis or Major Hackett, of course?"

"Nope. This is more of a private matter."

"Have to have clearance to use the communications center," said Stanley. "They don't need to see the nature of the message, but they have to clear it."

Weiss shrugged as if it wasn't all that important, and asked, "Where is Commander Lewis?"

"He's in the command module getting familiar with the systems."

"And where is that?"

She gave him directions, and said, "I could take you there if you'd like."

"No, I don't want to take you from your duties. The communications center is where, from here?"

Again she gave instructions. She smiled, and said, "See you later." Then she wandered off to be of assistance to others who might require it.

As soon as her attention was drawn to some other project or some other person, Weiss exited through the hatch that would lead him to the communications center. When he found it, he cycled open the hatch and stepped through. He was surprised, and delighted, to find it empty. As he thought about it, he realized that the computers could alert anyone, anywhere, at any time, that an important message had arrived. Computers would stand a twenty-four-hour watch without complaint and would be as alert in the twenty-fourth hour as in the first.

He sat down and looked at the array of communications gear. It was intimidating. There were few labels, and he could see no manuals stored anywhere. He then realized that the manuals would be stored in the library computer. Easy access for all and no additional weight of paper.

He found the proper manuals in the computer, scanned them, and learned what he needed to know. He had just begun to turn on the equipment when the hatch cycled open and Hackett stepped through. Bakker followed him.

"You were right," said Hackett. "He can't be trusted."

"I was just going to call my father," said Weiss. "What's wrong with that?"

"Then why not follow the procedures?" asked Bakker.

"I didn't think anyone would mind. No one was using the equipment."

"And you don't think that we're not monitoring the fluctuations in the electrical power. You suddenly come on-line to transmit, you might adversely affect some other electrical equipment," said Hackett. "So, you are restricted from the communications center with the single exception of notification of your family that you have arrived safely."

"That's not fair. I wasn't doing anything wrong."

Bakker shook her head. "First you go through the latest messages from New Mexico, then you come here, in violation of the rules, and you weren't doing anything wrong."

Weiss shrugged, and said, "You're going to believe whatever you want."

"All too true," said Hackett. "Now, please vacate the communications center."

[2]

PRESIDENT BUSKIRK SAT BEHIND HIS DESK, this one in the Oval Office, and read the message that had come to him from the White House Communications Center. It had been filtered down to White Sands for comment by Lieutenant General George Greenstein, then transmitted, intact, to the White House. Within minutes of the decrypting, it had been placed in a leather folder that was stamped "TOP SECRET" and hand-carried up to the Oval Office.

Buskirk opened the folder, scanned the sheets, then touched a button on the telephone/intercom/communications net, and said, "I want to see Heywood Bloom in here inside of thirty minutes. I know he's in Washington, and I don't want to be kept waiting."

The only response from the other end was, "Yes, Mr. President."

Buskirk turned back and looked out the window, across the expanse of lawn, to the sidewalks where the tourists circulated. Today there were no signs that ordered him to do something about the aliens coming toward Earth. Today there were no demonstrators demanding some action—any action—on his part. For the moment, at least, the public had calmed; but he didn't know how long that would last, especially with someone stirring the pot at every opportunity.

While he waited for word of Bloom, he watched the news channels, looking for signs of rioting and chaos in reaction to the alien vessel. Although there were reports on the aftermath of those riots, scenes of blackened stores and burned-out cars, at the moment, everything and everyone around the world were calm. The people were at home, or at their jobs, or trying to clean up some of the mess they had made the night before.

He took a telephone call from the Speaker of the House about the probability that some bit of legislation was going to pass, then turned his attention to the short report the science advisor had brought in. Buskirk's head spun as he tried to figure out the problems that went with a faster-than-light drive and how a single ship could, in fact, be broadcasting from two different locations at once.

The intercom in the outer office buzzed, and he heard his personal secretary, Shirley Hartwell, talking quietly. A moment later there was a quiet knock at the door, and Hartwell stuck her head in.

"Mr. Bloom, Mr. President."

Buskirk stood and walked forward, his right hand extended. "Please show him in."

The two men shook hands, and Buskirk pointed at one of the couches. "Please. Have a seat. Would you care for some sort of a refreshment?"

"Thank you, no, Mr. President."

"Then, Shirley, would you see that we're not disturbed for about thirty minutes."

"Yes, sir." She closed the door as she left.

Bloom was a middle-aged man with a thick head of graying hair, slightly rounded shoulders, and an enormous belly that came from eating too much food provided by those who wanted party support in various local, state, and federal elections. Bloom hit the circuit, cultivating candidates that he thought could beat the opposition, and often held meetings at the best restaurants. He knew he was overweight, but the food was always so good and there was always so much of it.

Now Bloom was feeling uncomfortable, because, while he was the national chairman of the party, the president, because he was the president, was the actual leader of the party. When the president said something, it had the force of an order. When he demanded an appearance, then someone was about to have his head handed to him, and Bloom was afraid that he had somehow offended the president in the last few days. He felt the sweat blossom on his forehead and drip down his sides. He felt slightly sick to his stomach and hoped he wouldn't throw up.

Buskirk sat down opposite Bloom and looked at him. He asked, conversationally, "Are you enjoying Washington this time around?"

"Yes, sir. Little warm for my taste, but I have had a number of useful and productive meetings."

"And the wife? Is she with you?"

"No, I had to leave Natalie at home this time. Our youngest, Wally, is sick."

"Nothing serious, I hope."

"Oh, no, sir. She just didn't want to leave home with the child sick. I thought it best."

"Well, if there is anything that I can do, you'll let me know, of course."

"Yes, Mr. President. Thank you."

"What can you tell me about this Jason Parker who has decided that he would like to be a United States senator?"

Bloom leaned back and relaxed slightly. "Ambitious man. Fairly good party man. Supports our national platform, though we disagree on abortion and gun control."

Buskirk laughed. "The two most controversial issues and the ones on which we need party unity."

"Yes, sir. He supports the platform and while his rhetoric is at times at odds with us, he votes the party line something like 95, 96 percent of the time. He's a good party man."

"Then maybe you can explain why he is creating this chaos about the alien ship."

"It was an issue that he believed would get him some

national exposure. He thought it would help his bid for the Senate when he announces it."

"Didn't he foresee the consequences?"

Bloom reached into his jacket and retrieved a handkerchief. He mopped his face with it, then seemed to dry his hands with it before he put it back into his pocket.

"I believe he was just thinking of the exposure on the national front that he could use in a statewide election."

"You're telling me that this man created this panic, then stirred the pot later, so that people in his home state would know his name."

Bloom had the almost irrational desire to tell the president that the plan had worked because they were now sitting in the Oval Office discussing Parker, but held his tongue. Instead, he said, "I don't believe he knew what would happen."

"I will grant you that it might have been impossible to predict the reaction of the general public. I'm not sure that a sane man could have predicted the riots; but after the first night, everyone, and I mean everyone, understood that further announcements would not be met with calm."

"Yes, sir."

"And we have him on the air with that picture that is highly speculative at best."

"Yes, sir."

"And he had to understand that people would panic. That there would be a backlash."

"Well, I'm not sure that's fair . . ."

"For Christ's sake, man, if the mere announcement of an alien ship caused the first wave of riots, what in the hell do you think a picture would do, especially when it was learned that the ship was closer?"

"What would you have me do, Mr. President."

"I don't like to meddle in party politics at that level, but I want this guy crushed. You will find a candidate from the party to oppose him. He will get no funding from the national party, and I want pressure brought on the state party. I want it clear that Parker is no longer in favor, and those who support him are going to find themselves on the out-side along with him."

"He might retain his state senate seat," said Bloom.

"I thought about that. I want him out. Find someone to oppose him in that arena as well. Pour money into the op-position's campaign. And if he is elected at any level, make it clear that there will be no support from the party at any time. I want him buried."

"Yes, sir. Is there anything else?"

"Nope. That about covers it. But also understand that a failure here will be met with drastic change. I hope that I don't have to spell that out."

"No, sir. I understand."

The president stood up. "Then, Heywood, don't be a stranger. We'll talk again."

[3]

JASON PARKER SAT AT HIS DESK, STARING AT the telephone, trying to understand what had happened. Nothing had gone right for more than two days. The party leadership, which had eagerly returned his telephone calls, were nowhere to be found. Party officials didn't seem to know who he was, and the staff for his election campaign began to slip away.

He stood up and walked to the wet bar and poured him-self a stiff drink. He tossed it down, feeling the satisfying burn of the alcohol and the sudden light-headedness of a full, straight shot of bourbon. He took a deep breath and walked to the door of his office.

Cairnes was still there, but she had given him her two weeks' notice. She had been offered a better-paying job, with shorter hours, and Parker had not been able to match the deal. She said that it was nothing personal, but she was going to take it. She needed the money and wanted the time off.

So Parker found himself nearly alone. Weiss had not

called to update him on the situation in space, though both
had believed that it would be possible for him to make
some sort of contact from the station. And Cairnes was
nearly out the door.

He said, as he watched her, "How about I take you to
dinner tonight as sort of a going-away reward?"

She looked at him and smiled, but said, "I already have
some plans, but that's very nice."

So, he thought, she doesn't want to be seen with me.
One minute I'm counting the votes into the Senate, with
her as the office manager, and the next, my campaign is
evaporating, and she doesn't want people to know that I'm
her boss. Or rather, I was her boss.

He closed the door quietly, walked first toward his desk,
then detoured toward the bar. There was nothing at his
desk that would do him any good. The telephone numbers
in his address book were now all as useful as the hiero-
glyphics on the pyramids in Egypt—meaning they were no
good at all.

He poured himself another shot of bourbon, and then
reached over for a drinking glass. He poured the alcohol
into it and used the bottle to nearly fill the glass. Something had gone horribly wrong, and he didn't know what it
was. All he knew was that the only solution for the day was
to get hammered. He took a strong pull at the alcohol, then
slowly walked back to his desk.

CHAPTER 15

[1]

IT HAD TAKEN A WEEK TO MOVE THE SUPPLIES
from the moon to the station. During that same week, more
people were brought up from Earth, and specialized supplies were added. The people were assigned quarters, and
some of those who had once had no roommate found
themselves living with someone else. Any system that ar-
bitrarily assigned people to pods was prone to mistakes.
But those were fixed as quickly as possible, and the only
person who didn't have a roommate, other than the top
commanders, was Steven Weiss. No one seemed to be able
to get along with him for more than a couple of hours.

Hackett was given the task of sorting and storing the
special equipment, but only because weapons were supposed to be kept out of space. That ideal had never been
followed, even after most of the governments on Earth had
signed a treaty to keep weapons out of space. Now, of

course, those weapons were not going to be directed at Earth but were there for the defense of the station and the Solar System.

The weapons brought to the station surprised Hackett. He had expected rockets and missiles, and there were some of those. They were, basically, air-to-air missiles and air-to-ground rockets that had been modified to work in space, which meant, simply, that an oxygen source was added so that the rocket motors would fire. The guidance systems were mostly heat-seeking because anything warm enough to support life would stand out against the frozen temperatures of deep space even if well insulated.

What really surprised Hackett was a battery of artillery. These were eight-inch guns that, on the ground, could throw a shell five or six miles. In space, with no gravity or friction, the shells would fly until they hit something. It seemed strange that anyone would think of putting artillery on the station, but it did make some kind of sense.

Hackett understood the problem, which was how to fire them. Clearly the barrels had to be pointed out, into space, and just as clearly, they were not airtight. He didn't know what the plans were for them.

There were also a couple of particle-beam weapons, but Hackett didn't think much of them. They had to be focused on a target for several seconds for it to cause any damage. Hackett couldn't see a situation in which that would be possible, especially if the two ships engaged one another at extreme distances. Their mere maneuvering should keep the beam from focusing properly.

The technicians who installed the larger engines, in a cluster of four pods far to the rear of the central pod, took the last shuttle back to Earth. The firing controls and the guidance system had already been installed and their operation adapted from the original controls built into the station. The only problem they detected could be easily remedied by simply accelerating slowly and steadily and careful maneuvering when close to a gravitational source.

If they hit nothing larger than a basketball once they were up to speed, the engine pods should all hang together.

Suddenly, almost too soon, the station was ready to begin its trip. During the initial acceleration, although nothing like that launching the old chemical rockets from Earth, all hands were required to be in their personal pods, strapped into the bunks bolted to the walls. Only the three people who would be watching the computer programs controlling the acceleration were allowed to be out and roaming around.

Hackett had thought about going to the command pod, where he could watch the operation, but then decided to avoid it so that he wouldn't get in the way. And if he really wanted to watch, the computer would display whatever he asked to see on the flat screen in his own cabin. In other words, he could watch the whole operation from the safety of his bunk, switching the scene as the mood moved him.

So Hackett watched as the rockets were fired but felt nothing and heard nothing. He watched as Lewis and two other Navy men monitored the operation from their command pod. He even watched the news coverage of the event as it was broadcast to Earth in real time though there was a delay built in because of the distance they were from Earth.

After an hour, with everything hanging together, and with the station accelerating out of orbit, Hackett decided that he didn't have to remain in his bunk. He unstrapped, swung his legs out, and was surprised to feel, ever so slightly, what he thought, at first, was gravity. Then he realized that it was only the slightest result of acceleration, pushing him toward the rear of the pod and the rear of the ship. Finally, he felt something that gave a hint that they were in motion.

As he opened the hatch and stepped out into the corridor, there was a quiet bong signaling an announcement and a voice he didn't recognize said, "We have stabilized our acceleration. You are free to move about the station."

[2]

RACHEL DAVIES, NOW DRESSED JUST AS
those who had welcomed her had been dressed, that is, in
T-shirt and shorts, though hers were abbreviated to the
point of nonexistence, wandered from one end of the central pod to the other, looking for something that would be
interesting to the people left on Earth. There were a dozen
people scattered around the pod, four of whom were standing on the wall, which was somewhat disconcerting. The
sight of them, standing at a ninety-degree angle to what
she considered the floor, engaging in casual conversation,
made her a little sick and somewhat dizzy. She decided not
to look at them if she didn't have to.

Sitting alone, in a strange-looking chair that sort of
wrapped around the occupant, holding him or her in place
so that the lack of gravity didn't allow anyone to drift
away, was Jonathan Travis. A low coffee table with a
metallic top that was magnetic sat in front of him. It held a
metallic cup with a cover on it. Travis looked as if he was
asleep.

Davies walked over, and said, "Not what I expected."

Travis, caught off guard and unsure of what she meant,
said, "You expected what?"

Without waiting for an invitation, she sat down across
the table so that she could look at him. "I thought we
would be subjected to great pressures and uncomfortable
stresses when we began to accelerate."

"You've been watching too many of those old space
movies. Besides, we're here, in space already. Don't need
a sudden, heavy boost to throw us into space, we can accelerate slowly so that there is no real discomfort."

"Well, we're on our way."

Travis nodded, and said, "I wish I knew what I was supposed to be doing here."

"I thought you were the expert on aliens."

Travis tried to smile and failed. He shrugged, and said,
"What I do is study reports by people who might have

misidentified any of a number of natural objects, or air-craft, or who believe they have had some sort of contact with alien creatures. I look at the physical evidence, which is limited, and I search for corroboration, which is often lacking. I can tell you more than you care to know about those subjects, but when you get to the bottom line, most of it is speculation based on less-than- exciting and maybe erroneous observation. I often deal with the anecdotal rather than the empirical."

"But they did ask you here."

"Yes, because I supposedly know something, and even if everything I know and believe is true, it just might not apply here. There is no evidence that the aliens we're now rushing to meet are the same ones who have been visiting Earth. It might be that those creatures on that ship out there haven't come anywhere near the Earth before now."

"Well, if nothing else, you get to ride out to the edge of the Solar System."

"And fall off the edge into what? A gigantic abyss filled with dragons and demons?"

Now she smiled. "No. But you'll be as far out as any other human has been."

He waved a hand. "Yes, with fifty or sixty others. Not much of a spot for me in the history books."

"Is that what you're after? A spot in the history books?"

"Don't know, really. I had thought that my studies would be of some value, but now, sitting here, I just can't see it. Looking at it with a skeptical eye, I now see how things should have progressed; but we were all so busy fighting with one another, and with scientists who refused to look at anything because they didn't want to be associated with UFOs, that we accomplished nothing. Good, solid material, eyewitness reports from technically trained people, physical evidence from radars and cameras were all buried by opinion and fabrication. I don't like you so I find the slightest thing wrong with your research or your witness and use it to hammer the information into the ground. Doesn't matter if the flaw, real or otherwise, is basically irrelevant. I have found it, and now I can ignore you."

"Sounds like journalism to me," said Davies.

"Actually, it reflects most of what happens in academia, or just about any other human endeavor. The difference is, if two scientists are arguing over the demise of the dinosaurs, for example, they both start with the facts that dinosaurs existed and they went extinct sixty-five million years ago. We start, for the most part, from a premise that UFOs are extraterrestrial, and we can even debate that point. We have little in the way of factual information. We have nowhere to begin, and we have no common ground."

Davies leaned back and crossed her legs. She thought for a moment, and said, "You know, this might make an interesting story for me. UFO expert who admits the truth about the study while trying to move it into the real world. The man who attempts to move UFOs into a scientific environment."

"Nope," said Travis, "I don't think that is such a good idea. Why attack the whole field and put myself on the outside looking in? Why alienate, and I use the word advisedly, everyone else who studies UFOs and similar phenomena. I think it best to let the sleeping dogs lie."

"Meaning?"

"Just that I'm not going to make the skeptical arguments for them, nor am I going to suggest that my function here is somewhat fantasy-oriented. I'm going to provide my insights, few that I might have, when asked to provide them."

"We could put together something that you would find useful. Maybe define your role here a little better."

Travis shook his head, then looked again at Davies. She didn't strike him as the brightest bulb in the display, but then, she didn't seem to be mean-spirited. She might be ambitious, but that didn't make her a bad person. If he cooperated, he would have something to do on the way out of the Solar System. Finally, he said, "Sure. Why not?"

[3]

BAKKER WANDERED AMONG THE PODS, JUST trying to get herself oriented because she was going to spend the next several months of her life living in the station. She liked knowing where things were and how to move from one place to another. She also wanted to get used to walking in Velcro slippers so that she didn't go floating off the deck.

The station itself, according to what she had seen personally, the photographs and video clips available in the computer system, and now from her own exploration, was a cluster of pods, she thought there were twenty of them, attached to a long and wide central pod that housed the meeting rooms, the galley and kitchen, the recycling center, and the communal bathrooms. Although separate bathing facilities were provided for men and women, there wasn't much in the way of privacy.

Many of the pods had a single function, and the equipment needed for that function was stored, attached, arrayed, and displayed there. Although there was a control room of sorts in the communications pod, for example, much of the equipment for that function was arranged around access shafts that allowed maintenance and replacement.

She found there was a pod that looked for all the world like one of the control rooms at the VLA in New Mexico. It was, in fact, a radio astronomy lab set up with the idea that Bakker, and any other astronomer, would have the equipment needed to monitor not only the happenings and discoveries on Earth, but would be in a position to monitor the aliens when the two ships got closer. She had known that such a place had been planned, but she had not been told exactly where it was. There hadn't been time.

During her tour, she found what she thought of as the maintenance pod, which was sort of a large janitor's closet, the recycling pod, and even a couple of hydroponic pods, where some fresh food was being grown. It wasn't very large, and the crops were somewhat limited. It was more of an experiment in hydroponics as opposed to a functional farm designed to provide fresh vegetables for the population of the station.

There were also two somewhat large pods that reminded her of window boxes on apartment building balconies. There were dirt for growing food and lights to simulate the sun's rays. She thought she could see the beginnings of green plants pushing their way through the surface of the soil, giving it a slightly greenish tint, but she wasn't sure about that. This was just another experiment in growing plants in space.

She eventually looked into the control pod, which contained the navigation equipment and the flight controls. She looked in to see Lewis and a woman sitting in what she thought of as the captain's chairs, watching a huge display screen. Centered in it was a single bright red orb that she knew to be Mars. She stood there, watching for a moment, then slipped away, not wanting to bother either of the pilots.

She worked her way back to the central pod, saw Davies talking to the UFO guy, and Hackett as he entered from the other side. She walked across the pod, and said, "Good morning."

Hackett looked as if he had just awakened and was in a bad mood because of it. He said, "I need something to drink and I need a shower."

"Drink? This early?"

"Orange juice, for Christ's sake. Or coffee. Or tomato juice. Just something wet."

"Are you always this much fun in the morning?" she asked innocently.

He looked at her, then smiled. "No. Sometimes I'm in a bad mood."

They walked deeper into the pod and sat down. Hackett scrubbed at his face with both hands as if that would help him wake up. He said, "I feel really crappy. Sluggish."

"Effects of the last several days?" asked Bakker.

"Hell, you've gone through it too. How come you don't look bad or feel bad?"

"I got a lot of sleep on the craft on the way up here, and nobody expects me to do a thing for another several days. I have the chance to relax."

"Still," said Hackett.

"You'll feel better in a couple of days."

"Sure I will."

She looked at him carefully, then asked, "What do you think will happen?"

He was silent for a minute, as if trying to form a reply, then said, "I don't know. Who has any experience in this kind of a thing?"

"I think if we go in with a confrontational attitude, then we're going to get a confrontation, and that can't be good for us. They have spaceflight, and we don't."

Hackett laughed, and said, "Actually we do. What we don't have is interstellar flight, but they won't know that. All they'll know is that we met them outside the limits of the Solar System, on neutral ground. And, their supply lines will be impossibly long while ours are relatively short."

"You're talking as if a fight is a foregone conclusion here. I don't see that."

"You brought up confrontation. I don't know what's going to happen. I don't even know how we're going to communicate with them. I don't know if we can. I just think that it's important that we meet them as far from the sun as possible. Let them think we have a technology that is farther advanced than it is. If they are hostile, if they have invasion on their minds, make them think they will fail here."

"I don't think I like this line of thought. You keep making assumptions that aren't in evidence. You seem to think that the aliens are evil."

Hackett rubbed his head as if it hurt. He said, "I don't know what to think, but I want us to be prepared for the worst. That way we don't get caught with our dicks in a wringer."

"You think that's is what is going to happen?"

Hackett looked at her closely, surprised by the question. Finally, he said, "No. I think we're basically going to pass in the night without either one of us making a hostile move. Neither side can afford to do anything like that until we learn a great deal more about each other."

Bakker sat back and sighed deeply. "I don't like the idea that we finally make contact with an alien race, and all our thoughts are of violence. Maybe they have no violent tendencies. Maybe they're a peace-loving race."

"We can always hope for that," said Hackett, "but it strikes me that we have to be prepared for the confrontation."

"Be prepared, but not initiate it," said Bakker.

Hackett shook his head. "It is too early for deep philosophical conversation. I need to get some juice or coffee. Then we can talk."

Bakker grinned. "As I understand it, we'll have plenty of time. We're not due to arrive at our destination for a very long time."

"Then I suggest we find something to drink," said Hackett. "That's what I need now."

CHAPTER 16

[1]

THE MARTIAN LANDSCAPE HAD BEEN PARTIALLY terraformed using huge glass-and-plastic domes constructed from the sand and soil found on Mars and chemical-processing plants that created enough oxygen for human habitation. The domes that had been erected for agriculture also produced oxygen, as did the trees, bushes and flowers that lined every street, filled every empty space, and were even grown in pots and window boxes of the human domes. Mars had been fit for human habitation for nearly two decades.

Hackett, however, was glad that he was on the surface of Mars. Although he would have preferred to stay on Earth, where life wasn't the constant struggle that it was on Mars, this was better than on the station. There was room to move and breathe and a little privacy. That was the thing that he missed most on the station. The lack of privacy.

Hackett stood at the window and looked down into the street some thirty or forty feet below him. There were people walking along quietly and one electric bus moving down the center of what would have been a grass-covered street on Earth. None of them seemed to be worried about a catastrophic failure in a dome, which could kill them all. The domes, he had been told, were engineered so that the catastrophic failures were believed to happen once every one hundred thousand years and by the time that a hundred thousand years had passed, the dome would have been replaced by something else, something better that would have an even longer mean time to failure. Hackett thought such reasoning was as fuzzy as the Burlington Coat Factory.

He was listening to the conversation going on behind him, but didn't care to participate at the moment. It concerned the signals, as they had been detected just before they entered Mars orbit, and he already knew about them.

Bakker sat at the head of the small conference table, leaning on her elbows and staring at the glass of water in front of her. It was a strangely colored, cloudy liquid that tasted as if it had been carbonated. She was trying to decide if she liked it better than Earth water. She decided that she didn't.

Across from her sat Weiss, though she would have been happier if Weiss had remained on the station. There was no reason for him to be here, and then she remembered that there was a very important reason. She shot a glance at Hackett, who was still looking out the window.

Hackett finally turned and stepped to the table. He pulled his chair around and sat down. He looked at the others in the room, including the man standing near a chart on an easel rather than a display on a computer. Sometimes things on Mars looked as if they had come from the middle of the twentieth century. And sometimes they seemed to belong to the nineteenth.

The man, who had identified himself as James Stuart, said, "This is the very latest from various sites on Earth."

He pointed at the chart on the easel, which was little more than lines of computer-type code.

Stuart grinned, and said, "Yeah, it is a joke. We have been able to break it down and have a better feeling for what the messages are. Before I show you, let me just say that our assumption, and I'm sure that it is one of yours as well, is that the messages are not meant for us. They are, more or less, internal communications."

He took the chart off the easel and set it on the floor. Behind it was a photograph that had the same strange composition as the one that had been revealed earlier; but this one, in color, had more detail.

Stuart said, "This is, of course, classified, but I doubt that any of you will be communicating with anyone who hasn't already seen it. This does give us a better idea of what the alien creatures out there look like."

There were two objects in the foreground of the picture, one of them visible from what would be the waist upward and the second a sort of head-and-shoulders shot. Arms branched off the trunk that were thick, almost as big as the trunk. There might have been three of them, though the picture wasn't clear enough to be sure about that.

The face was a nightmare mask of misshapen features. The eyes seemed to be narrow ovals that were oriented up and down rather than sideways. There were protrusions on the side of the head that could have been ears, but were narrow and looked to be pointed. The nose looked like an inverted triangle, and if there was a mouth, it was not visible in the photograph. The head itself was shaped like a lightbulb.

Travis, who sat at the far end of the table, leaned forward, as if to get a better look, and then glancing, first at Bakker and then at Hackett, said, "Nope. It really matches nothing that I'm familiar with. Nothing at all."

"The other important point," said Stuart, "is that we have now detected a message from seven light-years out. It is, of course, stronger than the others, and therefore easier to detect. Everything we have to date suggests that the ship, or ships, are heading toward us, meaning the Solar System."

[2]

HACKETT AND BAKKER WERE AT THE STREET level, walking along one of the streets, taking in the local atmosphere. It was a strange mixture of third-world utility and high-tech extravagance. The buildings looked as if they were constructed of adobe, but it was a synthetic material developed from the abundant sands of the Martian surface.

There were few hovercraft humming along the grass-covered streets. Most people walked, and there was nothing inside the dome that couldn't be reached in half an hour on foot, or by using the escalators and moving sidewalks that were sprinkled about quite liberally. It wasn't difficult to get around, even if the hovercars were restricted to use by only a few.

They turned a corner and spotted a small restaurant that had just a few tables on the sidewalk outside, looking like a modern simulation of a Parisian café. The tables had brightly colored umbrellas, even though the dome filtered out the more harmful of the sun's rays, and the Martian day was about as bright as a cloudy day on Earth.

"You want to?" asked Hackett, pointing.

"Sure."

They walked up, pulled out chairs, and sat down. Bakker turned and looked through the window of the shop next door and was surprised to see it filled with books. Honest to God, real live, printed on paper and bound by leather, books. Everything from leather-bound first editions to the latest of the mass-market paperbacks.

"A bookstore?"

"For those who love books?" said Hackett.

"Yeah, I understand that on Earth. Some stories were

just meant to be in books. But that's on Earth and not on Mars. Think of the expense just to get them here."

"Unless the owner makes them himself. Printing wouldn't be much of a problem. Binding might be."

Bakker said, "But they look old."

"Well, you can't tell from here." He also said, "You can't tell a book by its cover."

"You order for me. I'm going to look."

She stood up and walked into the shop. The interior mimicked what she thought a rare and used bookstore would look like in London or New York, but on Mars it was surprising.

She picked a book off the shelf and opened it. The copyright date, if she read it right, was 1874. The paper felt old, and the ink looked faded. It hadn't been printed on a computer and then bound. Or rather, it didn't look as it had been.

"That is an interesting volume. It is one of the first histories of the American Civil War."

The voice was deep, but the English was slightly accented. Bakker looked and was surprised again. The man was tall, thin, but young. She had expected a man out of Dickens's old England, with long sideburns and a tweed coat and a British accent, of course.

"Is this a first edition?"

"Ah, you know your books," said the man. He shook his head. "No, sadly, it is my creation."

"It looks as if it is very old."

"Thank you. There are a few here who appreciate having books rather than electronic images to be decoded by a machine."

"Where do you get the paper?"

"I make that myself. It's synthetic, composed of elements taken from the soil. Are you interested in that volume?"

Bakker put it back on the shelf carefully. "No, thank you."

"I have many others, if history is not your area of interest," he said.

"No, I was just curious about the books. Surprised to find them here, on Mars."

"A touch of home is often welcomed by those who have taken the leap into space."

"Yes, I suppose so."

"I can prepare for you anything that you might like. I have an extensive electronic library."

"Copyright?" said Bakker.

"Well, the oldest are all out of copyright. The newer volumes, the fiction and the like, must be paid for. The author receives a royalty for each volume I create."

"Well, thank you. My friend has ordered my lunch, so I must go."

"Please come back when you have the chance."

"Yes, of course." Bakker left the shop. It was the last thing that she would have expected on Mars, but then, a computer program that could be transmitted from Earth would have allowed him to set everything up. The only problem was the binding of the books, and he seemed to have solved that problem.

She returned to the table to find the food there and Hackett waiting patiently for her. As she sat down, he picked up his glass of beer, held it high, and said, "Here's to us and the Galaxy Exploration Team."

Bakker nodded, then took a drink, her eyes focused on Hackett's.

[3]

THE HOTEL ROOM WAS MADE OF SOMETHING that looked like molded plastic. With a touch of a button, it could be made airtight in case of a catastrophic failure of the dome. Of course, that should automatically happen if the dome failed, and the button was a backup system.

The furnishings were made of plastic and were surprisingly comfortable. Across from the double bed, which to Hackett and Bakker seemed luxuriously large when compared to the bunks that they had on the station, was a window that looked out into the city and onto the dome. There was a dim red tint to the sky outside the window that probably was a function of the dome.

Hackett tossed the thin sheet off and stood up. He walked to the window and looked down, fifteen or twenty feet, into the street. There were already people circulating, and Hackett suspected that there were people on the street all night. He had noticed an underclass of people who seemed to be as rootless as those he had seen on Earth. They survived on Mars the same way that those on Earth survived.

Bakker sat up, and asked, "What time do we have to leave?"

"Couple of hours yet."

"What are the plans?"

Hackett turned and looked at her. She hadn't bothered to find her clothes. She stood up and joined him at the window. "I think I could get used to living here."

"In the hotel or on Mars."

"Either one. It's more comfortable than on the station."

Hackett didn't understand that. Sure, they could take long showers on Mars, and there was gravity, which made life a little easier, but there wasn't much difference. It wasn't as if they had been limited to a small cabin with no space to move around and no place to find a little privacy. Hackett didn't really see any difference between where they were on Mars and the life they had on the station.

"You think that Weiss is going to be pissed?"

Hackett had to laugh. "Would you be?"

"Given the circumstances, yeah, I suppose so. But, like I said. It's more comfortable here."

Hackett picked up his shirt and put it on. He found his pants and donned them. Bakker had made no move to find her clothes. She just didn't care.

"I'm thinking," said Hackett, "that it would be nice to find some place for breakfast."

Bakker grinned. "And I'm thinking that I really don't want to leave here until we absolutely have to."

"I understand," said Hackett, taking off his shirt again.

[4]

THE SHUTTLE PORT WAS, OF COURSE, SEParated from the main dome by a couple of miles just in case something exploded. An electric train ran back and forth through a long plastic tube that held the air in but let the exhaust out, such as it was. The train ran on a regular schedule, so there was no trouble in getting to the spaceport.

Hackett and Bakker exited the train and walked to the long, low building that was used as the terminal, for conferences, and even had a couple of small restaurants, a gaming parlor, and a few shops selling the last chance for Martian souvenirs. It was modeled after the airports on Earth at about the turn of the century.

They walked into the terminal, strolled along the concourse, and found their way to the Conference Room D. Without knocking, Hackett opened the door and stepped back so that Bakker could enter first.

"You finally made it," said Weiss.

Hackett shot him a hasty glance.

Bakker pulled out a chair and sat down opposite Travis and Davies.

Hackett said, "There are a few things that we need to talk about before some of us get on the shuttle and head back to the station."

He glanced from one to the other. Weiss looked angry. Travis and Davies looked as if they had suddenly found each other. Their chairs were just a little closer to one another than they should be. First Lieutenant Harold Dobbs, a youngish man with short-cropped hair and huge, wide-set eyes, was looking down, at the table, as if afraid that looking anywhere else would call attention to himself.

Next to him was a junior female scientist whose name Hackett didn't know. He thought she was Judy, or Julie, or something like that. He hadn't met her officially on the trip from Earth orbit to Mars.

"Before we left Earth," said Hackett by way of preamble, "we were given an additional task. The president, and, I believe, General Greenstein concurred, thought that our base of operations should not be on Earth. They believed that we should establish, on Mars, a headquarters operation that would filter our message traffic to and from Earth. Something that could divert attention from Earth to Mars, in case such a diversion was needed."

"We're staying here?" asked Weiss, his voice high and tight.

"Not all of us," said Hackett, "which explains why we're meeting here. Some of us must catch the shuttle and some of us will catch the train."

"Catch the train?" asked Weiss.

Hackett ignored him, and said, "Lieutenant Dobbs, I'm afraid that you'll have the unenviable task of finding office space, basic equipment, and establishing the communications link with our facility at White Sands."

"Yes, sir."

"You'll have about two Earth weeks to get up and running. Assisting you will be," Hackett looked at the young scientist and said, "I'm afraid I don't have your last name."

"McCoy. I'm Julie McCoy."

"Yes, of course. Your function, quite naturally, will be to interpret the information that passes through the office. I think that General Greenstein's thinking was that you would have a first crack at it and that your analysis wouldn't be clouded by those conducted on Earth. A fresh set of eyes."

"Okay," she said dubiously.

"You're not to worry about right or wrong but simply

supply what you think. It'll help those left behind on Earth establish a baseline for their thinking."

"I would be more use on the station," she said.

"Possibly true," said Hackett, "but we need some good people here, on Mars."

He turned his attention to Weiss. He grinned evilly, and said, "And you have guessed correctly. You're to remain here and provide support to both Dobbs and McCoy. You are to supply your own analysis of the data and pass it along, just as McCoy will be doing. I think the idea is that you are to work independently, but I doubt that anyone will complain if you confer, especially after you have transmitted your reports."

"Nope," said Weiss. "I'm not going to remain here. You can't do anything about it."

"Actually, I can," said Hackett. "If I have to, I'll just ask a couple of the military police—I'm sure that you saw them—to restrain you until the shuttle has departed."

"I'm not staying here," said Weiss. "I'll pay for my own passage back to Earth."

"That is, of course, your option. However, there isn't another scheduled passenger ship for about a year, so go right ahead. By that time, this crisis will have been resolved, one way or another."

"Why?" asked Weiss.

Bakker looked at him surprised, and said, "You really think what you were doing with Parker went unnoticed? You pissed off everyone at the university. You pissed off the military. You leaked material that should have been held and gave opinions that were founded on the shakiest of science. You created trouble at every turn and seemed oblivious to it, which explains why you so willingly boarded the station."

"If I had my way," said Hackett, "you'd be with us so that I could keep an eye on you. This is the next best thing."

Bakker softened, and said, "It gives you a chance to redeem yourself. Do a good job here and when we get back to Earth, I'll give you a good recommendation if you wish to leave the university. If you wish to stay, I'll live up to the deal I made with you in New Mexico. I'll help you get your doctorate."

"And if I raise a stink?"

"Again, your choice. But you won't be able to raise this stink until this crisis is over, and I suspect that by that time no one will really care."

Weiss looked as if he wanted to say something else, but Dobbs interrupted. "What do I do with him?"

"Use him as you see fit," said Hackett.

"Listen to his scientific advice," said Bakker. "He actually can think well when his mind isn't clouded with ambition and trickery."

"General Greenstein has transmitted his instructions, and you should be able to download them. Once the office is up and running, there will be new instructions and staff. Maybe some of it from the station on our return."

"What are we going to call this operation," asked McCoy.

"Galaxy Exploration Team."

"Sort of grandiose, isn't it?" asked Dobbs.

Hackett said, "We're just beginning. Later I hope that it will be appropriate."

CHAPTER 17

[1]

THE STATION, WHICH HADN'T DECELERATED all that much in orbit around Mars, used the little gravitational advantage it offered to slingshot itself back into deep space. From that point on, it would continue slowly to accelerate, finally passing close to Saturn and using the planet's gravitation field to generate more speed. The station would then continue, moving ever faster, away from the sun and deeper into space, eventually crossing the orbit of Pluto.

Power was generated by a combination of chemical rockets, which were fueled by huge pods that had been attached in Mars orbit, and electrical energy, generated by the solar panels. Of course, as they moved farther from the sun, the ability of the solar panels would be degraded simply because there would be less solar energy to gather.

Although untried, they would attempt to gather, as they

moved, the hydrogen that was spread throughout the galaxy. Collectors would concentrate the hydrogen, and it would be used to fuel cells that would supplement the solar panels and the chemical rockets. Power was being drawn from every source available.

It was believed that the station would be self-sufficient, at least from an energy standpoint. Food was a different matter, and they had more pods affixed that carried those supplies. Calculations had suggested how long the journey, from Mars and back, would last, and the rations had been doubled. It was planned that they would have more than enough food, even if they had to wait several months for the alien ship to arrive.

That left only air and water, and all of that had to be carefully recycled. Hackett understood what that meant, but he wasn't sure that others thought much about it. Maybe they didn't want to. If they did, there might have been some psychological problems.

Hackett himself tried not to think about the water. True, some of it had been replaced when they were on Mars, but the weight of water was such that it made little sense to boost it into orbit when all they had to do was carefully recycle what they had. Of course they had to recycle it from everywhere, which meant the showers and other such facilities.

They also reduced the food waste in recycling pods, which did add to the water and provided them with an additional source of food. It was a dark brown cracker that tasted a little better than cardboard, but was, in fact, quite nutritious. It could sustain life without any other source of food. To survive, the person just needed to find water, which brought him back to that. Recycled water.

And the air was the same. Recycled, not only through filters and scrubbers, but also through the lungs of everyone in the station. The fact that he was breathing air that had been breathed by someone else didn't bother him much. He couldn't see the air and, for the most part, he couldn't taste it. Air was just out there, and he breathed it in without thinking about it.

Water, however, had to be gathered in a glass and he had to make a conscious effort to drink it. He had to think about it, and he could see it. Usually, people added an artificial flavor to it, such as strawberry or orange, and then it looked like any other beverage. No one thought about where it might have been the day before.

So the station, gathering energy as it flew, gathering speed as it moved through the Solar System, and recycling everything, headed toward the Oort Cloud. It was aimed, more or less, at the point that someone on the ground on Earth, or in the navigational center on the station, thought would eventually hold the alien craft.

[2]

BAKKER WAS IN THE SCIENCE POD, SITTING IN front of a monitor using a keyboard to access the computer. Like her counterparts at the VLA, she was studying the alien signal. She had the latest data uploaded from the VLA so that she knew the signal was now four and a half light-years from Earth, just a little farther than the closest star system.

She was looking for a way to understand the signal, assuming, as they had for a long time, that it was not designed to communicate with another intelligent race. And she was having no luck in figuring out anything.

There was a tapping on the wall, and she turned, looking through the open hatch. "Yes, Major Hackett," she said, formally, "you are welcome to join me."

Hackett entered and slipped into the chair beside her. "Anything that I should know about?"

"Well, I think it's pretty much a foregone conclusion that they have a faster-than-light drive or they'd have a fleet of ships out there."

"Why not a fleet?"

"Because I think if there was a fleet, we would have found something else long ago. The first signal we detected was right at the limits of our capabilities. Now, we are getting stronger signals from a ship that is closer. Our capabilities have improved somewhat, but we're finding nothing else out at fifty light-years. Now that we know what to look for, the task is simpler. We just haven't found anything."

"Travis said that we've been visited for about a hundred years."

"Yes, I know what he thinks, but I just don't see it, unless it is another race, and they're working to conceal their electromagnetic signals from us."

Hackett nodded, and said, "How do you know that everyone communicates through some form of electromagnetic radiation? Maybe they do it another way and we just haven't found it because we haven't been looking for it."

"Ah, the flaw in SETI that no one ever mentions. We assume that all civilizations will develop radio, and we assume that all civilizations will assume that all others will use radio in an attempt to communicate. The problem is that radio might not be the only, or even best method of communication, it's just the one we assume they would use."

"But we did find a radio signal."

Bakker laughed and said, "Well, not really. We have an electromagnetic signal that has revealed to us, with great speculation and manipulation, a partial video picture. Sort of the same thing, but . . ."

Hackett waved a hand. "That's okay. I don't need a lecture. Have you got anything new and interesting?"

"No."

"I have a question that has been bothering me for a while. Have they spotted us?"

"You mean us us, or do you mean Earth?"

"Let's go with Earth first."

"Well, Earth has been radiating electromagnetic waves,

first as radio and later as television, for more than 175 years. We have sent out signals in an attempt to communicate with other intelligent civilizations, off and on, for 70 or 80 years."

Hackett nodded, and said, "And obviously there has been no response."

"Well, if the civilization was far enough away, and they figured out the message, and if they wanted to respond, we might not have gotten that response. A civilization just a hundred light-years from Earth would take a hundred years to get the message, a year or two to figure it out and decide to respond, then another hundred years for their message to get back to us. So, we wouldn't have yet heard from them."

"Unless, of course, that ship is their response."

Bakker turned away from the computer monitor and looked at Hackett. "Well, yes, but I don't think so."

"Why?"

"The line of flight hasn't been direct. They are aimed, generally in our direction, but they're not aimed at us precisely. I think, if that was their response, the ship would have been coming right at us at high speed. That just isn't the case. This seems more of an exploration of the area than something coming to us."

Hackett nodded, and said, "I just wish that UFO guy had some better information."

"Meaning?"

"Well, think about it. If he knows what he's talking about, then there have been visitors to Earth since, hell, I don't know when but from the middle of the twentieth century, at least. They know where we are. That gives us one set of data."

"Yes," said Bakker, slowly, "but it wouldn't be the same group."

"Now how can you say that?"

"Because if it was, we would have spotted them long before we did. The problem before was a combination of a weak signal and the distance. As the distance shrinks, the odds of our detecting the signal increase dramatically. If they had been operating inside our solar system, or even within a light-year or two, we would have spotted them before now. This has got to be a different group of aliens."

"Which means anything the UFO guy could tell us isn't worth much."

"No," said Bakker. "Our point of reference has always been through human eyes. If he has been studying actual alien visitation, then he has a perspective that would be different than ours."

"So we go talk to him."

"I was wondering," said Bakker, "if they had ever established any sort of a protocol for contact with the aliens."

"Who?"

"The UFO groups."

"So, let's go ask."

[3]

TRAVIS WAS SITTING IN THE CENTRAL POD, A covered glass sitting in front of him, and talking to Rachel Davies. She was without her camera. They seemed to be sitting quite close to one another, their heads nearly touching as they talked. They seemed unaware of anyone else in the pod.

Hackett and Bakker approached and stood there, waiting until one or the other noticed them. When Davies finally looked up, Hackett, trying to keep the sarcasm from his voice, though he couldn't have explained why he was irritated, asked, "You two busy?"

Travis straightened, then blushed, as if he had been caught doing something that he shouldn't. He said, "No. We're just talking."

Hackett pointed at the couch on the other side of the coffee table, and asked, "Mind if we join you?"

"Sure," said Davies, though she didn't look very happy about it.

"John," said Hackett, "we"—he pointed at Bakker and himself—"have a couple of questions for you."

"Shoot."

Suddenly Hackett was unsure of what he wanted to know, or how to ask any questions without sounding condescending. He started to speak, stopped, then asked, "Are you absolutely certain that we have been visited?"

"If you mean do I consider some UFOs as extraterrestrial spacecraft, then the answer is yes."

"Based on what?" asked Bakker.

Travis looked at her, and shrugged. "We've gone over that. You asked my opinion, and I gave it to you. If you don't like it, then go somewhere else."

Bakker started to snap at him, then grinned, "Fair enough. We did ask for your opinion."

"Besides," said Travis, "I would have thought that craft out there would have suggested that there are spacefaring, intelligent races in the universe, some of them coming toward Earth."

"Point taken," said Bakker.

"Okay," said Hackett. "We," and again he indicated Bakker and himself, "don't think that the craft out there is one of those that has visited Earth before. But that isn't the point. What we wondered is if there has been any contact between humans and the aliens."

Travis shook his head. "I talk and talk. I hear the words, so I know that others can hear, but we go right back to the same things over and over."

"Meaning?" asked Hackett.

"Dr. Bakker sat on a panel with a woman who said that she had been abducted by alien creatures."

"Sure. But . . ."

"But what? You don't like her story. You think she is deluded? We sit here, flying out to intercept an alien vessel, and you want to disbelieve a woman who said she has already had some contact with an alien race."

"This is different."

"How?"

"Well, for one thing, others have been able to intercept the signals."

"Yes, but as I understand it, there are some alternative interpretations for the signal that don't necessarily imply an intelligence, yet here we are."

Hackett waved a hand as if to wipe a slate. "Look. Here's where we are. In several weeks we're going to be in a position to make contact with the aliens. The distance between us, with any luck, will be something that would allow two-way communication in a fairly convenient manner. We just don't know how to initiate that contact. Has that question ever been tackled by any of your people?"

"My people? You mean the flying saucer nuts?"

Hackett looked at him closely. "Okay. I phrased that badly. I am interested in gathering some data here."

"There has been precious little in the way of two-way communication," said Hackett. "There are those who have said they engaged in a dialogue with the aliens, people we called the contactees, meaning they were in contact, but they never offered anything in the way of corroborative evidence. Their stories are not accepted as accurate."

"What about these abductees?"

"They don't initiate the contact, and it is usually one-sided. The aliens gather the data they want and give us little in the way of information in return. Some of the researchers believe the aliens lie as a way of hiding what they're really doing. But the point is, the abductees are more like victims of a random shooting. They don't want to be involved, they just happen to be there."

"Then there is nothing that you can tell us that would be helpful," said Bakker.

"Well, not really. What we have learned is that there is a common factor, even if we have no common ancestors and we have no common evolution. That common factor is simply that we are all intelligent creatures, and that gives us one basis for communications."

"That's not much," said Hackett.

"Actually, it's quite a bit. Look, the aliens that have

been reported are all, basically, humanoid, meaning two arms, two legs and single head. That suggests more in common. Similar environmental pressures that produce an intelligent creature structured in the same basic way. That, I would think, would supply some commonality."

"That could mean," said Hackett, "that their past is as bloody as ours."

"But, they might have already unified their worlds," said Travis. "Or, it might not have been as fragmented as ours to begin with, but I doubt that. Until you have a means of communication over great distances, different groups will react to environmental stress in different ways, and competition for resources, meaning food and mates, will set up a situation in which their evolution toward civilization should match ours to some extent, meaning it was just as fragmented."

"Speculation," said Bakker.

"Yes, but speculation based on what has happened in the past with the visitors," said Travis. "Hints have been dropped here and there."

"Speculation," repeated Bakker.

"So, what do you want?" asked Travis.

"A plan to contact that other ship," said Hackett.

[4]

WITH THE STATION MOVING TOWARD THE OUTER edges of the Solar System, there wasn't much to be done at White Sands. Control of, or rather communications with, the station had shifted to the VLA. Greenstein did not need to be in New Mexico any longer. But before he left, he decided that he wanted to see the facilities at the Very Large Array.

Used to entering military installations, Greenstein was a little disturbed by the lack of security, but then, this was an isolated scientific area that didn't belong to the Army.

They just drove up the long road and stopped outside what appeared to be the main building.

A moment later the door opened and two people, a man and woman, exited. As Greenstein, dressed in civilian clothes, began to climb out of the car, the man said, "I'm sorry, but this is a closed facility."

Greenstein asked, "Are you Gibson?"

"Yes. And you are?"

"Greenstein."

"Ah, the general."

"I thought I would drop by for a briefing before I return to Washington."

Gibson pointed, and said, "This is Liz Taylor, and we would be happy to show you around."

"Nice to meet you, Ms. Taylor," said Greenstein.

"Actually, it's doctor."

"Forgive me, Doctor."

"Let's get inside, out of this heat."

Inside, they walked past the conference room and into the main radio room. Greenstein stood in the middle of it, while Gibson pointed to various pieces of electronic equipment and explained what each did.

Greenstein nodded, pretending that he understood, and finally asked, "What's new in the way of signals?"

Taylor, grinning broadly, said, "Let's go into the conference room."

Greenstein was surprised to find the conference room looking like the dorm room of two college freshman, neither of whom had ever thought to pick up anything. Books, disks, computers, printouts, soda cans, pizza boxes, and even some clothes were scattered over the table, the chairs, and the floor. Stacked along one wall were more books.

Gibson moved a pizza box and two shirts and a skirt from a chair, and said, "Please have a seat. Please direct your attention to the monitor on the wall, and we'll give you a show."

"All right," said Greenstein somewhat dubiously.

"First up, you'll see, with the scale wildly out of

proportion, a map of the outer edge of the Solar System. Our ship has passed beyond the orbit of Pluto and is more than five light-weeks from the sun."

"I hadn't realized that they had gotten so far out."

"It is the deepest penetration into space by any ship carrying a human crew."

"Score one for us."

"The alien ship," said Gibson, "has been located again. It is just over eighteen light-months from the sun, and is closing more or less on us. Given what we know, the two ships should meet one another in about six weeks or so. That depends on their wanting to meet us and their having located our ship."

"Why their locating us?"

"They have the maneuvering capability and the speed. We certainly couldn't overtake them."

Greenstein stared at the map, at the two glowing dots that represented the relative positions of the two ships, and wondered if this was important enough to bother the president. Nothing was going to happen for weeks unless one ship, or the other, sped up. He knew that the station was not going to speed up, and was probably decelerating as it moved deeper into space. He had no idea what the alien ship would do.

"Is there just one alien ship out there?"

Gibson sat back in his chair and rubbed his chin as if thinking about it. Finally, he said, "I don't know. Liz, what do you think?"

"I think that it is very unlikely they have more than one ship in this part of the galaxy. I think there is one ship that has faster-than-light capability."

Greenstein said, almost as if he wasn't aware that he had spoken out loud, "If we could capture that ship, then we would have faster-than-light drive, too."

"You aren't seriously thinking about a military action against the first alien race that we encounter, are you?"

Greenstein looked up suddenly, and said, "No. I don't have the authority to make such a decision."

"And even if we captured the ship," said Gibson, "that doesn't mean that we would understand how it flies faster than light. The technology might be so far advanced that we simply couldn't figure it out."

"We're not contemplating anything at all like that," said Greenstein.

"I would hope not," said Taylor. "That would be an act of war and interstellar piracy."

CHAPTER 18

[1]

LEWIS LEFT THE COMMAND POD, WALKING through the connecting corridors until he came to the central pod. He stopped at the hatch and watched as the people circulated. Working hours were pretty much what the individual decided they were as long as the necessary work was done. Given that, there were always people in the central pod relaxing.

Lewis entered, found himself a soda, then sat down for the first time in several hours, in a location where he could relax. He had no screens to watch, no instruments that regulated the life support for the station, no instruments to monitor the output of electrical energy, and nothing that provided a clue about the navigation of the station. All he had to do was sit there, sip his soda through the straw, and relax.

He had nearly fallen asleep, the soda can in his hand,

when he felt the couch shift, and that woke him. He was so in tune with the various vibrations, noises, and conditions of the station that he noticed the smallest change. Sometimes it was just an air filter that was working a little harder, or the firing of a positional jet that set the orientation of the station, and sometimes it was an electrical motor that burned out. Any little change caught his attention.

He opened his eyes and looked at Hackett. He closed his eyes again.

"Thought we should talk for a moment," said Hackett.

"Do we need to do this right now?" asked Lewis, but he knew it was too late for him to go back to sleep. He was already wide-awake.

"We're getting close to the destination," said Hackett. "We're beginning to slow down."

"Yeah, so?"

"Look," he said. "I have the same orders that you do."

"How do you know?"

"Because I can't do my job unless you help, and the only way for you to help is to know what has been asked."

"You're getting pretty cryptic here," said Lewis. "I really don't need that." He lifted the soda so that he could take a drink of it.

"I want to know what you plan to do. I want to know what I can expect when we're finally there."

"Well, first, there is no 'there' there. We have no specific point, just a general area of space in which we'll, what? Orbit? At least for a time."

"As the alien ship comes closer . . ."

"You know, there isn't much I can do about it. All our instruments, all our sensors, are based on the speed of light. If the alien is traveling faster than that, we'll have no real warning. He'll be here and by us before I can push a button or make a radio call."

"Just what are we going to do?" asked Hackett.

"There really isn't much I can do. We don't know exactly where the alien ship is, but we know where it's been.

We don't know how fast it's traveling, only that it's moving faster than light. If it gets by us, there is no way I can intercept it."

Hackett sat back, and said, "I really hadn't thought about this at all."

"Well, I've thought about it since I was given this assignment, and all I can tell you is that all the advantages belong to the alien, if he really is moving faster than light. Hell, we won't even see him until he's long gone."

"Then there is no way that we'll be able to engage him or to board him."

"Not unless he invites us on board. Faster-than-light speed is a hell of a defense when you think about it. Especially against those of us who can't even come close."

"Then our mission is a failure," said Hackett.

Lewis sat up straight and looked at Hackett. "Nope. Our original mission was to meet the enemy out here, far from Earth. Let him know that we aren't restricted to the surface of our planet. Let him think that we also have interstellar travel."

"But now we can't do that?"

"I hadn't counted on faster-than-light travel, but here's what we don't know, and there is a lot of it. Do they slow down near a star? Do they have to slow down as they approach a star? Do they monitor space around them? Will their sensors allow them to see us?"

"And?"

"Well, once we get out, close to where their path might be, we begin radiating—light, radar, radio, television, everything. We become a beacon and hope they want to take a look at us," said Lewis.

"Which gives the initiative to them," said Hackett, disgustedly.

"Yeah, it does, but if we're going to put our coded orders into operation, then we're going to have to do something like that. We have no choice."

"How long to intercept?"

Lewis laughed. "I think you're being overly optimistic

here. We're not really going to be able to intercept them. All we can do is hope that we're enough of a curiosity that they'll slow down to take a look at us. We have to make them want to look at us, and that's about all we can do."

"Crap," said Hackett.

"That sums it up very nicely."

[2]

GREENSTEIN'S CAR PULLED UP UNDER THE overhang outside the White House. A Marine guard, in a perfect uniform, hurried down the steps and opened the rear door, stepping back and rendering the hand salute. Greenstein, as he exited the car, straightened, returned the salute, and then walked up the steps where another guard, in an equally perfect uniform, opened the door.

Inside there was a man in a light brown suit, a brilliant white shirt, and dark tie. As he came forward, he said, "Good morning, General. The president is waiting for you."

Together, without a further word, they walked down the wide, thickly carpeted corridor. Oil paintings of other presidents, some of the first ladies, and even historic moments decorated the walls. A few had small spotlights focused on them, drawing attention to the presidents who had been members of Buskirk's party.

They reached a door where a single man, in a suit, stood, almost as if he was a guard. A woman, dressed in pants and a suit coat, appeared, opened the door, then stepped back, out of the way so that Greenstein could enter the Oval Office. Neither of them spoke.

Greenstein's escort gestured at the door, and said, "The president is waiting for you, General."

"Good morning, General," said the president, standing up and moving forward.

"Good morning, Mr. President."

The president pointed at a couch, and said, "Please, have a seat. Would you care for a beverage? Coffee?"

"No, thank you, Mr. President."

Buskirk took a seat opposite Greenstein, studied him for a moment, then asked, "Have you issued the orders?"

"Coded instructions have been sent, yes, sir."

Buskirk took a deep breath, and said, "I'm not sure this is such a good idea."

Greenstein felt his stomach knot. He didn't like to argue with the president, who, if he wanted, could end Greenstein's career in a matter of minutes. He said, "Mr. President, our scientists, surveyed quietly, have suggested that faster-than-light travel is theoretically possible, but they see nothing that suggests how to do it or if we'll have it within the next hundred years. Given our belief that the alien ship is traveling faster than light, their opinions might change, but I don't think that's going to speed the process."

"Grabbing the alien ship . . ."

"Mr. President, if I may. We are under a threat here. The aliens have all the advantages. They know where we live, but we don't know where they live. They have a technology that is far superior to ours, and if they decide to invade Earth, or to exterminate us, the advantages are theirs. The best we can hope for is that they'll be surprised by our ship, so far out into space, and believe that we have capabilities that we simply don't possess. We do, however, have the opportunity to grab some of those capabilities."

"General," said Buskirk, "I am aware of all that, but we are about to engage in an act of interstellar war and I would like something a little more solid than the assumption that they might have hostile intent by coming here."

"We have a moral imperative, sir. We must act to preserve, not only the United States, but the human race. There are times when we have no choice but to act in a certain way to preserve what we have and what we are."

"General, I don't need a lecture on the responsibilities of this office."

"Yes, sir. Sorry."

"I am looking for an alternative here. Anything that we can do to change the situation."

"Yes, sir. But I see no alternative. We must act."

Buskirk fell silent. He stood up and walked to the windows so that he could look out into the gardens of the White House. He stood there for a long time.

Greenstein sat, watching. Although he could argue the point, and he believed that there was no choice but to try to learn the secret of faster-than-light drive from the aliens, in the end the decision wasn't his. History would record Buskirk as the man who had made the decision, and history would judge whether it was right or wrong.

But historians often judged acts, not by the times in which they took place but by the standards set by the histories, fifty, a hundred, a thousand years later. Would a historian, a thousand years in the future, with the human race spread over portions of the galaxy, understand that a single man believed that it was right to steal the secret from an alien race. If the confrontation turned violent, would that historian understand that the decision was made based on what that man believed to be in the best interest of the world? Would anyone a thousand years in the future be able to understand the danger that the mere existence of the aliens presented?

The president turned, and asked, "You believe we are doing the right thing?"

"Mr. President, I don't believe we have any other choice. We must act decisively."

Buskirk smiled, and said, "Thank you for indulging an old man. I'll inform you of my decision. Thank you for coming."

Greenstein leaped to his feet, nearly coming to attention. "Thank you, Mr. President."

[3]

BAKKER SAT AT THE CONFERENCE TABLE, looking first at Lewis, then at Hackett. She pointed to the monitor mounted on the bulkhead to her left. She said, "I have plotted, as best I could, the alien's course as we have deduced it. I have to say that it is highly speculative and assumes that we are dealing with a single ship."

"Have you spotted any indications that there is more than one ship?" asked Lewis.

"Well," said Bakker, "that's kind of a hard one. Given they have a faster-than-light drive, everything we have observed could be the result of a single ship."

"How far away are they?"

"I can't say for sure. We have detected them in the last few days, but I'm not sure how old the signals are. I haven't gotten a good reading on the distance."

"Are we going to get close to them?" asked Lewis.

Bakker studied the display for a few moments and shook her head. "I don't really know. Depends on their speed and how old the signals are. Given our heading now, I think that we're going to get close, but I can't tell you when without a lot more work and communications with the VLA . . . but the time delay is now beginning to inhibit the work. They're far enough away that our signal takes a couple of months to get there."

Lewis held up a hand, and said, "And their answer takes a couple of months to get back here. We are essentially on our own. We're going to get no help from Earth."

"Until we figure out a way to transmit messages faster than light, we have now moved into an area where anything we get from them, any response they make to our queries is going to be several months out of date."

"Can you determine the location of the alien signal and how far away it is?" asked Lewis.

"Yeah, as long as I have the computer time to use, and as long as I can get a good fix on their signal. You realize, of course, that the problem is complicated by their speed and by ours. It's like trying to figure out where a bullet is from a platform that is moving like another bullet."

"How long?"

Bakker shrugged. "If I don't stop to eat . . . I think I can tell you where they were in a couple of hours."

Lewis stood up to signal the end of the meeting. He said, "Sarah, I know this is a complicated problem, and I'll give you all the help you need, but I have to have an answer here in very short order. I have to make some decisions."

"I'll do the best I can."

[4]

ALTHOUGH SHE BEAMED HER STORIES BACK TO Earth on a regular basis, and she kept coming up with new ideas for even better stories, Davies had not realized that the distances were such that no one was seeing what she reported. She thought that she was getting regular exposure. In a couple of months she might get regular exposure again, but at the moment, she hadn't been seen on the air in five weeks.

She did a report on the hydroponics and how they used the freshly grown food to supplement their diets. She reported on their efforts to track the alien ship, and she did personal profiles on some of the more interesting of the crew. She edited the reports on the station, then used the communications center to beam them back toward Earth.

Now, she turned her attention to Travis. She set up her camera, in her own cabin, and used the metallic bulkhead as the backdrop. She wished there was some way that she could make it look more like they were traveling in space, but the ship was a closed system, with only a few tiny windows that looked out into blackness.

Travis entered and stood for a moment, looking first at the camera, then at the chair. A single light was shining on it, making it, and the cabin, brighter.

"That where you want me to sit?" he asked.

She looked at his wardrobe, which consisted of the standard uniform of T-shirt and shorts, and thought that it wouldn't make a good impression.

"Maybe you should change."

"Into what?"

Davies sat down on the edge of the bunk and crossed her legs. She said, "Into something a little more formal."

"Why?"

"I think you should look professional when you do this interview."

"I've seen the others, and none of them changed. All were wearing the same basic thing. We all look professional wearing just what everyone else is wearing. Besides, what real difference does it make?"

Davies lowered her eyes and stared at the deck. The difference was that she didn't really care about the professionalism or the perception or impression that those others made. She did want Travis to look good and professional because he talked about UFOs as if it was proven they were extraterrestrial and because she liked him. She liked him quite a lot.

"What did you have in mind?" he asked, finally.

Now she looked up and smiled. "I thought I'd do an interview about how you feel now that your work has been validated. We know that there are other intelligent civilizations, and we know that they can get here from there."

Travis laughed. Then, seriously, he said, "I don't think that this validates my work. It just makes some of the underlying premises more likely."

She reached up and turned on the camera because she had learned that you always had the camera rolling in case something was said that you wished had been on disk. "But you aren't afraid of what we're going to see. What we're going to find."

Travis stopped and looked up at a corner of the cabin, lost in thought. Finally, he said, "I believe that any civilization that has reached the technological point where it can defeat the huge problems of interstellar travel is going to be somewhat enlightened. I know that Parker, back on Earth, talked about Earth's history and what has happened when two societies meet, one with a technological advantage over the other; but I'm not sure that applies here."

"Why?"

"Well, because we're dealing with a technological achievement that suggests a sophistication of thought. That implies some enlightened thinking."

"But we are now moving out into space, and our planet is as fragmented as ever."

"Yes, but those societies that engage in reprehensible acts, in terrorism and violence, are not those who are making this trip. The scientific achievement is being accomplished by the more advanced of the Earth-based civilizations."

Davies nodded, smiled, then asked, "But we have weapons on board here. Weapons designed to work in space and attack the enemy."

"The difference," said Travis, "is that these weapons are here as a defensive measure. We don't plan to initiate a hostile action."

Davies, without realizing it, had found the contradiction in his argument. She said, "But the weapons suggest that we expect the worst from the alien society." As she said that, she was afraid that he would get angry.

Instead of anger, he grinned. "What it really suggests is that all of this is speculation. If we listen to one of the researchers who studies the reports of alien abduction, we find that the aliens are evil creatures that want to take the Earth from us and replace us with hybrids. Another suggests the aliens are really just scientists conducting research on Earth, not unlike that which we ourselves conduct, and a third tells us the aliens have a wonderful Eastern-style philosophy."

"What do you think is going to happen?"

"I don't know," said Travis. "I'm here as the expert on

alien intelligence and I know so very little. Everything is just speculation."

Davies nodded as if to indicate the interview was over, then reached up and turned off the camera. She pushed the front of it so that the lens was pointing up, then she stood. Without another word, she grabbed the bottom of her T-shirt with her right hand on the left side and her left hand on the right and lifted slowly. She freed the garment from her hands and just let it float away. She stood in front of Travis in just her shorts and knee socks.

He just sat quietly, watching her. He was enjoying the show and had suddenly forgotten all about UFOs, alien creatures, and space flight. The only reminder was her shirt, as it drifted around her cabin.

She sat down on the bed, leaned back gripping the edge, and looked right into his eyes. "Care to join me?"

CHAPTER 19

[1]

LEWIS SAT IN THE CONTROL POD, FACING THE
screen that was showing him space as it looked around
him. Hackett sat next to him, where the copilot would normally sit, and Bakker was in a jump seat set back but between the two so that she could see everything that they
did and everything that was displayed on the instruments
and the screen.

"We have slowed," said Lewis, "to nearly a crawl. We
are maintaining enough speed so that we aren't drawn back
toward the sun, and we are maneuvering to avoid the
cometary debris of the Oort Cloud."

Bakker said, "I have attempted to orient the cameras so
that they are scanning space where I think the alien ship
will appear. I have to stress that. I think."

"When?" asked Hackett, though he had heard her make
her estimates a dozen times.

"Anytime now."

Lewis checked the instruments. They had turned on all the outside lights so that the station glowed. The sun was so far away it looked like little more than a bright dot. They could barely see the disk shape, meaning that it was larger and brighter than the other stars and provided nothing in the way of heat or light. The solar panels, so useful in Earth orbit, or as they began their trip out of the Solar System, were now nearly useless.

He had also turned on the radars, knowing that they would probably never detect the alien ship using that old system. It didn't matter because the radiation would provide an electromagnetic beacon if the aliens were looking for something of that nature.

Hackett leaned back in his seat and stretched. "We could be here for days."

"We could be here forever," said Bakker. "They might just fly right past us. If they don't slow down, we might never know they were around."

"You know," said Hackett, "if they enter the Solar System and slow down near Earth, it's going to be months before we know anything about that."

"I'll keep looking for their signals," said Bakker. "If they get past us, I think I'll get an indication from that, but I don't know how good it will be."

"We're not going to sit around here for days are we?" asked Hackett.

Lewis laughed. "You have something else to do?"

There was a quiet tapping at the hatch, and Rachel Davies looked in. "I would like to record this," she said.

Lewis waved at her, telling her to enter. He said, "There isn't anything to record, and we don't know if there is ever going to be anything."

She thought about that, and said, "I would like to leave my camera here."

"Everything going on in here is being recorded now," said Lewis. "Standard procedure."

"Yes, but that's your recording which belongs to the

government, which means that everyone can use it. I would like something that is exclusive to me. A little different angle and with some of my questions or observations on it that won't be in the public domain."

The screen in front of them showed nothing. Space was empty. No sign of the alien ship. No indications that anything was close to them. Even the Oort Cloud was a disappointment. There were hundreds of the big icebergs in orbit around the sun, but relatively few of them scattered inside the cloud. Cloud just wasn't the right word.

Davies brought her camera into the cabin, set it up where it showed both Lewis and Hackett and also had a view of the screen in front of them. Bakker was just out of the frame, but Davies didn't care. She wanted the two men in command and the scene on the screen as it unfolded.

Hackett wanted to ask what they should be looking for, but Bakker had explained it to them. She thought it was unlikely that they would spot the alien ship visually. There wasn't much light to reflect from the surface. If the aliens had used any sort of stealth, the rounded surfaces and light-absorbing composites, then the best they could hope to see would be a dark mass moving against a background that was only a little lighter.

Hackett turned in the seat and looked at Bakker. "Isn't there anything you can do?"

"Running out of patience?" asked Lewis.

"I don't like having no idea how long something is going to last, especially when there is a chance that we won't even see it when it flies by."

"All I can do is scan the sky around us, limit the range of my search, and see what I can see. Might tell us that nothing is close and might not." She looked directly at Hackett. "But you have to understand that we have only seen them, so to speak, by their radio signals. Without that we are effectively blind."

[2]

"I THINK WE FOUND IT AGAIN."

Taylor turned from the computer monitor and looked at the main display. "Got it where?"

Gibson leaned closer, as if that would help him see the monitor better, and said, "Preliminary seems to indicate maybe a little outside of the Oort Cloud. What? A light-year and a quarter, maybe a half, away."

Taylor spun around so that she was facing the main monitor and looked at the glowing dot. With the ship that close, and moving as quickly as it did, calculations for the distance didn't take months to verify. They could do it in a couple of hours.

"How far are they from the station?"

Gibson grinned, and said, "I make it a light-week or so, depending on how closely Lewis and the boys followed the syllabus. If they were careful, then the alien ship can't be all that far from them."

"How fast is it traveling?"

Gibson shrugged. "All I know is that this is where it was a year and a half ago."

Taylor nodded and leaned back. If the aliens were within a light-year of Earth, and if they could, in fact, travel faster than the speed of light, then when the sun set tonight, they could look up into the sky and see the alien ship. Or, if the ship was big enough and bright enough, they could look up now and see it.

"We heard anything from the outposts in the asteroids? Or Mars for that matter?"

Gibson understood what she was asking, and said, "Message traffic has all been quiet. I don't think anything has been detected inside the Solar System."

"The key word is 'detected,'" said Taylor.

"Well, all we can do is check the logs again, but the messages have all been read. I know there is nothing in them."

"We need to call Avilson, too. Let him know that we have the ship that close to Earth."

Gibson turned back to face the monitor. "And we need to let the military know."

"Yes," said Taylor. "That we do. I just wish there was a way that we could tell those people on the station."

"If we transmit now," said Gibson, looking at his watch. "They should have the message in about what, a year or so?"

"Yeah. That's the bitch, ain't it."

[3]

AFTER TWENTY-FOUR HOURS, HACKETT WANTED to give up. They had been in position, lights burning, radars and sensors and radios radiating, and even the engines producing heat that should have stood out in the coldness of space. If they couldn't find the aliens, the aliens should have been able to spot them.

He had left the control pod to stretch his legs, to eat, and to catch a nap that was little more than a long doze, with him waking up every five or ten minutes. The sleep wasn't restful, and he just couldn't go to sleep for any longer.

He watched Lewis, who seemed to take it all in stride. The man was relaxed, sitting for hours in front of the control panel and the instruments, looking at them, searching for any change that would indicate trouble.

But the alien ship, wherever it was, still didn't show. The screens were blank, the radars empty, and the sensors without any sort of a return. The only thing they detected were the comets, huge iceberg-sized, dirty snowballs that periodically dropped out of orbit and fell toward the sun. Most of them were so unspectacular that only the truly dedicated stargazers ever saw them.

And while it might have been scientifically beneficial to make some observations from part of the Oort Cloud, only Bakker expressed any interest in it. She went through the motions, making recordings of everything in space around them, but her heart wasn't in it. She, just like all the others, was looking for the alien ship that had to be close to them but had somehow avoided them.

With the recordings finished, Bakker strolled to the control pod and took her seat just behind those of Hackett and Lewis. She leaned forward, her hands on the backs of their chairs, and said, "We should have seen something."

Lewis took a deep breath, and said, "This is just like fishing, except that we have but one fish and the pond is awfully damned large."

Hackett was going to protest, but then realized they had set out the bait, which was themselves, and they had done everything they could to attract the attention of the aliens just as fishermen tied bits of bright string and fastened little propellers and other whirligigs to the line to attract the fish. Now, all they could do was wait until they got a bite.

But Hackett didn't want to wait. He turned to look at Bakker, and asked, "Isn't there anything you can do?"

"Just what would that be?"

"Well, how far away are they?"

"I can't tell you," she said. "All I know is that they're in the vicinity. We've been sitting here for about fifty hours trying to attract their attention. If they are within fifty light-hours of us, they should have detected us."

Hackett fell silent because no one could give him the information he wanted. He needed to have some sort of deadline. If the alien ship hadn't appeared by some arbitrary number, then it wasn't going to show, but, of course, there was no such magical number just as the fisherman, waiting on the pond didn't know when the fish would get hungry, when it would be close enough to spot the hook and bait, and then if it decided that the bait looked like something that it wanted to eat. Hackett was growing as impatient as a dozen five-year-olds waiting for Santa Claus at the local mall.

Finally, he blurted, "Just how in the hell can you stand this?"

Lewis just grinned, and said, "A space pilot has little to do but sit quietly and monitor the instruments, realizing that the ship will spot anything wrong with it long before he does. Except, sometimes, it doesn't, then quick action by the pilot saves everything."

Bakker added, "And searching for an intelligent signal doesn't exactly result in any sort of find. Took us, and by that I mean, it took hundreds of astronomers nearly a century to find the first one."

"Yeah, yeah," snapped Hackett, "patience is its own reward, but I'm damned tired of waiting."

"Then go find something to drink," said Lewis. "You're making me nervous."

"What really gets me," said Hackett, "is that we won't know when this is over if the aliens don't appear. They could flash right by us, and we wouldn't know."

"Actually, we would," said Bakker. "Their signal pops up all the time, and if we detect it on the other side of the Solar System, we'll know that we can punch out of here."

"Great," said Hackett.

Lewis leaned forward suddenly, touched a control, and turned his attention to the flat screen. "There," he said, pointing. "There."

Something was flickering on the edge of the screen, maybe a hundred thousand miles away, but big enough to register. It didn't look like another of the comets or other debris scattered in the Oort Cloud.

"Is that it?" asked Hackett, stunned.

Bakker had stood up and was leaning across them to get a better look. She nodded, and with a voice filled with awe, said, "Yeah. That's them."

"Christ," said Hackett.

And with a voice that sounded calm, devoid of emotion, Lewis said, "Good things come to he who waits."

CHAPTER 20

[1]

WHATEVER IT WAS, ALL AGREED THAT IT WAS gigantic, more than five miles long, maybe even bigger. There were a couple of lights glowing on it, but the surface itself was dark, maybe black, creating a charcoal shape against the background of space. It gave the impression of a ship assembled in space, as the station had been, because it had none of the sleek, smooth surfaces that suggested aerodynamic design.

"Can you get a better picture?" asked Hackett.

Lewis touched a button, moved a mouse, then clicked. The alien ship filled the screen. They could now see the bumps and protrusions on it. There seemed to be no front or back, top or bottom. Of course, in space, those sorts of considerations were not all that important. With a faster-than-light drive, the orientation of the engines and the direction of thrust might mean nothing at all.

The design seemed to be asymmetrical, which gave it an alien look. They could see nothing on the alien ship that looked human, which made sense. The ship hadn't been created by humans. It was designed by aliens for faster-than-light travel, and no one on the station knew what those considerations might be or how they would affect the design.

"It's big," said Hackett.

"What did you expect?" asked Lewis.

Hackett slumped back in his seat and almost shrugged. He had no idea what he had expected. Maybe the needle-thin ships with smoke coming from the back that had been the staple of Buck Rogers and Flash Gordon. Maybe something that looked like the flying saucers that Travis had described to them more than once. Or maybe something like a floating city in the James Blish tradition of science fiction.

Lewis manipulated the controls, almost as if he were controlling a camera, to give them a better look at the alien craft. There were splotches on it. Discolored portions that were a light gray and gave the impression of wood ash.

"I don't see any signs of ports or windows or anything like that," said Bakker.

"We don't need windows to see out," said Lewis. "The original astronauts insisted on windows, so we have been designing the spacecraft since then with windows in them, but there is no need for them."

On what would be considered the top, given the craft's orientation to the station, there was a cluster of bright lights that had a greenish tinge. Hackett pointed it out, and said, "Little green men?"

"Maybe we should get Travis up here. He might have some useful insights."

Lewis grinned, and said, "And that reporter. She's going to be highly pissed that she missed the first appearance of the alien ship."

Hackett just sat, quietly, looking at that alien ship, looking for something that was unusual, strange, or out of

place. He was looking for something that would give him
a clue about the aliens and who they were.

"Maybe we'd better check the communications bands,"
said Hackett.

Bakker said, "Yeah. Let me get with the communications people and see what we have."

"And tell the communications officer to begin to broadcast everything we see back to Earth. That way, if something happens to us, they'll know what happened."

As Bakker left the control pod, both Travis and Davies
pushed their way in. Davies spotted the ship on the screen
and gasped suddenly. "Shit."

"It's them," said Lewis unnecessarily.

Travis reached out, searching with his hand for the back
of a chair. Without looking at it, he sat down. He said,
"Looks nothing like I thought it would."

"Meaning?"

Travis glanced at Lewis, and said, "We've had reports,
since nearly the beginning of the modern UFO era, of alien
ships in orbit around Earth. High-flying things that
dropped down to dispatch the smaller, disk-shaped craft.
But the descriptions were of huge, cigar-shaped things that
looked more like the rocket ships seen in the old movies
rather than a real interstellar craft."

"Does that mean all your UFO stuff is wrong?" asked
Davies.

Travis didn't seem to hear her until she repeated the
question. He said, "No, I wouldn't think so. If we have one
alien race that can travel interstellar distances, then there is
no reason there couldn't be two, or four, or a hundred."

"Not much in the way of interesting surface detail,"
said Lewis.

"Is it moving?" asked Davies.

"Coming at us," said Lewis.

"Then they've seen us?"

"I would think so. They slowed to below light speed
close to us, meaning, to me, that they saw us and have
stopped to investigate."

"That might not be a good thing," said Travis.

Lewis looked at him, and said, "I don't think we have anything to fear. They recognize us as an artificial ship and know that it means we are intelligent. Otherwise, we couldn't be here."

[2]

HACKETT LEFT THE CONTROL POD, WALKED through the connecting corridors, and found himself at one of the weapons pods. He touched the panel beside the hatch, waited as it scanned his handprint, then entered when it opened automatically.

He moved to the control panel and sat down. He touched a button, and it lighted. On the screen he saw the alien ship, but under it was a series of numbers giving the range to it in miles, the length of time it would take a weapon to reach it, or if it was out of range of that particular weapon system.

Using the screen, he studied the enemy. The ship was just large and black and ill shaped. According to his instruments, it wasn't radiating anything, including radio signals. There was, naturally, a heat signature, and using the infrared, he got a different view of the craft, including a huge heat source at what he considered the bottom of it, given his perspective.

Like Lewis in the control pod, Hackett began to run recordings of everything and beamed the information back to Earth. If something happened that prevented their return home, then a record would exist. Someone would be able to figure it all out.

He could detect nothing that looked like the shields that had protected so many science fiction ships. He could launch one of his missiles and, as far as he knew, it would run straight and true to impact against the skin of the alien ship.

The beam weapons, the lasers, would dance across the

skin, but he didn't know if the ship could absorb the energy and dissipate it the way the heat tiles on one of the old shuttles had deflected and dissipated the heat of reentry.

What it boiled down to was that Hackett knew nothing about the enemy ship, how it was constructed, what weapons it might carry, and what its retaliatory capabilities might be. He was as confused as a drunk standing in front of a maze. He had no idea how he had gotten there, why he was there, or how to get out of it.

Hackett knew there were trigger-happy soldiers who would use any excuse to open fire. And, in the back of his mind was the order that he had been given to learn the secret of faster-than-light travel. Such knowledge would spread the human race through the galaxy faster than the Black Death had overrun Europe.

But the problem was that he could learn it only through contact with the aliens, and there seemed to be no way to initiate that communication unless the aliens did it. He could see nothing on any of the displays that would give him a clue about how to communicate.

Still, he had to prepare. He touched a couple of buttons, which opened a limited circuit. Facing the camera, he said, "Weapons specialists to the weapons pod. Weapons specialists to the weapons pod."

A few moments later two men and one woman appeared. The oldest was the lead weapons specialist, Sergeant Michael Garner. He had not yet reached his thirtieth birthday, was short, stout, and had a neatly shaved head. His features were blunt and spread across a bullet-shaped head. He didn't look like an intellectual, but was very smart and had graduated near the top of his class.

Sergeant Katherine Griffin, known as Kate, was twenty-eight but looked younger. She was tall and thin and had her long hair pulled back into a bun. She was happy with her job and didn't mind that she was not in command. She believed that she was not qualified to be the lead weapons specialist but, in reality, was even smarter than Garner.

Last was the youngest, Specialist Bruce Howe, who thought he was smarter than he was. Like Griffin, he was tall, but he was also very thin. His hair was as long as regulations allowed. He was not a handsome man, with sharp, pointed features that were scattered across his face in an almost haphazard manner.

As they entered, Garner asked, "What's up?"

"We have the ship in sight."

None of them reacted to that news. It was as if they expected nothing else and were not particularly interested in anything about it. They were at the farthest reaches of the Solar System and were uninterested in what was going on around them.

Garner slipped into one of the command chairs, picked a thread microphone and headset off the shelf in front of him, and put it on. He reached over and flipped on the control panel.

Griffin sat down beside him and buckled herself into her chair. She reached out and pulled the screen around slightly so that she could see it better. She focused her attention on it, then touched the screen four times to activate the various weapons systems.

Howe took a seat behind both of them. His role was that of a backup. If one of them was somehow injured, became ill, or irrational, it was his job to take over as the assistant. He had to know what was going on, but he had no job if everything went according to plan.

Garner said, "We're set."

"You realize that you are to launch nothing unless ordered to do so and only I, or Lewis, have the authority to order such a launch."

"Yes, sir. But what if you are incapacitated?"

"You have your instructions," said Hackett. He realized the flaw, but he just didn't want to be responsible for starting a war by accident.

"Damn. That thing's big," said Griffin.

"Observations?" asked Hackett.

None of them had anything else to say. They studied the

monitor, they looked at the range markings to the aliens, and searched for a sign that there was something radiating from the ship, but they had no insights.

"Okay," said Hackett. "I'm going back to the control pod. You remain on duty here until relieved."

"Yes, sir," said Garner.

[3]

"IT'S STOPPED," SAID BAKKER.

She was standing in one of the instrumentation pods, using the computers to study the ship. With her were two technicians, both who had some knowledge of astronomy. They sat off to one side, using their own equipment.

Ruth Mason was the younger of the two. She was a small, delicate woman who was a superb athlete. She had minored in astronomy, though her real love was history.

Next to her was Jo Phillips, who was, in contrast, a large woman who had virtually no athletic ability. She was, however, one of the smartest people on the station. She had fine hair and a large nose that didn't seem suited to her face.

"The first thing I want," said Bakker, "is to see if there are any indications of the ship attempting to communicate with us. I want to look at the normal electromagnetic radiation bands, but I want us to go beyond that. Look for light in both the visible spectrum and the invisible. I want us to be able to say, with confidence, that they attempted no communication."

"What if they attempt through some other method?" asked Phillips.

"Such as?"

"Telepathy."

Bakker was going to snap out an answer, but thought better of it. Although science had been unable to establish the existence of something like telepathy, it didn't mean that an alien species might not have developed some sort of telepathic ability. Of course, there was no way for them to test for, or listen for, telepathic messages.

"Keep your search in the range of our instrumentation," said Bakker.

She sat down and let the technicians do their work. If they found a signal, then she would apply the techniques they had used to understand the first of the signals. Maybe that way they could learn something more about the aliens.

"I think we're being scanned," said Mason.

Bakker turned to look at the screen. There was a sudden burst of radiation across the electromagnetic band. It included the wavelengths used for radars and radio, but went far beyond that as well. It was almost as if the aliens wanted to jam any signal emitted by the station and didn't want to take the time to find it. They'd just jam everything.

But, as quickly as it had come, it was gone. It was as if they had turned off their equipment. Bakker had thought they might be attempting to stop the station's communication with Earth, but that clearly was not the reason for the radiation burst.

"Heat signature has increased slightly," said Phillips.

Bakker wondered if the changing in the heat signature could be an attempt at communication. In the cold of space, such a change would be easily detected. The problem was, even if it was an attempt to communicate, Bakker would have no idea of how to reply. No one on Earth used heat to talk.

"I'm going to meet with Lewis and Hackett," Bakker said. "You get anything, and I mean anything, you let me know."

[4]

THE ALIEN SHIP WAS HANGING IN SPACE, maintaining its distance. If the station altered its path, the aliens mirrored that alteration. It kept one side to the station so that no one knew what the other side looked like. It could be the same, could be covered with lights or windows or hatches. Hundreds of tiny ships could be stored there, clinging to the side of the ship like baby spiders hanging on to their mother.

Lewis, Hackett, Bakker, Davies, and Travis had moved into the conference pod. There were four screens there, each providing updated information about the alien ship. If anything changed, they would know it as quickly as anyone else. They could initiate their response from that pod.

Lewis, in his role as the station's commander, asked, "Anything I should know about that we haven't mentioned?"

No one said anything.

"Okay. I have to tell you that I'm at a loss here. I don't know what I expected when we finally found them, and I don't know what we should be doing."

"I have found no indication of a signal," said Bakker. "Just a massive burst of radiation, then nothing."

Hackett said, "I have the weapons ready to go if we need them, but I have told the crew not to fire without specific orders from either me or you."

Lewis nodded, and said, "Good." He looked at Travis. "Okay. The ball is now in your court."

"There are any number of stories of attempted contact, overlooking the tales of telepathy and channeling . . ."

"Why reject telepathy?" asked Bakker

"Because there was never a way to verify it. Had the aliens sent a message that they would appear at some location at some specified time and actually arrived, well, then, I guess we could say there was some telepathic contact. And even though those sorts of claims have been made, when the appointed hour came, at the appointed location, there were no aliens. Given that, I think we can reject telepathic communication."

"Serious attempts?"

"Well, there is anecdotal testimony from a number of reports. In one of the last cases in the Air Force's official investigation, a guy claimed that, with a flashlight, he established a momentary contact. He said that when he flashed the numerical equivalent of *pi*, the lights on the UFO responded. There really was no trading of information but a claim that there had been a response, which, I guess, is communication."

"Come on," said Lewis. "I don't need a lecture here. I need some information."

"When we look at the history, we find claims, but we don't have any solid evidence."

"Christ," snapped Lewis. "You were brought on this mission because of your expertise in alien communication."

"Well, I'm not sure that's quite right, but I am providing you with what I know about this. There are claims of communication, but there is no solid evidence that any of the claims are grounded in reality."

Lewis glared at Travis in disgust, then turned his attention to Bakker. "So what can you tell us?"

"Not much more. The signals that we have received from the aliens are not similar to those we have been able to, in a very limited sense, translate. We have nothing."

"Okay. So we can't communicate with them. What is our next option?"

"Without advocating it as a position," said Hackett, "we do have the missiles."

Now Bakker sounded disgusted. "Oh for crying out loud, Tom, you can't launch a missile."

"Actually, I was thinking of it as a way of communication," said Hackett.

"It communicates hostile intent, and that is the last thing we want," said Bakker.

"Again, that might not be right. We have the alien ship at the threshold of our system. It might be the best thing we could do," said Hackett. "Let them know that we can travel in space and that we understand weapons."

Bakker looked to Lewis. "You're not going to allow this, are you?"

"Of course not. I'm not going to start some kind of interstellar war."

"So," said Hackett, "all we can do is sit around, on our butts, unable to do anything."

"We could probe them with out scanners and sensors," said Bakker.

"We've taken that as far as we can," said Lewis. "We have tried all the passive systems we have."

Hackett said, "Now this is just thinking out loud, but we could take the warhead out of a missile, cut the thrust, and launch it. See what the aliens do. We're not attacking them, we're just dropping a missile into space that is headed, more or less in their direction."

"I don't like it," said Bakker. "I think that it's way too overt."

"Well," countered Hackett, "it's not an attack, it gives us the initiative, which we haven't held for a long time, and it could induce a response from the aliens."

"Sure, they open fire with everything they have and we find ourselves trying to breathe in a vacuum."

"Our options are limited," said Lewis. "We need to do something."

"Why?" asked Bakker.

Lewis looked at her for a moment, and said, "Because we're human, and we're here."

CHAPTER 21

[1]

THEY TRIED TO FIGURE OUT A WAY OF COMMU-
nicating with the aliens. They flashed their lights in sequence. They flashed *pi* because Travis had said that a man
who saw a UFO on Earth had tried it and gotten a response. They beamed signals using a mathematical base
for them, hoping that the dots and dashes would be recognized for what they were. And every hour or so, they
broadcast a voice signal and sometimes they tried television.

The alien ship, however, remained as it had been, floating an exact distance away, some of the lights on its side
flashing, but with no discernible signal. If the station
began to drift toward it, the alien ship moved away, maintaining a precise distance between the two.

After twenty-four hours, Lewis was ready to launch one

of the smaller shuttles to see what would happen if humans approached the aliens. He could think of nothing else.

And then the alien ship brightened, turned as if pointing itself at the station, and there was a sudden, massive burst of electromagnetic radiation. Station monitors, recorders, and electronics, recorded it.

Lewis announced the burst of energy over the intercom. Bakker ran to her pod and dropped into one of the chairs next to Mason. She said, "You got all that?"

"Isn't much different than the first burst."

"But it was different," said Bakker.

"Yes."

"Show me."

Mason's hands worked the keyboard and the mouse, and the screen showed a breakdown of the various wavelengths that had been in the signal. "You can see," she said, "that they're all over the spectrum."

"Any embedded signal?"

Mason turned back to the keyboard, and said, "We've got something there. Strong."

"Let's see what you've got."

Before she did anything, Mason said, "I would have thought that if they were responding to us, they would respond on the same frequency we used."

"Except that we broadcast all over the spectrum as well," said Bakker. "We weren't sure what their receiving capability was, so this might be the response."

"Shouldn't we have narrowed the band, figuring that they would be able to detect the signal at their end?" said Mason.

"Maybe. If we find anything here, then we can do that as well."

While Bakker sat quietly, Mason worked at the keyboard and with the voice input. Bakker wanted to reach over and take the keyboard away from Mason, but she knew that the best management technique was to allow the people to do their jobs. Mason might take a little longer to complete the task, but the delay would be only a couple of minutes.

"Got it," said Mason.

"Show me."

"This is rough. I can refine it."

There was a flickering on the screen, looking as if someone had videoed a candle, or group of candles through a thick film of petroleum jelly. The colors ranged from a deep, dark, burgundy red to a muddy greenish brown. Nothing could be seen that made any sense to Bakker.

"Okay," said Mason. "Let me do this. I've got to compensate for the signal strength."

Waves seemed to pass over the image on the screen, sharpening it, and altering the colors so that the red faded and the muddiness of the green cleared. Mason's fingers manipulated the keys and the mouse. She looked up periodically, grunted as if pleased, then looked down at her fingers.

Bakker watched as the image cleared. There were two figures on the screen, one behind and to the left of the other. She had no clue about their size because there was nothing in the image that she recognized and therefore had no frame of reference. The aliens could be tiny, no larger than an infant, or they could be the size of a house. There was no way for her to tell.

Both looked to be the same, just as two humans would look to be the same. There were differences in coloring. One seemed to be ashen, with a yellow tint, and the other, standing or sitting slightly behind the first, had a more bluish look.

Bakker leaned forward to study the image, unaware that she was looking at the first solid photograph of an alien species. She was just studying it, looking for anything that she thought of as out of the ordinary when the whole thing was out of the ordinary.

"Geez, they look human," said Mason.

She was right. The heads were bullet-shaped, coming to

a round point at the crown, and, for some reason, Bakker thought of the coneheads. But the point wasn't all that pronounced and certainly more round, like the slug from a .45-caliber pistol rather than a bullet from a rifle.

There was no evidence of hair, and the eyes seemed to be farther up the forehead than they should be. They were larger than human eyes, given the dimensions of the head, and much rounder, nearly circular.

There was no hint of a nose, giving the face a flat look. There was a mouth—an elongated slit that had no lips. The chin was round and protruding, and gave way into a neck that thickened into shoulders.

"They're hideous," said Mason.

"What'd you expect?" snapped Bakker.

She tried to see detail in the background, but it was lost in shadows. There was a single rounded point that could have been a light glowing, but she just didn't know.

Finally, she leaned over and touched a button for the intercom. She said, "Lewis. Hackett. We've got something."

[2]

NEITHER LEWIS NOR HACKETT WANTED TO leave the command pod. Hackett responded, saying, "Link the data here."

Bakker responded, "Wait one."

Hackett looked over to Lewis, and said, "Now what's that all about."

Several minutes later, Bakker pushed through the hatch and dropped into a seat. "Wait until you see what we've got."

An instant later the image appeared on the screen in front of Hackett and Lewis. Hackett sat there for a moment, then felt his stomach turn over. Icy fingers massaged his spine, and he felt slightly sick. It was not the reaction he had expected when seeing the aliens for the first time.

"This accurate?" asked Lewis.

"This is what they broadcast to us. I would assume that it is an accurate representation of what they look like. I can't see them sending us something fake."

"What if they're, I don't know, squids," said Hackett, "but they know what we look like, or believe they know. Maybe they came up with something they thought we would find . . . pleasing?"

"How would they know what we look like?" asked Lewis.

Bakker didn't wait for Hackett to answer. She said, "We've been broadcasting all sorts of signals for the last century. They might have intercepted some of those and created the image based on a flawed, captured signal."

"That's speculation," said Lewis.

"Of course," agreed Bakker. "I was just suggesting a scenario in which they might know, in general, what humans look like. This image we have of them might be based on that. I don't think it is. I think we've got an accurate representation, but there is always the possibility they created it for us."

Hackett sat with his eyes on the screen. To him the aliens were a nightmarish horror. He suddenly thought of them as the enemy. Such ugly things could only be ready to invade and destroy the Earth.

He sat there, his head spinning. He wasn't sure what he wanted to do, but thought they had to attack the enemy ship immediately. The enemy aliens had to know that Earth would not be dominated easily and the way to do that was attack.

Bakker leaned forward, and said, "Tom? Are you all right? You look sick."

He shook his head and bent at the waist, as if to put his head between his knees. He felt sweaty, first hot, then cold. He felt as if he was going to be sick, but then suddenly the nausea passed, and he felt better.

"Tom?"

He waved a hand. "I'm fine. I'm fine."

"Okay," said Lewis. "We've got to send this information back to Earth. Now."

"Copies have already been broadcast by narrow beam," said Bakker. "They won't have anything for months, you understand, but the information is on its way."

"Next question," said Lewis. "Do we respond?"

"Of course," said Bakker. "We send them the same sort of thing they sent us, on the same frequencies they used. That demonstrates our intelligence and capabilities."

"I thought our ship, out here, did that," said Hackett.

"It does. But we now show that we have not only received their message, we have, after a fashion, decoded it, and are responding in kind."

"So it's a kind of intelligence test for us," said Lewis.

"Well, I suppose you could think of it as something like that," said Bakker.

"I don't think this is a good idea," said Hackett.

"Why not?" asked Bakker. "It's not as if we're telling them something that they don't already know or can't find out for themselves fairly easily. They knew we were here. They found us. They should have an idea about what we look like. We're not giving them secrets."

Hackett, whose training had always made him wary of providing information to those who didn't have it and had no real need to have it, was still hesitant. But then he realized that he wasn't thinking things through. He was reacting to a photograph that he had found personally disturbing. And he was forgetting his additional assignment of learning the secret of faster-than-light travel. Without additional communications, he would have no opportunity to discover anything.

To Bakker, he asked, "Just what did you have in mind?"

"Similar picture to theirs. Let them see a couple of humans sitting in front of the camera. Or standing. Let them see the whole body from the top of the head to the bottom of the feet."

"That's more than they gave us."

"But it doesn't reveal anything to them that they couldn't extrapolate anyway."

Lewis broke in. "I think we should do it. Why don't you set it up, Sarah. Tom and I will stay here and keep an eye on the alien ship."

"It won't take all that long. I'll review the photograph to make sure there is nothing in it that we don't want there, but I think we could be ready to transmit in about five or ten minutes at the most."

"Who will be the test subjects?"

"I'll just grab a couple of people."

[3]

IT WAS NO SECRET THAT BAKKER AND HER AS-tronomers had been able to reproduce a photograph sent from the alien ship. Travis wanted to see it because he was curious as to how closely it matched the descriptions given by witnesses on Earth. It seemed to him that if the witness's descriptions were accurate, or rather, matched those of these aliens, then he would be able to offer some advice about motivations and reactions.

With Davies, they tapped into the mainframe and pulled up the picture. Travis, who had been used to seeing drawings of aliens, who had seen the few photographs offered by witnesses, and who believed that aliens had visited the Earth, was not shocked, surprised, or overwhelmed by what he was seeing. To him, it was just another picture.

Had he thought about it, he would have realized that all those other pictures, especially the drawings, provided little evidence. This photograph, transmitted by the aliens themselves, had a provenance that none of the others had. This was the first documented exchange of information.

Davies, who had set up her camera to record his reactions and impressions, turned on her camera and told him to go ahead and look.

Travis watched the image develop but had no overt reaction. It didn't match much of what he had seen, with a couple of exceptions. One had been a fur-covered beast that had a bullet-shaped head but that also had a triangular nose.

"Don't recognize it," said Travis.

"What do you think?" asked Davies.

"It's pretty ugly."

"That's it?" she asked exasperated. "You get a look at an alien, and your only comment is that it's ugly."

"What do you expect? I have a picture here that gives me nothing but a look at the head and shoulders. There is nothing to see, and for all I know these creatures have not interacted with anyone on Earth."

"A reaction," challenged Davies. "Tell me what you feel about seeing this."

Travis turned and looked at her. She was crouching beside her camera, looking at the video display. She wasn't paying much attention to what was on the monitor.

"What do you think?" he asked.

She glanced up, looked at the monitor, and shrugged. "I have no reaction. I'm the reporter here. I'm observing history in the making."

"What crap," said Travis.

"How does this fit in with your view of the universe?" asked Davies.

"It changes nothing except maybe meaning that some of the UFO reports we have studied for the last century certainly have a basis in reality. It means that there is other intelligent life in the galaxy."

Davies straightened up and looked at Travis. "This interview sucks. You aren't giving me anything here."

"What do you want? Shock? I mean, it's not as if I haven't been looking at pictures of aliens for my whole life. This is just one more."

And as he said that he began to realize the significance of the event. It wasn't really just one more, but it was the only one. The others could be figments of the imagination. They could be the creations of a deluded mind. They could be a combination of half-remembered creatures from old movies, the horrors of nightmares, and the folklore of a dozen cultures.

But what he was looking at now was clearly something from another world. Something that had crossed space in a ship that had capabilities that humans dreamed of only in science fiction, and scientists said, basically, was impossible. He felt the blood drain from his face and felt his head begin to spin.

And, while Davies might have been able to video his reactions, there was nothing he could say now. He didn't know what to say because he didn't know what he felt. His world had been turned upside down, and he was only just beginning to realize it.

[4]

"OKAY," SAID LEWIS. "LET'S GET READY TO broadcast our picture, but I don't want some wimpy little radio signal. I want something robust that suggests power to the aliens. I want them to think that we are much stronger than we are."

Bakker laughed, and said, "We can boost the power but the signal might be lost that way."

Hackett said, "I have an idea if we're into head games here. Why embed a picture at all? Why not just leave it out and let them try to figure out what we've done. Give them a puzzle."

Bakker was about to protest, then stopped. Instead, she said, "You know, there is something to that."

"They don't know why we're here," said Hackett. "All they know is that as they slowed from faster-than-light speed, they found us. They may have spotted us because we wanted them to, but they just know we're here."

"So we react to their signal with one of our own. They know they put a picture in it. We don't, but they will expect it. We have a psychological advantage," said Bakker.

"This sounds like we're overthinking the problem," said Lewis. "I don't think I want to do that. Maybe the less guile, the better for us."

Hackett said, "But maybe if we do, it will provide a new and better way for communications. That's what we need to do. Open a better line of communication."

"We can go either way," said Bakker. "Take about five minutes to set everything up, and to make sure that we're broadcasting the strongest signal possible."

Lewis sat quietly for a minute, thinking about the situation. Hackett could tell that Lewis was intrigued by the possibility of throwing the aliens a curve. It would give them, meaning the humans, an edge, and, frankly, Hackett couldn't see that they had any other edge.

Finally, Lewis said, "Let's try it and see if we get any response from them. If we don't, then I think we send the message again, with the photograph embedded."

Bakker said, "I'll be transmitting from the communications pod. I'll need as much power routed there as possible, and I'll put in a narrow bead."

"Call when ready, but don't transmit until then."

Bakker stood, and said, "I'll let you know."

As she moved through the hatch, Lewis said to Hackett, "I'm not sure this is such a hot idea."

CHAPTER 22

[1]

HACKETT NOW SAT IN THE COMMAND POD, EX-
cited and worried. They were about to make a move, the
first they had thought through and the first they had initiated. The aliens, even if they were unaware, had been controlling the game from the beginning. Everything flowed
from that first message discovered what seemed like a century ago. They had tracked the aliens across the sky, had
sacrificed so much just to meet them at the fringes of the
Solar System, and now, finally, they were going to make a
move.

Over the intercom, Bakker said, "We are now ready to
reply to them."

Lewis hesitated and finally leaned forward so that his
lips were near the microphone. The motion was unnecessary.

He said, "Go ahead."

Then, suddenly the lights dimmed slightly and the image on the screen flickered as if there was a sudden dip in power. The lights brightened again.

"Message sent," said Bakker.

"Now what?" asked Lewis.

"We wait," said Bakker. "See if they respond. They should have received our signal by now."

Hackett kept his eyes on the alien ship almost as if he expected it to light up or explosions to ripple across the surface. Of course, there was no visible reaction.

Sitting up, Lewis said, "There. That something?"

Hackett looked to see where Lewis was pointing, toward the rear of the alien ship, but he saw nothing. The alien ship held its position in space, keeping its distance from the station.

"What?"

"There." Lewis touched the screen.

The rear, or what they considered the rear of the alien ship, seemed to brighten. There wasn't much there, just a hint of illumination.

"Don't know," said Hackett.

Bakker poked her head in the hatch, and said, "Anything happening?"

"Come on in, Sarah," said Hackett. "Yeah. We have something going on here."

"Range is increasing," said Lewis.

"They're turning away from us," said Bakker.

Hackett touched a button, and said, quietly, "Weapons?"

"Yes, sir."

"Arm the weapons but do not fire. I repeat, I don't want anyone to shoot unless I give the order."

"Understood, Major."

Now Hackett turned his attention back to the alien ship. The glow at one end had brightened so that it looked as if the rear had caught fire. The ship had turned so that almost all they could see was the fiery glow.

"What's happening?" asked Lewis.

"I think they're preparing to depart," said Bakker.

"Going where?"

Bakker moved around to study the screen. "Can we pull back a ways?" she asked.

Lewis touched the controls and the scene vanished, then rapidly rebuilt itself. Now the alien ship was a dime-sized shape in the center of the screen. Beyond it, farther out from the sun, was a single, large comet that had to be twenty or thirty miles across, glowing dimly in the starlight.

"I think they're maneuvering out of the Solar System," said Bakker. "Maybe getting back on their original course."

"You sure?"

"Oh, hell. Of course not. I'm just telling you what I can see there."

The alien ship was picking up speed, widening the gap between it and the station. It turned again, but not so that it moved toward either the sun or the station. It was almost as if the alien pilots were maneuvering so that they could get out of the Solar System.

"Now what?" asked Bakker.

"Well, we sure as hell can't follow them," said Lewis. "They're much too fast for us. Not to mention that we can't get much farther from Earth with any hope of ever getting back alive."

"But they're getting away," said Bakker.

Hackett laughed. "That they are. What would you have us do about it?"

"I don't know."

Lewis said, "Maybe they're preparing for an attack run."

"I have alerted the weapons pod, but they won't fire unless I authorize it."

Bakker looked horrified. "You can't just shoot at them."

"I'm not going to. We'll return fire for fire received and nothing more."

"But . . ."

"Sarah, if they shoot, we have to shoot back. We have no choice."

Bakker fell silent, her eyes on the screen.

"They're still accelerating," said Lewis. "I think they're just leaving."

Hackett, his attention focused on the aliens, felt the first tingle of relief. They had traveled about a light-year from Earth, had intercepted the alien ship, seen them, and now the aliens were retreating. They weren't going to attack the station and seemed to be avoiding moving deeper into the Solar System.

Space around the ship seemed to change. The images began to flicker, almost as if they were seeing through the heat waves rising from a sun-hot highway in the desert. The alien ship became indistinct, as the glow from the rear became as bright as the sun seen from Earth.

"Can we stop it?" asked Lewis.

Hackett shook his head. "If it jumps to faster-than-light, even the beam weapon won't be able to catch it. It can out-run all our weapons."

"Fire now," said Lewis.

But rather than giving the order, Hackett sat there. He didn't use the intercom.

Almost immediately, Lewis said, "Belay that. We can't just open fire."

As they watched, the alien ship seemed to burst into flames, or rather, the glow from the rear spread across the ship like St. Elmo's fire surrounding an old sailing ship. As the glow brightened, the details of the ship began to fade, then suddenly, without any warning, it vanished.

"What the hell?" said Lewis.

"They jumped to faster-than-light speed."

"You mean they don't accelerate?" said Lewis.

Bakker said, "Apparently not. They generate some kind of a field, and that propels them beyond the speed of light."

Hackett sat back in his seat. "We got all that recorded? We can see it again?"

"It's all recorded," said Lewis. "I have some of the

instrument readings as well. We got everything so that we can review it."

"Damn," said Bakker. "Who would have thought?"

[2]

THEY HAD THOUGHT ABOUT USING THE CON-ference pod with video access to all those who were interested, but Lewis decided that would tie up too many of the station's resources. Instead they sat in the central pod, around what looked like a large coffee table. Those who were interested sat around the perimeter, listening, and, occasionally, throwing in a comment.

Lewis, when he entered, sat down in one of the chairs at one end of the table, almost as if he was taking over the meeting, and said, "Without further orders and with the contact terminated by the aliens, I have ordered a return to Earth."

There was a momentary silence, then one man began to applaud. A woman shrieked with delight and others began to cheer. Lewis sat stone-faced for a moment, then broke into a broad smile.

Bakker held up her hand, trying to restore order. The cheering subsided slowly and finally died out. She looked from face to face, and said, "Do any of you remember how long it took us to get out here? The trip back will take just as long. Maybe longer because we have to compensate for the gravitational pull of the sun. It's a long way."

Lewis said, "The trip home is never as long as the trip out because we're going home."

That brought another round of cheering. One man held his glass high, and yelled, repeatedly, "To the Earth. To the Earth," until others picked up on the chant. Hackett didn't know if the man was toasting Earth or suggesting that they head back to Earth as quickly as they could. Maybe he wanted the trip to begin immediately.

This time Bakker waited until the cheering, and the

drinking, died down. She said, a touch of annoyance in her voice, "I thought we were going to discuss our observations of the aliens and their ship."

Grinning broadly, Hackett said, "Why? We have plenty of time to do that. You just said that."

"We need to discuss this while everything is fresh in our minds. I want to get these impressions logged."

"Sarah, nothing is going to change overnight. We've all been under a strain here, and now the reason for that stress has just blasted out of here. You have to give people a chance to decompress."

"Yeah," said Bakker, ignoring him. "Did you wonder why, once they had found evidence of another intelligent, spacefaring race, they would just blast off?"

"Because they had another mission to complete," said someone in the rear.

Bakker searched for the man who had spoken. She asked, "What does that mean?"

"It means," said Hackett, "that the Solar System was never their destination. They had orders to explore somewhere else. They were passing close when they spotted us. They swung by us, meaning the Solar System and not the station, to gather a little data. They wanted to see who we were and what our capabilities were. They got that information, then returned to their original mission, whatever it was."

"You really believe that?"

"That's what we would do. If it didn't take us too far out of our way, sure, we'd check out the anomaly, then return to the scheduled mission."

"What we would do is not necessarily what an alien race would do."

Hackett shrugged. "No, but there is nothing to suggest otherwise."

"Then they'll be back," said Bakker.

"Oh, yeah," said Hackett. "They'll be back. That goes without saying."

EPILOGUE

IT WAS A YEAR AND A HALF AFTER THEY HAD intercepted the alien ship inside the Oort Cloud before the first of the shuttles landed at the White Sands Spaceport. Major (lieutenant colonel designee) Hackett and Dr. Sarah Bakker were on that shuttle, but Lewis, as commander of the station, believed it was his responsibility to wait for the change of command ceremony on board before he left his post.

Rachel Davies, her network job assured, along with a weekly science program for public television, knew that she had to be on that first shuttle, and arranged it so that she could record the trip from the station to the Earth, then get off first so that she would have her own footage of the debarkation. She also made sure that Jonathan Travis would cohost her weekly science show, and that one segment a week would explain something about UFOs and alien life.

As the shuttle touched down, and Hackett stood up, for

the first time in years in the standard, one-G environment of Earth, he felt old, weak, and more than a little faint. He steadied himself using the back of a seat and watched as the others seemed to creep toward the hatch so that they could exit. This was no rush to get out that sometimes infected those on an airliner. Even knowing that friends, families, and loved ones were now just beyond the sealed hatch, the people were moving slowly. They weren't accustomed to the gravity or the thickness of the air.

Bakker waited for Hackett at the hatch and, together, they stepped out into the blazing sunlight and the overwhelming heat of a late New Mexico morning. Hackett squeezed his eyes tightly shut, realizing that he wasn't prepared for the sun after more than two years in an environment of dimmed artificial light that radiated little in the way of heat.

The air was heavy, as if it were thicker than water. He saw that others, at the bottom of the short flight of stairs that led from the hatch to the ground, were being helped into something that looked like modified golf carts painted red, white, and blue. Everyone seemed to have been caught by surprise by the sudden gravity, sudden brightness, and the sudden task of breathing. They had tried to compensate on the station, requiring everyone to spend time in the gym pod, but somehow that exercise didn't prepare them for their return to the original one-G world.

Holding Bakker's hand, more for the support that it offered than out of affection, and using the handholds, he slowly, cautiously, began the task of getting to the bottom of the steps. He said nothing to Bakker because he wasn't up to the task of speaking while fighting the atmosphere and trying not to fall into a heap.

Then, somewhere, a band began to play. There was a rumbling overhead as a flight of fighters appeared, flashed by, and headed south so fast that they were gone before anyone had much of a chance to see them. As the roar faded there was a rippling of applause that built until it thundered through the valley, out over the desert and echoed back toward the shuttle.

Hackett, now sitting on the rear of the golf cart, Bakker next to him, leaned close to her, and said, "This I didn't expect." He kept his eyes shut against the burning of the desert sun and wondered why they hadn't landed at night, or at the very least, dusk.

They were driven a short distance, to a reviewing stand situated so that those on the backs of the carts would not be forced to stare into the sun. They stopped, facing bleachers that had been hastily erected for the occasion. They were filled with people. There were thousands more standing around the perimeter, even people standing near the fences that were a good five hundred yards away.

When those on the shuttle had been moved to the reviewing area, the band fell silent, and Lieutenant General (full general designee) George Greenstein stepped to a microphone that looked as if it belonged to the middle of the twentieth century. There was a pop, a momentary buzz, then Greenstein's voice boomed over the loudspeakers that sounded as if they had been installed by a teenager who loved bass and little else.

"On behalf of the president, Congress, the United States, and the people of the world, I would like to welcome you all home and to thank you all for a job well-done."

There was wild cheering at that. People were on their feet, screaming their approval. Slowly, after two or three minutes, the crowd began to run out of steam, and the cheering subsided.

"These men and women," started Greenstein. He stopped, waited, and then began again. "These men and women turned back a threat that was coming toward us. They risked their lives to travel to the very edge of the Solar System, to a point that no other human has ever reached, met, and engaged the enemy."

Again there was cheering and this time it went on and on. Hackett became embarrassed, knowing that they hadn't engaged an enemy, but had exchanged coded messages with an alien race, before the aliens decided to return to their original mission, whatever it might have been. They had done nothing to turn the threat and had been at the mercy of the aliens if the aliens had decided to attack.

He leaned close to Bakker, and whispered, "Well, he's not exactly telling them truth, the whole truth, and nothing but the truth."

Bakker, squinting against the bright sunlight, tried to smile. The effort was nearly too much for her. She said, quietly, "Let the general have his say. It won't hurt us."

"You can never tell."

As the crowd cycled down and sat again, Greenstein said, "The human race has met the enemy and turned it back. Had the Aztecs, the Incas, or the Romans been as successful in protecting their empires and their homes, we might all be speaking Aztec, Incan, or Latin."

"Crap," whispered Hackett, embarrassed by the political incorrectness of the speech. He wondered if it offended anyone.

Bakker would have slapped at his leg to shut him up, if she had had the strength. The gravity was just too intense for her at the moment.

"But the job isn't finished," said Greenstein.

"Uh-oh."

"We have so much more to do, and we must move the human race from its single basket. We must spread throughout the galaxy so that we, as a species, survive and the threat from an alien race does not condemn all of humanity."

Greenstein waited, but there was no cheering here. Into the silence, he said, "We begin, immediately, the task of moving into new star systems and developing the galaxy around us. Our exploration teams will begin forming by the end of the week, and by the end of the year, the first of the colonists will be ready to leave Earth behind."

Hackett looked at Bakker, and asked, "What in the hell is this all about?"

Greenstein, at the microphone answered. He said, "Yes, we have the capability to begin our move outward from the Earth. Today we begin a new chapter in human history."

He raised his voice, and added, "But today is for the heroes. Ladies and gentlemen, one more time, let's give these heroes the welcome they deserve. Let them know that we appreciate their courage in facing the worst threat that has ever come toward the Earth."

This the crowd understood. They leaped to their feet, screaming, whistling, clapping, and cheering. They kept at it as, one by one, the men and women from the station slowly, carefully, and painfully stood as Greenstein called out their names.

Then the general left the reviewing stand and, followed by his aides, moved among returnees, shaking their hands and exchanging a few words with each of them. An aide would then hand the general a small, blue, oblong box, which he, in turn, handed to the space traveler.

When the general finished handing out the specially designed congressional medals, he returned to the reviewing stand and waited while the crowd applauded, cheered, whistled, and stomped their feet. The band began to play again, and then, slowly, the dignitaries who had been on the reviewing stand began to move among those near the golf carts.

Hackett, on his feet near Bakker, holding on to one of the steel rods that supported the tin roof of the golf cart with one hand and the blue box with the other, said quietly, almost under his breath, "This is really all I need."

"No," whispered Bakker, "it's what they need."